DEATH BEFORE COFFEE

DEATH BEFORE COFFEE

A MIKE O'SHEA NOVEL

DESMOND P. RYAN

To my children, Sam and Ben

Praise for Death Before Coffee

"Riveting. Edgy. Thrilling. Real. You enter the world of real policing, where personalities collide, emotions run high, and cops express how they really feel. You are in the thick of things, from personal lives to the daily grind. You have a front row seat to the investigative process and the conflicts that arise trying to do the right thing all while trying to find a decent cup of coffee."—Donato (Dan) Sinisi, CAPP, Security Management Professional and Instructor, author of *The Art of Private Patrol: What you Really Need to Know* and *Keep Yourself Safe*

"The details Desmond P. Ryan uses to describe the gritty city underbelly in Death Before Coffee could only be written by a police detective who has walked dark alleys, stood over bodies, and has more than a passing familiarity with seedy street lizards who hide in shadows. Ryan's flair for painting a vivid picture puts you right beside Detective Mike O'Shea and I found myself continually looking for parallels between Ryan's characters and the officers I have known over the years. A great read for crime fiction lovers."—Cal Miller, Crime Reporter - Retired, *Toronto Star,* Member Crime Stoppers Board of Directors, Honorary Toronto Police Service Detective.

Chapter One

Thursday, August 23, 2018 - 3:06 a.m.

Running. Always running. Getting closer, panting to catch up. Chest pounding. Mouth dry. At the door. Yank it open. The bang. And the click. Sal. Blood everywhere. Squealing tires. Standing. Helpless. The smell of Julia's perfume.

Mike O'Shea awoke from the dream he knew so well, his white T-shirt soaked with sweat clinging to his chest. He kicked the tangled sheets from his legs in an attempt to free himself from his lived nightmare. He hated these fucking sheets. Too rough. Carmen had paid a fortune for them. Like her, they were overpriced.

Looking over at the vintage clock radio on his nightstand, Mike sat up and rubbed his eyes. He steadied his breathing. *In like the vacuum, out like the wind.* Nice enough woman, that meditation teacher or whatever she called herself. Brought in by the Toronto Police Service to work with him and the other high-strung coppers they'd sent to the 'lunch-and-learn' sessions a few months ago.

He'd liked the idea of meditation. Might help with the panic attacks. Not that he *had* panic attacks, of course; 'panic attacks' were the shrink's words. Whatever you wanted to call them, though, they seemed to be getting worse over the last year or so. He was probably just tired. Worn-out. Overwhelmed.

In the moments when he was honest with himself, Mike had to admit that he was, in fact, completely, totally, and absolutely fucking exhausted. *I just need to catch a break,* he'd told himself many times. *Just need some time to regroup, to pause, to sleep. A few days—or months—would do the trick.*

It wasn't that he didn't like being a cop. Hell, he lived and breathed it, even if he didn't drink the corporate Kool-Aid. Even if Homicide still hadn't caught Malcom, the shooter.

Yeah, he still loved *The Job*. The people and their fucked-up stories. The chance to unfuck-up their stories. The chance to give people answers, closure, relief. Everything they hadn't given him.

Fucking Sal.

On nights like these, after dreams like these, he doubted himself, waking as he did with feelings that he'd carried with him even before his life all went to shit. Feelings that fed the stories echoing in his head, albeit in different iterations at different times. *Coulda caught up with Sal sooner. Shoulda pulled my gun. Woulda shot Malcolm on the first—if not my second—chance. But I didn't. I just let Sal get capped and that fucker get away.* It all just reminded him that he should have known better, done better, been better.

You're not helping anyone, Michael. Not even yourself.

He had spent five years in the Juvenile Prostitution Task Force. He and Sal had been tracking a prostitution ring that lured vulnerable young women and girls from shopping malls in Toronto. Once these fuckers had the girls, they broke them and then fed them to men hungry to screw something younger than their own daughters. To keep things fresh for the clients, these girls were rotated between Toronto, Niagara Falls, and Buffalo.

One girl in particular—Chelsea Hendricks—fit the profile and became the face of the investigation. She was a small-town girl pissed off at Mom and Dad for any number of teenaged-girl reasons, and she dealt with those reasons by running away to the Big City with no cash, no plan, no clue.

The two eager coppers had spent months tracing her disappearance, obsessed with finding her and cracking the ring. They were so close, so fucking close.

And then it all went to shit. And Sal.

Shot in the head, dying in Mike's arms. Shooter aimed at Mike. The gun jammed. Took off before Mike could get his own gun out of the holster. Or maybe he froze, depending on who was telling the story. Asshole was still out there somewhere.

Mike had refused time off after Sal's funeral. There was work to do. Someone had to catch the asshole, and he was the only witness. Homicide had stepped in, but after taking Mike's statement, they refused to speak to him about the case. *His* case. Fuckers threatened him with a host of Police Act charges if he didn't step aside. Stop *interfering*, as the head of Homicide called it.

Fuckers.

Now, as he sat in his room in the dark, it all flooded back. He could hear the gun, his ears ringing just like they did that night in the underground parking garage. He could feel the weight of Sal's body, still warm, slumped in his arms. His sweat felt the same as Sal's blood had, splattered all over him along with Sal's brain. He could smell the Armani perfume Julia wore, masking the smell of gunpowder, car exhaust, and death.

And he knew, as viscerally as he did then, that it was all his fault. Sal's mother knew. Chelsea's mother knew. Mike knew. Had he been a better copper, a better detective, a better partner, Sal would be alive today. He had his chance to make it right, and that chance had fucking run out.

He sat up, alone in the bed. Looking around himself, he was surprised at how quickly the feelings of abandonment rolled in. At the debrief of Sal's death, the therapist they brought in suggested that Mike had some underlying 'issues' triggered by the shooting. She'd used that word, too. *Triggered.* Nice fucking choice. The therapist apologized. Whatever.

And then he was sent to see her again after he started having nightmares about the girl Ron Roberts had accidentally shot at the warehouse.

Mike would just sit there, listening to her questions, mumbling one-word answers. Standing appointment. Went on for months. Then she took a week off. She told him to set something up for the following week. Mike shook her hand, left her office, and never called back.

And now, at 3:00 a.m., he tried to shrug it all off. The Hendricks case. Sal. Earlier still, his father's coffin being lowered into the barely frozen ground.

Teaszy and wee Katie clinging to their mother, whose radiant red hair blew across her stoic young face. Father Richard's comforting hand on his little brother's shoulder as his brother wept over the open hole in the ground.

And he, Michael—never Mike, always Michael—left alone to console himself.

Chapter Two

Thursday, August 23, 2018 - 3:25 a.m.

Mike's knees were stiff as he swung out of bed, shaking his head to try and silence his thoughts. It wasn't until after he pulled on yesterday's briefs that he noticed that Carmen hadn't been to bed yet.

He looked at the clock again. And listened.

Nothing.

Working late was one thing, but this?

His cell phone was flashing.

1:47 - Hey. It's me. Working late. Likely an all-nighter. Lucas is with Dad and Carol. Luv ya.

Mike turned on the lights as he made his way down the stairs to the dark living room. He wasn't a stupid man, and as he made his way through the living room to the kitchen, he began to see the writing on the wall.

All-nighter, my ass. She works in the main office of a bloody bank, not as an emergency room doc, for chrissakes!

Wide awake and angry now, he opened a cupboard door and then slammed it shut. Another night that she's not home. Like two nights ago. And three days before that. And… Hell, he'd lost track of the number of times.

"Fucker!" he yelled at no one in particular. At Carmen. At himself. At whoever she was undoubtedly snuggled up to while he actually considered, albeit momentarily, that she might be in trouble.

Thank Christ for Jameson.

He pulled the bottle from the cupboard above the fridge and poured himself a glass. Leaning back against the sink, aware of the dirty dishes behind him, he took a sip, then a gulp. He'd finished what was in the glass by the time he put it to his mouth for the third time. He poured himself another and then, thinking twice, brought both the glass and the bottle with him to the living room.

He collapsed into the red wingback chair, staring at the couch his wife recently seemed to prefer sleeping on instead of in their bed. He poured himself another glass and drank it. Then he stood, paced, looked at the family photos on the wall again.

I wasn't half bad-looking back then. And the other half isn't that bad-looking now.

He returned to his chair, chuckled, and poured himself another shot. Looking at the bottle, he saw that it was already closer to empty than full. He figured what the hell and kept pouring until it there was none left. Then he promptly fell asleep.

* * *

Sunlight flooded through the front windows, waking him.

Shit. Shit. Shit.

Mike pulled himself up from the chair and stumbled into the kitchen.

8:30 a.m.

Fuck! I'm supposed to be in court in less than an hour.

He looked at the empty Jameson bottle. Then, knowing that his son would be home after school while he was at work and that his mother would no doubt show up at some point in the day, searched for a place to stash it.

Above the fridge. Back where he had found it. Hiding in plain view.

He hurriedly gave the kitchen a quick once-over before opening the drawer where they kept the coffee. None there.

Shit! How am I supposed to survive without a coffee? It's just not right.

With no time to waste searching, Mike slammed the drawer shut and rushed up the stairs, his head beginning to pound.

The shower did not help.

Chapter Three

Thursday, August 23, 2018 - 2:55 p.m.

The stuffy courtroom and the curmudgeonly judge who presided over it were not helping Mike's present condition. He had become increasingly ravenous as the morning wore on, and the shitty café sandwich he'd grabbed during the lunch recess was sitting like a weight in his gut.

And there was no coffee. Order didn't go in last night, the girl had said. Juice and water only.

Fucking millennials and their fucking six-dollar-a-bottle freshly squeezed organic bullshit juice.

He had been forced to settle on bottles of much-needed water instead.

Court having reconvened after the late lunch and a brief recess, Mike was finally being summonsed to the stand as the first witness. The chugging of the window air conditioner matched the beating of the hammers in his pounding head, and when he looked over at the jury, they seemed as tired as he was. He tightened the tie around his neck, feeling the stubble he had neglected to shave off that morning, and fastened the top button of his suit jacket.

Then taking a deep breath, he straightened his back to make himself appear bigger than he felt and stepped into the witness box to the left of the judge. He was just so damn tired and had to dig deep to find the confidence he knew the jury required of him as lead investigator. He took another deep breath, pushed his broad shoulders back, and took on the weight of the trial.

The court clerk did not look up from her keyboard as she swore him in. Instead, she sounded bored, like a tired waitress reciting the list of drafts on tap for the thirty-sixth time that day. Mike looked down at the smarmy bastard sitting at the defence table to his right and whispering into his lawyer's ear.

"Good afternoon, Detective." Crown Attorney Bridget Calloway glanced up at the officer in charge of her case and tried not to gasp. Mike looked more like an angry version of something the cat had dragged in than the level-headed police detective she knew him to be.

Mike nodded slightly to her.

"Detective," she let the mystique of Mike's title hang in the air just long enough for it to waft over to the jury box, "I understand that you have twenty-seven years of police service behind you, the last ten of which you have completed as a district investigator. Is that correct?"

"Yes." Mike took a deep breath, tasting stale whiskey on his exhale. "That is correct."

"And as I understand it, the matter that brings you here today involves a young child named Jessica Sanderson and a sexual assault causing bodily harm. Is that correct?" She pivoted on her heels to face the jury.

"Yes. That is correct."

"And what specifically qualifies you to investigate sexual assaults involving children?"

Mike's mind shot back to his life before the funeral, before his subsequent hurried transfer out of the squad, back to the time when he felt on top of his game.

He cleared his throat, nodded subtly to the jury, and listed off a number of what were considered, even in policing circles, a very impressive series of courses, experiences, and job titles. He glanced occasionally over to the jury, whose members seemed to be hanging off his every word. He smiled slightly; he was still that guy every woman trusted and every man wanted as a buddy.

He finished reciting his credentials and concluded, "And the courts have given me Expert Witness designation as a result of my years in the Juvenile Prostitution Task Force, where I dealt exclusively with sexually exploited children."

"Very good, Detective. Do you see in the courtroom today the person responsible for the sexual assault causing bodily harm on a minor?" Bridget let her words linger.

"Objection," the greasy mouthpiece seated behind the defence table mumbled, half-rising from his chair. The defendant seated next to him inhaled loudly, his newly pressed shirt and too-short tie expanding with him.

"Sustained. Rephrase, Ms. Calloway," the judge sighed, not lifting his eyes as he continued typing on the laptop in front of him, seemingly oblivious, or so Mike hoped, to the condition of the officer in the witness stand beside him.

"Of course, Your Honour," Bridget nodded, knowing that she had already succeeded in planting the seeds of guilt in the jurors' minds. "Detective O'Shea, do you see the man your investigation identified as the accused perpetrator of the sexual assault causing bodily harm in the courtroom today?"

"Yes, I do." Mike felt his jaw clench and his tongue pushing hard against the roof of his mouth, any and all traces of a night spent emptying a bottle to fill a void dissipating. "The gentleman in the white shirt with the red tie seated behind the defence table."

"You are referring to the accused, Gregory Sanderson. Is that correct, Detective?"

"That is correct."

Bridget switched gears. "Now, Detective, sexual assault causing bodily harm is a particularly heinous crime—"

"Objection."

"Sustained. Watch your step, Ms. Calloway," the judge cautioned as he peered at Bridget over his reading glasses and the screen of his laptop.

"Of course." Bridget smiled. "Detective, tell us how you came to lay the charge you did."

"On Wednesday, February 13th of last year, as a result of my regular duties as a detective, I was made aware of an incident involving a twelve-year-old girl who visited the school nurse's office with stomach cramps."

Mike paused to take a breath. Bridget stepped away from her podium and walked towards the jury as if to join them for the unveiling of some dark secret. Just as she came within whispering distance of the front row, she stopped, turned to face Mike, and furrowed her brow.

"Is that common, Detective?" she asked, as if chatting with Mike over an early-evening cocktail. "I mean, is it common for the police, a detective, no less, to be called to a school about a twelve-year-old with a belly-ache?"

Bridget glanced at the jury.

"No," Mike continued. "The school also called an ambulance and the youngster was taken to The Hospital for Sick Children. After further investigation at Sick Kids, doctors confirmed that the young girl was in the early stages of labour."

Bridget glanced over her shoulder at the jury, seeing the looks of disgust, horror, and empathy that she had hoped Mike's disclosure would elicit. Then tilting her head slightly to one side, she locked eyes with Mike, wordlessly cuing him for his next line.

"The child, Jessica, gave birth to a baby girl seven hours later," Mike obliged her. "On February 14th."

The crown attorney returned to her podium, poked at the notes in front of her, and waited for the jury to absorb the full impact of the emotional trigger Mike had just pulled.

"A Valentine's Day baby. I see. Is that all, Detective?"

"No. Doctors at Sick Kids also determined that the victim, that is, Jessica Sanderson, had also contracted genital herpes."

An audible gasp from the jurors overrode the chugging of the dying air conditioning unit.

"I apologize for jumping ahead, Your Honour, but…" Bridget paused. It was late afternoon, and she wanted to give the jurors all night to stew over Mike's next answer. "Detective, what did your subsequent investigation reveal about the health status of the accused, Gregory Sanderson?"

Mike looked directly at the jurors one by one before looking over to the judge, and then to Bridget. "That the accused, Gregory Sanderson, the victim's father, also has herpes."

The entire jury box recoiled as if the words were as foul as the smell of a full johnny-on-the-spot on a scorching August afternoon. Mike glanced at defence counsel, surprised he had not jumped out of his seat with objections. Instead, the mouthpiece pushed a yellow legal pad over to his client, who nodded like a frantic bobble-head.

Good, Mike thought, glaring at Sanderson. *You'd better fucking panic, you piece of shit.*

Bridget waited for the jury to digest this latest revelation and to quiet down before continuing.

"Detective, was the sexual assault of Jessica Sanderson your—the police's—first encounter with Gregory Sanderson?"

"Objection. Relevance?"

"Yes, Ms. Calloway. Relevance?" The judge lowered the screen of his laptop as he angled his glasses down his nose to look at the prosecutor.

"No," Mike replied, not waiting for Bridget to respond. First encounter? No fucking way. A series of late-night vehicle stops with young girls with him in his car on file. A report from Children's Aid that had come through the school. Two or three domestic incident reports that gave no reason for the argument between husband and wife. A sexual preference for young girls? Unproven. A sexual preference acted upon with back-page 'escorts'? Unproven. That sexual preference expressed closer to home? Absolutely.

"Detective O'Shea. I am going to pre-emptively incaution you now—"

"My apologies, Your Honour," Mike mumbled. It was Chelsea Hendricks all over again. Supply and demand. Was this fucker just feeding the demand, or did he create that demand in the first place? Which part of that equation was fucking his own daughter about? He wouldn't be the first shithead to put his little girl out.

Not my job anymore. Made very clear after I got the boot.

Beads of sweat crawled down Mike's chest and stomach. His collar tightened, and he stretched his neck to wriggle free from its constricting grasp.

Bridget said something that Mike did not hear. He was back in the inter-view room with Gregory Sanderson and his lawyer—the same mouthpiece sitting beside him now.

"I am suggesting to you that these traffic stops with known prostitutes are as a result of your sexual activities with these underaged girls. Is that a fair suggestion?"

"I don't know."

"My client chooses to remain silent."

"I am suggesting to you that you have been having sexual relations with your daughter for some time now."

"I have no comment."

"My client will not be answering that question."

"Given your knowledge of prostitution and your sexual activities with your daughter, I am suggesting that you are grooming Jessica—"

"My client vehemently denies any such suggestion, Detective."

"Tell me about Malcolm."

"This interrogation is over, Detective O'Shea. You've got my card. Any and all communications with or about my client will go through me or my office. Let's go, Greg."

Mike re-emerged into a silent courtroom, all eyes on him, anticipating a response to something. The air conditioner was useless against the heat of too many people in too small a room. He gasped for the air that was smothering him as his mind's eye saw Malcolm pull the trigger, smelled the gunpowder over the fumes in the underground garage, felt the warm oozy pieces of Sal's brain in his hand instead of the cold grip of his service revolver.

"Detective O'Shea, Ms. Calloway was asking you...?" The judge looked over his shoulder at Mike for the first time today.

"I'm sorry." Mike tried to pull some saliva into his dry mouth, forcing his shoulders down again, feeling his undershirt sticking to his body. "Can you repeat the question?"

"What led you to believe that the accused, the father of the victim, also fathered the victim's child—his own grandchild?"

"Your Honour." The mouthpiece finally rose from behind the defence table, straightened his tie, and smoothed back the gelled strands of hair strewn across his high forehead. "I find Ms. Calloway's line of questioning to be highly prejudicial against my client. In fact, I find Ms. Calloway's conduct—"

"Mr. Reiner," the judge began, "I am going to suggest to you that this is neither the time nor the place to begin questioning your colleague's conduct. I have listened to both of you argue like children over what has been shown to be irrelevant or insignificant points of law for the past few days. I understand that the good detective is the first of many witnesses to be called, and he's already following your leads. I have no interest in watching either of you— or *you*, Detective—prance around for the remainder of our time together. Now, it would appear that this officer's testimony will be more involved than I had been led to believe before we launched into this trial."

The judge furrowed his unruly eyebrows and glared at Bridget before the deep creases in his forehead unfolded. He turned back to the defence counsel. "While we had anticipated that this trial would be completed in a two-week span, I would suggest that we will be lucky to get through the detective's testimony before end of day tomorrow, which will put us quite behind schedule. Having so said, looking at the time now and the faces of our jury members, I'm going to suggest that we recess for the day and begin again, bright-eyed and bushy-tailed, at ten sharp tomorrow morning with Detective O'Shea continuing his evidence. Court adjourned."

With that, the judge slammed his laptop shut, stood up, and disappeared through a door behind the bench into his chambers.

"All rise," the court clerk called out as quickly as she could.

Chapter Four

Thursday, August 23, 2018 - 3:20 p.m.

As always, Mike accompanied Bridget to the Crown offices, a ritual developed over their years of shared trials. Usually, there was energy—electricity, even—between them that those inclined to gossip said went beyond intellectual. Truth be told, the closest they'd ever come to meeting outside of work was at the annual Crown/Police Christmas parties, where well-oiled lawyers and coppers with bad haircuts surrounded Bridget, no doubt hoping to score a little extra Christmas cheer. The drinks were too expensive for Mike's liking, and the lawyers and cops were too cheap for Bridget's liking. Neither stayed long. Neither even said hello to the other.

"What the hell is wrong with you?" Bridget snapped at Mike as she stopped at the door to the offices, the knot of stress that had taken up residence at the base of her neck over the past few days unraveling slightly.

"We need to talk," Mike said. There had to be a way to suspend the trial until he could find the piece that would tie Gregory Sanderson into a much darker world.

"What? You pregnant and your parents kicked you out? Is that why you look like a bum?"

"No."

"Phew! Oh, and make sure you put on plenty of cologne before you go in to work tonight. You reek of booze."

"Yeah, well," Mike's shoulders slumped as he looked away, "it was a long night."

"Or morning came rather quickly, you mean?"

Mike bit his lower lip and looked around the near-deserted hallway.

"Oh, Christ," Bridget said, smiling slightly as she shook her head. "How the hell did you do so many years in undercover with a tell like that?"

"I was much younger then. And things were different." Mike paused, not sure where to start. "Bridget, I think there's more to Sanderson than meets the eye."

"I don't have time for a crime novel now, Mike," Bridget snapped, mechanically punching in the numeric code on the door, the knot in her neck tightening again. "Cut to the chase."

"I think he is or was part of the crew that murdered Sal."

"Let it go, Mike. Not your investigation. Homicide has it. I'm sure—"

The door clicked as she turned the handle.

"No, Bridget, listen. He was grooming her. There's no doubt in my mind. Except he knocked her up. Or who knows? Maybe thought he could make more from her as a preggo—"

"Stop!" She pushed the door open. "Sounds like one helluva longshot—"

"Not a long shot. Happens all the time. Daddy likes little girls. Knows other guys who like little girls. Daddy likes his little girl first, then figures other guys will, too, and—"

"Mike—" Bridget interrupted, a shiver catching the knot in her neck.

"I know. There are hundreds…thousands…of guys involved, but I've got a feeling—"

"No, Mike!" Bridget rotated her head, releasing a tiny bit of tension as she leaned against the open door. "Feelings are great. So are hunches. So are instincts. Save them for your cronies in the pub."

"Really? That's what you think I'm all about?"

Bridget looked inside the open-concept office at the clerks hurriedly photocopying bits and pieces of cases while her colleagues' ears were glued to phones, fingers tapping on keyboards, words filling the screens in front of them. "We're not going there. Not your job any more."

"Like fuck," Mike muttered.

"It's over, Mike. Let the young guys who are in the JPTF now do their thing. And Homicide has the murder investigation—"

"*Has had* the investigation, you mean," Mike corrected. "For thirteen fucking years. Cop killer. Name known. Description known. Last direction of travel known. All the resources on the fucking planet at their disposal and—"

"Mike, for Christ's sake, you've done your bit." Bridget slumped against the doorframe, the weight of her own life bearing down on her. "If you're that sure, forward whatever you have—"

"Into the vortex, you mean," Mike shot back at her.

"Listen," Bridget continued, "we are lucky to have coppers like you. *I'm* lucky to have you—dedicated, smart, strong, not bad-looking—but you know how these things go. We can't mess around with it now, not when we're so close. We need to focus on *this* trial to put Sanderson behind bars. That's our job. They'll know where to find him if he is tied in with anything else, and you know we have special Crowns to prosecute those cases if and when they arise, but..."

God, she is such a lawyer, Mike thought, and not as a compliment.

"...there is absolutely no way in hell that I will suggest to His Honour that we suspend the trial for a fishing expedition. It won't fly, and you know it."

Mike sighed, any colour left in his tired face draining away, the laugh lines in his cheeks deepening as his jowls drooped. At that moment, he felt as if he had aged about twenty years.

"Listen, Mike. I'm not saying you're wrong. Nor am I saying that this isn't worth pursuing by the appropriate unit."

"Fuck that."

"What I *am* saying is that you need to suck it up. There is a protocol in place, and I need you to be solid for this trial."

Bridget moved out of the doorway as a clerk popped out, whizzing past Mike, a piece of paper in one hand, coffee mug in the other, rushing down the hall muttering to herself.

"I need you," Bridget continued, deciding it was now time to pull out the big guns.

"I'm not one of your fan-boys," Mike squawked, much to his own surprise. "I mean, I know what has to happen here, and I know how to get it done—"

"Oh, do you? I'm practically blushing, Detective." She tilted her head just enough and placed one hand on her hip.

"You've just made my day."

"The bar was pretty low, let's be honest here," she replied, giving him a reassuring squeeze on the arm. She stepped back. "You're not blushing, are you, Detective O'Shea? Big tough copper like you? Come on. It can't be that easy."

"Did you just call me easy?"

"You are many things, Michael O'Shea, but *easy* is not likely one of them."

The tired cop looked down at his glistening shoes with a smirk as the crown attorney stepped into the office.

"Oh, and Mike?" Bridget called over her shoulder at him. "Don't forget: bright-eyed and bushy-tailed for tomorrow morning. No wild parties. No visits from Mr. Jameson or any of his other ne'er-do-well friends. And please, don't be late. This judge already hates me and would love a reason to tear a strip off me."

She winked as the heavy metal door closed behind her. Mike stood in front of it for a good minute or two before glancing down at his watch. He was late for his first shift with the man who had once saved his life.

Mike hustled down the courthouse steps, beginning to take stock of the thoughts floating around his still-throbbing head. He smirked in spite of himself.

Bridget. Prettier than she was smart, and she could run legalistic circles around her colleagues blindfolded. Unfortunately, her true abilities were seldom showcased in the run-of-the-mill criminal cases she was assigned. The senior Crowns—all men at this downtown courthouse—took the sexiest cases.

The case Mike desperately wanted to pull together wasn't sexy. It was stale. Old news. As old as a case of a pimp-turned-cop-killer could be. Fucking Homicide had dropped the ball. Was still dropping the ball. And the JPTF?

A bunch of clubbing pretty boys living out some gamer fantasy better suited to teenaged boys who played videogames on their laptops late into the night than to the hardcore investigators they were supposed to be.

Not like when Mike and Sal were there.

Fuck. Bridget was likely right. The best he could do was drop a dime—another dime—to the Ds in charge of Sal's murder investigation. Maybe they had something. Maybe they'd want something. His hopes weren't high on either count.

He settled himself behind the wheel of his old pickup truck, one of the few things he refused to give up or change for Carmen. Thank Christ.

Then he looked down at his watch. *Fuck. Late. Too late.*

Five minutes. Just five fucking minutes of peace to enjoy a good fucking cup of coffee.

Is that really so much to ask? he muttered aloud.

Chapter Five

Thursday, August 23, 2018 - 4:35 p.m.

"Body in a laneway. Might be a homicide, might not be. Either way, we have to attend," Detective Ron Roberts advised as Mike walked into the 6th District detective office. "I'll go get the printout of the call from the front desk if you want to get the car."

"No 'Hello, welcome to the platoon, Mike. Can I buy you a coffee?'"

"Oh. Right. I'm not good with this partner thing. We work alone in Traffic. I miss that. Always will. Even after five years of working as a district D."

"Which part tdo you miss: working alone or doing traffic enforcement?"

"Both."

* * *

Mike popped the top button of his shirt, loosened his tie, and folded himself into the driver's seat of the unmarked police car, ignoring the man sitting quietly in the passenger seat. Despite now working in the same district out of the same office, both he and Ron Roberts had actively avoided one another. They had been on opposite shifts, so their paths had had no reason to cross again. Just as well. Bad memories for both of them. Nothing to talk about. Best left alone.

And now, the cop whose partner had been killed almost fifteen years ago and the cop who had shot two people later that same night were working together. Mike's situation—and where he would end up—had been the subject of constant speculation and Monday morning quarterbacking amongst the rank and file for years, but too many other incidents had occurred to keep his fate at the top of the pile. And Ron's? First kill was clean: no issues and no gossip. The second—the girl—was not at all clean and was resurrected by the media every time there was a questionable police shooting. So was Sal's murder. Mike wondered if Ron ever thought about the girl. He himself never stopped thinking about Sal. Or Malcolm.

Mike wished he hadn't transferred to B platoon to work with Roberts. He wished those fuckers in Homicide had done their job back then. And he wished that Carmen had come home last night. But here he was, and there they were. All beyond his control, or so he had to believe.

Mike thought again about the Sanderson case. With or without any new revelations, it was much more challenging than he or Bridget had anticipated, and his working the two-to-midnight evening shift for the next seven days wasn't going to make things any easier. It wasn't the 2 p.m. start that was the problem. It was the shift ending at midnight, a lie for detectives like Mike who actually did their jobs. Their shifts finished when the investigation was complete, not when the clock struck twelve. And with a body in a laneway to start the shift, there was no telling when this day would end.

But Sanderson. Was his theory just a long shot? Mike wondered. Was he obsessed? Or was this asshole somehow tied in to the ring that had murdered his partner? And if so, who knew about it? Who cared?

Mike's thoughts blocked out any chance of conversation that might have taken place between him and Ron, new partners sitting twelve inches from one another for the first time since that night. Not that Mike had anything to say to Ron.

Ron Roberts hadn't initiated conversation either, suggesting that the silence suited him just as well.

Mike navigated the car out of the packed lot behind the station, only now becoming aware that Ron was staring out the passenger window. As he pulled onto the otherwise residential street, a man walking his dog looked over and gave Mike the stink-eye.

Bridget's right. Let's just get this conviction and see what happens from there. It's still anyone's game.

Chapter Six

Thursday, August 23, 2018 - 4:50 p.m.

Mike dropped the engine into park in front of the closest coffee shop. He breathed an audible sigh of relief, suddenly aware that he'd been clenching his jaw for the whole goddamned day.

"Why you don't just use the drive-through?" Ron said, uttering the first words spoken since the men had got in the car together fifteen minutes earlier. "It would be a lot quicker."

"Too confusing," Mike muttered back.

After almost three decades on the job, and after a day—and a night—like he had just had, Mike was feeling every moment of his forty-eight and then some years. Four straight days in court, a two-week trial that looked as if it would turn into three, witnesses lined up who would almost definitely break down on the stand, a home life that was crumbling around him: It was safe to say that he was in need of some caffeine and a decent night's sleep. Sleep was unlikely, so the coffee would have to do.

Mike glanced in the side mirror and got a good look at himself. His shirt was wrinkled, his tie askew, and his navy pinstriped suit looked lived in. The stubble on his face was becoming increasingly obvious. His blue eyes blinked back at him, tired and bloodshot. His still-dark hair looked as if it had not seen a comb in weeks.

Mike could hear his mother's lilting voice chastising him. He had taken Bridget's advice to clean up a bit, dousing himself with enough cologne to mask a night's worth of whiskey and a day's worth of sweat. Now, in the confines of the car, he realized that he stank like a teenaged boy on a first date.

"Really? I've never found drive-throughs confusing at all," Ron said, interrupting Mike's self-abasement.

"Good for you." *Fuck you.*

Mike stepped out of the car into a full -body stretch. His old partners all knew about his drive-through issues and had always just left it at that. He hated having to get to know new partners, having to train them to tolerate all his little idiosyncrasies, and even worse, having to put up with all of theirs.

"Want a coffee?" he called back. An olive branch.

"No, thanks," Ron replied, preening as he settled further into his seat. "I had one before I came in. Another one would make me too jumpy."

"Suit yourself," Mike yawned as he slammed the car door shut. *Still a fucking idiot.*

* * *

It was evening shift in the city, and any district detectives out on the street would stand out like a pair of mismatched socks in the cutlery drawer. They would be the two guys who didn't look like they belonged together, the kind of guys driving mid-sized, nondescript sedans that screamed 'cop' to every low-life in the city. They all had neatly trimmed hair, flashy ties, and spit-shined shoes. Most were cleanshaven, having given up the signature moustache they may have sported during their uniformed days in favour of a more refined look. Regardless of the weather, these district detectives always wore the jacket of their conservative suits to cover their issued handguns secured in shoulder holsters or on their belts. Back in the day, Mike used to have his snubby tucked into the small of his back. Not now. He had his issued Glock in his shoulder holster, just like every other district D.

The work of a district D was never-ending, often thankless, with terrible hours. Most of the guys—and it was mostly guys in the districts—were either there for the money, afraid of the road, or occasionally the oddballs who actually believed they were making a difference, one case at a time.

Mike O'Shea and Ron Roberts were the oddballs. They both thought, in their own little way, that they could make a difference. This belief, however misguided, was where their similarities ended. The only reason they were partners now was because, quite frankly, Mike was the only one in the office who didn't flat-out refuse to work with Ron after Ron's last partnership imploded. The only condition Mike had was that they not discuss what had happened that night thirteen years before. It was a condition they were both fine with.

And now here they were, going to look at a body found in a laneway just after 4:30 p.m. Homicide? Overdose? A simple sudden death?

Having started his shift at the courthouse at 9:30 that morning, Mike felt as if he'd already worked a full day. In fact, as the sun continued to shine brightly, he already had. While he was used to working long evening shifts, it was knowing that he had to be back, *bright-eyed and bushy-tailed,* in court and ready to testify at 9:30 the next morning that troubled him.

He'd have to pace himself, and getting this coffee was an integral part of that pacing.

He had decided long ago that there was something universal about coffee shops and cops, and especially the coffee shops that were frequented by cops. They were the clean, crisp, cookie -cutter–predictable places where the coffee was often free for the men and women in uniform.

Like this shop.

Mike remembered hearing about the evils of the free cup of coffee, how it was the slippery slope to corruption that every senior officer warned every new recruit under his command about. A free cup of coffee. A free donut. A free meal. A free car rental. A free weekend getaway. And then the phone call for help. A parking ticket that needed to be withdrawn. A kid who needed a caution. A criminal charge that needed to disappear. An investigation that needed to never have happened.

A cop killer who should never get caught? They never talked about that, did they?

It all started with that free cup of coffee, they said.

Like fuck.

Mike was surprised to see no uniforms in the place, although he suspected that most were in the alley with the body. He ordered his usual coffee with milk, no sugar, and the girl smiled and slid it across the counter without ringing it in.

"Thanks," he said.

As Mike reached for the coffee, something pushed him. Stumbling forward, he felt the man behind him drop as if he'd been taken out at the knees. The girl behind the counter screamed, and time seemed to stand still just for the briefest of moments as even the cash register's incessant song was silenced.

As the other patrons just stood there, stunned and motionless, until they heard the crack of the man's head hitting the floor, Mike dropped to the ground, kneeling beside the stranger, forgetting his coffee that was still on the counter. But he was a fraction of a second too late to catch the man and to have prevented the gash on his head, a gash that did not spew blood as it should have. In fact, there was barely a splattering of red on the cold, grey tile floor. The man's heart had stopped pumping before he'd even hit the ground. Mike had seen this often enough to know, and without hesitation, he put his ear to the man's mouth.

Nothing.

The man was starting to turn blue.

"Call an ambulance," Mike ordered over his shoulder as he began doing chest compressions.

No one moved.

"I said call a fucking ambulance! Now!"

Momentarily stunned by the lack of action on the part of the young people working the counter, Mike had to remind himself that they weren't police officers. They were, by the looks of them, college kids working a few hours a week to pay for tuition and beer.

Sitting in the car, Ron had been watching his partner through the open coffee shop door, and having had more experience with death than most, he had already summoned help on the radio.

"Ambulance is on the way," the former Traffic man advised as he joined Mike inside. "You look like you're straining. Let me cut in."

I just fucking got started, Mike wanted to yell, but as the offer sank in, he had to admit that he was grateful. Sweat was pouring down his face, and he was surprisingly out of breath, perhaps the fallout of too many long days. Or too much whiskey the night before. Or too many dreams where…. In any event, he counted out the final compressions, checked for breathing, and pulled away from the dead man.

Ron moved into place and continued the compressions, his body heaving as he forced his weight down through the palms of his hands onto the man's chest.

In what seemed like hours but was not, the distinctive wail of an ambulance siren sang in Mike's ears, followed by the familiar *woop-woop* of a police car's horn. One of the beauties of working downtown was that there was always help close by.

As Ron continued chest compressions, Mike reached around and pulled the dead man's wallet out of his back pocket. They would need a name, age, and next-of-kin information sooner rather than later.

The driver's licence was the first card visible. Alvin Chedoba. Forty-seven years of age. Out-of-town home address. Mike dug a little further into the wallet. A few credit cards. No cash. Three pictures.

Mike's heart sank as he looked at a picture of the man—this man—standing over a pretty woman and two little girls. He barely glanced at the two single photos. School pictures, most likely. The younger girl still had her baby teeth.

Family man. Just a regular guy grabbing a mid-afternoon coffee.

"Let me jump in," Mike said to Ron, who had yet to break into a sweat.

"I'm good. The ambulance must be pretty close. Why don't you go out and tell them what you know."

As he watched the ambulance pull up, Mike couldn't help thinking how death and coffee were the only two sure things in policing. Only difference was, you never acquired a taste for death.

Mike briefed the paramedics outside. The younger medic nodded as her older male partner hauled the kit bag with the defibrillator past them and into the coffee shop, placing it beside the deceased's body.

The staff had retreated back behind the counter. Some patrons were making their way out the door, and Mike could see Ron almost bristling as they practically stepped over him to do so. Others absently sipped their coffee, eyes on phones and computer screens, oblivious to the drama playing out in front of them.

The paramedics placed the paddles on Alvin's chest asnd Ron felt a rib crack under the weight of the compressions.

"Clear!" the young paramedic hollered.

"Clear," Ron called back, leaning away from the body.

Bounce.

Pause.

The paramedics listened. Then listened some more.

"Clear!"

Bounce.

"You good to continue?" the paramedic at the defibrillator asked Ron.

"Sure," Ron leaned in, resuming the rhythm and the count.

"Let's try some adrenaline and see what happens," the young paramedic advised, reaching into her bag of tricks to pull out a huge syringe.

See what happens, Mike thought. *Inspiring.*

He looked up through the open door to see two uniformed officers sprinting towards the coffee shop, slowing down as they saw the two paramedics alongside the two men that they recognized as their own crouching around a body on the floor.

"Holy shit. You okay, Detective Roberts?" one of them asked.

Ron looked up at the officer as he continued with the compressions. Mike thought he saw Ron rolling his eyes slightly.

"I'm fine. This fellow… not so much."

The officers stood motionless, looking back and forth at each other and then at Ron.

"So, gentlemen," Ron said between compressions, still not having broken a sweat, "which one of you wants to take over for me?"

One of the officers dropped to his knees and took over from Ron.

"Got your coffee?" Ron looked over to Mike, brushing off the knees of his pants as he stood up.

"On the counter behind you," Mike responded.

"Either grab it or leave it. We have to go."

The paramedics looked up at the two detectives.

"We have another body to attend to," Ron advised, adjusting his tie and straightening his jacket. "If you need names or badge numbers, just ask these two fine officers."

With his now-tepid coffee in hand, Mike followed Ron as the two detectives walked out into the early evening sunshine.

Chapter Seven

Thursday, August 23, 2018 - 5:14 p.m.

Settling back into the familiarity of the car, Mike took a deep breath before wheeling out of the lot. After snapping his seatbelt on, Ron pulled out a steno pad and began to write.

"Need the guy's info?" Mike asked, taking a gulp from his cup, relishing the bitter taste of the coffee as it made its way down his throat.

"No. Not our concern. We've got our own body to deal with."

"Fair enough." Mike glanced over at his partner. With not a feather ruffled, it appeared that Ron had filed this incident away and was moving on to the task at hand. His partner had been this calm that night in the burning warehouse, too. Mike could still feel the flames from that fire on his skin, still feel the despair he had felt when it had struck him he might not be able to escape.

"He was dead when he hit the floor," he said now. *In like the vacuum, two, three, four.*

"Definitely. Nothing you could have done."

Out like the wind, six, seven, eight.

And those little girls no longer have a father.

In like the vacuum, two, three, four.

And their mother will manage, just like mine did.

"Out like the wind, six, seven, eight," Mike muttered under his breath.

"What's that?" Ron asked, looking up from his notes.

"Nothing. Nothing at all," Mike sputtered.

"Suit yourself. I wonder if he had life insurance," Ron mused.

"What?"

"Guy in the coffee shop. I wonder if—"

"I heard. Dunno." Mike did not need to know, nor did he want to. How to get those fuckers at Homicide to do their fucking jobs was enough for him to think about now. Or how to prove that there were more victims in the Sanderson case. Or how to get a simple fucking cup of coffee that wasn't cold and didn't taste like shit. That was enough for him to think about now.

"He didn't look that old," Ron continued, almost cheerily. "Probably had a family. A mortgage. Some debts. You know. Would be unfortunate to die and leave the wife and kids destitute."

"Yep." Mike knew this to be true. He could feel his temples throbbing.

"My father left my mother and me when I was a baby, you know."

"Huh." *Did not know. Do not want to know. Shut up.*

"He didn't die. Might just as well have. It was just as hard."

"I bet."

"Not a dime in support."

"Huh."

"I hope this guy had life insurance."

The barrage of lights in front of them was a welcome sight to Mike. He was not in the mood to listen to whatever Ron Roberts had to say about the merits of life insurance or anything else that did not have to do with this particular call. In fact, he was increasingly not in the mood for Ron Roberts.

"You've never worked in Traffic, have you?" Ron suddenly asked.

"Nope."

"I can tell. Park here," his partner directed, pointing to a spot behind a marked scout car just a few feet from the entrance to the alleyway.

Mike wheeled the car around and took a couple more deep breaths.

"You okay?" Ron asked.

"Right as rain," Mike said, not taking his eyes off the flashing lights on the roof of the car in front of him.

"If not—"

"I'm fine," Mike snapped, turning his attentions to the task at hand. The first look at a crime scene was critical. It set the tone of the investigation and dictated the likelihood of a successful outcome. That's what Mike had been taught, that's what experience had proven, and that's what he was going to do now.

"You don't look fine," Ron pressed.

"Your concern is touching." Mike did not bother hiding his annoyance as he glared at his partner.

"I'm not concerned about you. I'm concerned about this investigation. We've got a young platoon with more weaknesses than strengths, and the quality of direction they'll be getting from their sergeant is less than adequate," Ron shot back, sounding equally annoyed. Then he added, "In my opinion."

"Fair enough."

"Not like this in Traffic. No accidents, just preventable collisions. Fatalities. Here, it's anyone's call. I suppose the outcome is the same. Death."

"Very profound."

"Regardless, the rules are very clear, and so are our responsibilities. Both are unforgiving, and neither allow for a lot of wiggle room. These young ones are relying on us—"

"If this your idea of a pep-talk—"

"I don't do 'pep.'"

"I didn't imagine you would," Mike replied into his coffee cup.

"Look at that," Ron pointed to the alleyway, shaking his head in disgust. "Not even taped off."

"Yeah. I noticed." Mike knew the area well, and if he remembered correctly, it was a popular thoroughfare. And that meant lots of opportunity for cross-contamination.

"I wonder how many people have walked through our crime scene since our boys got here," Ron huffed, noting the number of uniformed officers milling around aimlessly in the laneway ten or so houses from where Mike had parked.

"Or delivery trucks," Mike said, shaking his head at the sloppy police work and good evidence lost.

"Not their fault," Ron said.

"Then whose fault is it?"

"The road sergeant's. He knows how little these kids know. He should have had that laneway taped off from the get-go."

Mike looked at the alley and then back at Ron, who he figured must look to any civilians like the ideal detective in contrast to what he himself must be looking like about now. The guy was even wearing a fucking fedora, for chrissakes.

"It's going to be a long night, isn't it?" he finally sighed.

"Depending on whether or not it's a homicide and who they send, it could be a long few days" were Ron's less-than-encouraging words.

Chapter Eight

Thursday, August 23, 2018 - 5:21 p.m.

"I don't suppose anyone has told them to turn off their lights, or they'll run the batteries down?" Ron sniffed. "It was never like this in Traffic."

Mike ignored the comment, too focused on taking in the scene to respond to his new partner. Strip mall on the right, backyards on the left. What about people? Dog-walkers? Drug addicts? Prostitutes and johns? Little old Polish ladies on their way to Mass who used this lane as a shortcut to the church on the corner.

And what about the dead guy? A botched robbery or drug deal gone bad? A random wrong-place-wrong-time? Or just time to go, just like Alvin in the coffee shop?

While his preference was to take a moment to jot down his initial impressions, time was not on their side. Mike gulped some of his now-cold coffee and pulled himself out of the car, annoyed at the thought of evidence being destroyed by the incompetence of the officers—especially the sergeant, he had to agree—on the scene.

"Here." Ron retrieved a small attaché case from the back seat as he stepped out of the car. He passed it over the hood to Mike.

"What's this?"

"Crime fighting kit. I give one to all my new partners. Has property receipts, rubber gloves, police tape, some pens, and a couple of flash drives. One of them is loaded up with templates of all our forms. Just a few things

I've found over the years that I've always needed but nobody seemed to have."

"Just like Christmas," Mike said as he looked inside. Pulling out one of the many steno pads and a pen, he tossed the case back into the car before closing his door. "You do know that I was a D on the other platoon, right? And a squad guy—"

"It'll come in handy. You'll see."

"Traffic man prompting an old squad guy. World has gone insane."

"Sorry?"

"Nothing. Never mind."

"No, seriously. Something you need to know. I'm a bit deaf in my left ear. Began after…"

Ron's voice died away when he saw a look of boredom on Mike's face. The two men looked at each other and then looked away.

The alley was unremarkable. A couple of rusted, green dumpsters had been tagged by adolescent self-proclaimed artists, while overgrown weeds sprouted amidst the cracked chunks of the once-solid asphalt. Loading docks for the strip mall were on one side of the alley, with residential garages attached to long narrow backyards along the other. The original immigrant homeowners were selling off their semi-detached houses to the thirty-something professionals with burgeoning families for well over the asking prices. It was easy to tell which house was which: The post-hipsters would likely have rock gardens in front of their houses while the pre-gentrification immigrant homes had lush green lawns out front. From where he stood, Mike assumed the backyards with patchy lawns sprinkled with strollers, tricycles, and abandoned toys belonged to the former group, while the yard with full vegetable gardens in the back belonged to the older residents. Some of those older places still had pigeon coops or illegal chicken sheds out back as well.

Judging by the condition of the garage with the police tape on it, their body was behind a post-hipster house.

Mike took a closer look at the litter in the alley: a couple of beer cans, likely from a local hound looking for a quiet place to quench his thirst, a few piles of dog shit, some spent condoms of various sizes and colours suggesting that back street sex-for-money was still in high demand. Nothing out of the ordinary. Mike scratched down some notes on the steno pad as he and Ron made their way to the scene.

An ageless man pushing a bundle buggy full of empty beer cans and liquor bottles rattled past the two detectives.

"Hey, buddy," Mike called out. "Leave it."

"But—" The man froze,; the can he had picked up held mid-air.

"I said," Mike pulled out his tin, "leave it. This is a crime scene. Did you not see the flashing lights at the top of the street or the police officers everywhere?"

"Oh. Oh. Oh," the man mumbled apologetically, dropping the can and scurrying along through the laneway, a couple of empty beer cans spilling out of his buggy as he went.

"Fucking idiot," Mike muttered, shaking his head, frustrated all over again at the incompetent police work. "We gotta get this laneway sealed off. No wonder lawyers think cops are fucking idiots." bumble-heads."

Ron, with his crime -fighting kit in hand, didn't write anything down as he almost ran, chin up, looking like a bird sniffing in the wind, his head moving rapidly back and forth as his eyes narrowed to scan the alley. He kicked at the gravel, then wiped the dust off the toe of his glistening shoe on the calf of his other leg without missing a step. Occasionally, he would stop as if he wanted to say something or listen, and then start walking again.

As they got closer to the body, a uniformed officer walked up to them. Mike was new to the platoon, so the uniform acknowledged him with a nod, but addressed Ron.

"Hello, Detective Roberts," said the young uniform, almost out of breath. Ron never allowed the young officers to call him by his first name. He was Old School, where formality was a privilege held by rank and earned by experience. At least, that's how he saw it.

"Ah, Constable Preston McAfee. One of our finest. Lose your hat?" Ron looked the officer up and down.

"I see you haven't," the officer laughed, glancing at Ron's fedora.

"Pardon?"

"Er… No, sir. It's in my car." The officer shrank back before jutting out his jaw and pumping out his chest simultaneously.

"Well, you might want to get it. Never know when the media or the duty inspector are going to show up." Ron turned, walking towards the only area in the entire alley to have any police tape around it. "Who put the tape up?"

"I did," the officer said.

"Did the deceased drop from the sky, Preston?"

Mike glanced sideways at his partner.

"No, sir." McAfee looked down at his feet.

Ron stood facing the tape, and then looked back along the alley to the street, his hands down at his side. He looked back at the young uniform.

"I'm assuming, then, Preston, that this whole laneway has been contaminated. Get the sergeant to assign somebody to tape off the top of this alley, right where it meets the road. And get the sergeant to have someone tape off the bottom of the alley," he pointed, "over there where that bottle-collector just went. When the officer tapes off the top of the alley, get him to determine which is the least contaminated route in and out of the scene and tape off a path. Unless you need a sergeant to do that, too. I'm hoping not. In any event, that path is going to be the route everyone uses from now on. And for future reference, Preston, this whole alleyway is your scene."

"Yes, sir."

The young officer began talking into his radio as he turned to walk back up the alley to his scout car.

"Preston, wait."

"Sir?" McAfee stopped mid-transmission, turning back to face the detectives.

"Establish the route *before* you contaminate the scene any more."

"Yes, sir."

"And since we're all here *now*, what have we got?" Ron's face above his snug collar was turning red as his annoyance with the young officer increased.

"People out walking their dog in the alleyway found him."

"When?"

"Um…" McAfee fingered through his memo book and began reciting robotically, "Call came in about an hour ago. They said they called about ten minutes before we arrived—"

"Do you have their information?" Ron interrupted.

"They're right over there," the uniform said, pointing to a young couple with a mangy old mongrel standing by the back of the strip mall. The man was sucking on a cigarette while the woman, her back to them, appeared to be talking on her cell phone.

"And why are they standing in the middle of your crime scene, Preston?"

"The, uh, sergeant told me to have them wait there."

"Get those people out of our scene and seize his cigarette and hold it so Forensics can eliminate the ashes from the scene. And hope to God, Preston, that the Crown doesn't tear you a new one when this goes to trial."

Ron's voice was eerily calm, but his face was now beet red. Mike, who had been making a sketch of the scene, was starting to get a bit concerned. Having already seen one man drop dead today, he didn't particularly want to place a bet on whether Ron or McAfee would be next at the rate they were going. So instead, he elected to extricate himself from the situation by going to speak to the two witnesses.

"Make sure you get a car to bring them to the station," Ron called out to Mike. "These people are all onside and excited when they find a body, but they never seem to be able to make it to the station when it comes time to give a statement."

"Not my first rodeo, buddy," Mike called back to Ron as he escorted the couple and their dog to the road along what he deemed to be the least contaminated route.

"What do we know about this body?" Ron asked McAfee as he watched Mike remove the human and canine contaminants from the scene.

"Um…" The young officer fumbled through his memo book again.

"I don't need an exact account. Just an overview is fine."

"Well, they said they walk through here with the dog all the time—"

"And let me guess? There's never been a body here before."

"No, sir. There…uh…hasn't. Been a body, that is," McAfee stammered.

"Go on," Ron invited with a faint smile. "By the way, is the sun getting hotter or is it just me?"

"I don't know, sir. I guess it's getting warmer. Yeah. So," McAfee returned to his notes, "they walk through here all the time, but today, they see this body in the corner over there by the garage. They think it's just a drunk passed out and don't really think much of it. But their dog is off leash and goes over and starts sniffing, and the drunk doesn't move. The guy gets kind of concerned, goes over, and that's when he discovers this."

"It *is* getting hotter, isn't it?" Ron said, taking off his fedora and wiping the sweat from his forehead with a tissue pulled from his pocket. "Suggests it's going to be a really hot night. Don't forget to make a note of the temperature when you arrived and the temperature when Forensics gets here. Could be a significant difference, if this sun is any indication."

"And how would I do that, sir?"

"Do what?"

"Note the temperature. I don't have—"

"Write down in your memo book that it appeared to be getting warmer and why."

"But I don't know why, sir."

"You *feel* it getting warmer, don't you?" Ron said. *God give me patience,* he thought.

"Oh. Right." McAfee smiled, and then furrowed his brow. "Why is that important?"

"Do you know when this man died?"

"No, sir."

"Neither do I, and that's not our job. Looking for witnesses, gathering evidence, generating persons of interest—that's what we do."

"Yes, sir, I know that, but—"

"The coroner will be the one estimating the time of death. Through the stages of rigor mortis. Based on ideal conditions."

"Of course, sir." Mc nodded, as if this was common knowledge.

"Does this scenario meet the standard for 'ideal conditions,' Preston?"

The officer paused for a second to think before sputtering out his answer.

"Yes, sir. I mean, no, sir. I mean—"

"No, Preston, it does not. Never mind. *I'll* make a note. As long as it's captured somewhere. So how did our witnesses know the deceased was, in fact, dead?" Ron replaced the fedora on his head, squaring it before pulling the brim down to shade his eyes from the late afternoon sun.

"I don't really know, sir. I, uh, never really asked. They just told me he was dead. I, uh, didn't really talk to the lady, and the guy, well, he didn't really say much except that the man was dead."

"All right, then, Preston," Ron sighed, trying not to let his increasing lack of patience impede the investigation. "I'm assuming that the Duty Desk has been notified. How about Homicide?"

"Not yet. Staff told us to have you come out first."

"Just to confirm that he's dead?" Ron chuckled silently, trying to find pockets of amusement where he could, if just for his own sanity. "I'm assuming that the paramedics contacted the coroner before they left?"

"Yes, sir, they did."

"Good. So call Homicide for me and tell them everything you just told me. Who was the first officer on scene?"

"I was."

"Well, then, don't call Homicide. I'll do it myself. And don't be going anywhere because you'll be guarding the body until it gets safely locked away in the morgue. But first things first." Ron looked back to see that the alley had been taped off, watching the uniformed officer making his way towards the body along the strip mall wall. "Go along the path that's being created, get your hat, and then come back and stand over the body. Make it quick. I'll wait here for you, but then I'd like to talk to some of the neighbours."

"Yes, sir." The young officer sprang over to the wall, then sprinted up the alley towards his scout car, where he would retrieve his hat and could perhaps have a gulp from the can of pop he had purchased just before being dispatched to this call. Then he would return to guard the body for the next several hours until Homicide released it to the morgue, something McAfee was confident that he could do.

A somewhat skeptical Ron watched him and sighed. "It was never like this in Traffic," he muttered.

Chapter Nine

Thursday, August 23, 2018 - 6:03 p.m.

For a homicide scene, there was a notable absence of blood around the body. At first blush, the witnesses' assumption that the victim was just some guy passed out in the laneway was reasonable. There was nothing immediately apparent to suggest a struggle. Indeed, except for being slightly over-dressed for the weather, the victim, from a distance, seemed quite peacefully settled in.

Mike stood for a good two or three minutes, breathing in the scene. Breathing in the stench. Breathing in death. Breathing in…?

He nodded to McAfee as he took a step closer to the body, sure that it was swelling right before his eyes. "Bodily gasses working their magic," he said. "This fucking heat is baking him like a stuffed pig."

"Sir?"

Ignoring McAfee for a moment, Mike looked at the pulpy face of the deceased. It was the colour of uncooked chicken, and the only real traces of blood were matted in his disheveled grey hair.

"I said this is definitely a homicide."

"Oh."

The man's right cheekbone was crushed, the rest of his face looking like mashed banana.

"Right cheekbone. Whoever did this was left-handed. Make a note."

"Of what, sir?"

"Never mind. I was talking to myself."

"Oh."

No bruising. Had he been so severely beaten that he had bled out before discolouration had a chance to occur? If so, there was another scene. Where?

"Dunno, but likely already bleached and cleaned. Shit."

"Sir?"

"Talking to myself again."

"No, not that, sir. I was just wondering. What was it like? You know, when…"

Mike wished he hadn't worn this suit today. While it was impressive in court, it was hot as hell at the best of times, and there was no way he could take the jacket off at a scene. He loosened his tie a bit more, wishing he could undo another button. He gave his shirt a tug in the hope of creating some airflow between it and the T-shirt that was stuck to his body.

"Rage."

"Sir?"

"Here. Now. Look. Not anger or surprise. Takes a lot to shatter a guy's head like this. Was it drugs? Desperation? A lover's jealousy…?"

"I see what you mean," McAfee said, scratching an itch on his forehead.

"And look at this," Mike went on, pointing to the man's throat. To suggest that it had been slit would be too polite. Too sterile. Too painless. "The raggedness of that gouge there suggests that a blunt instrument had hit the surface of this guy's neck so hard that it ruptured the jugular vein, causing the skin to explode."

"Okay."

"The poor sucker likely blew out his throat while the killer was pounding the shit out of his head. Would definitely speed up the dying process, popping the jugular like that. Lucky strike for both of them, then."

Looking at the man's torso, Mike could see that a jacket had been haphazardly pulled over the blood-soaked T-shirt. It didn't quite fit right.

"And this, Percy—"

"Preston, sir."

"Preston. Look at this jacket. Likely put on the body after our buddy was dead."

"How do you know that, sir?" McAfee asked, his eyes opening wider than even he thought possible.

Mike stopped and sniffed the air again. Slight odour of decomposition consistent with what he saw in front of him. No stale boozy smell. No sweet aroma of smoked crack. Odd. He had been expecting something.

"You pick up a few things over the years."

"Was it like that back in the day, sir?"

"Well?" Ron interjected from behind Mike, ignoring the young uniformed officer.

"Just looking. Some defensive injuries on the hands," Mike replied, still looking at the body.

"Pretty scarred hands. Looks like they're permanently puffy."

"Alcohol?" Mike asked.

"Or a boxer. One way to tell for sure. Look at his ears." Ron was now peering around Mike, like a scrawny little boy glancing over his big brother's shoulder at some wondrous sight.

Mike's checked out the exposed ear. His partner was right. Cauliflower ears. Synonymous with an Old School boxer or a serious street-scrapper.

"I used to box a bit in my day," Ron sighed, his thin chest puffing almost unnoticeably as he stepped back behind Mike. Without thinking, Mike found himself turning around and looking at Ron's ears. No cauliflowers there. His new partner had either been a very good boxer or was playing Mike as a fool. Looking at Ron's almost delicate hands, Mike assumed that he was being played.

Both men looked back at the body. A nice, albeit cheap, leather belt held up the modest black tailored pants. Professionally tailored, at that. Perhaps to accommodate the right leg, amputated somewhere around the knee? The street amputees Mike dealt with usually just had their pant legs mostly- cut off and the remnant pinned up with safety pins like an envelope. This guy was obviously not your average hound. It occurred to Mike that he might not be a hound at all.

And the shoes. Shoe. On the deceased's left foot. Plain shiny black slip-on.

Higher end. Clean. Incongruent with the situation its owner found himself in now.

Mike glanced down at his own usually impeccably shined shoes and noticed a covering of white dust on them. Ron's were the same, enveloped in gravel dust from the alley they had both walked through. The deceased's only shoe, then, had not walked on this gravel.

"Definitely dumped," Mike said. He stepped back and looked around. No sign of crutches, a walker, or canes anywhere in sight. Looking back down at the puddles of loose gravel, he didn't see any impressions suggestive of a walking aid having even been at the scene. He made a mental note to ask the uniforms if they had found anything of the like in their search of the area.

"Our deceased hasn't been here long enough for the bugs to move in," Ron stated, stepping forward to poke at the body with his pen before using it to draw a rough diagram of the body's position in his steno pad.

Mike winced before scribbling down a few notes in his own pad.

"How much do you figure he weighs?" Ron pondered aloud as he pressed the pen to his lips.

"Say two hundred pounds give or take, minus fifty for the leg, making him about a buck fifty," Mike responded, his eyes squinting in disgust, deciding not to remind his partner where that pen had just been.

"That's a decent weight to lift, drag, and dump," Ron said, scratching something down. "And if you're going to go to all that trouble, why here where everyone can see? Why not a more concealed or even a less obvious spot?"

The two men glanced around them. While it may or may not have been obvious from the street, the body would be highly visible to anyone looking out the second-floor window of the house on the property in front of them. Or from neighbours' houses on either side, for that matter.

"No idea, but the place where this guy was murdered is somewhere out there waiting to be found."

The two detectives stood in silence, lost in their thoughts for several minutes as the late afternoon sun continued to heat up the evening air. Preston McAfee stood guard over the body, hat on, sweat streaming down his face, shifting surreptitiously from foot to foot and wishing he had taken a piss when he had had the chance.

"Staff has been advised that you might run into some overtime on this, and he'll let the staff sergeant on the relieving platoon know," Ron said, turning to the young officer. "The duty inspector won't be around. There was a triple shooting in the east end this afternoon, and he's going to be tied up on that. As far as writing your report goes, just do a barebones Sudden Death occurrence. Don't head it up as Murder or anything like that."

"Yes, sir," McAfee nodded slightly, more to free the chin of his baby face from the starched uniform collar than in agreement. "What if I—"

"Head it up as a Sudden Death, Preston," Ron repeated.

"Yes, sir."

"Now, when they get here, Homicide will tell you who is in charge of the case and where to send the report. Make sure you leave a copy of it at the station so they can include it in the unit commander's report for the morning. Is there anything I'm forgetting, Mike?"

Ron looked over to see his partner speaking to another officer.

"Just if he needs to piss or get something to eat—?" Mike said over his shoulder.

"Oh, sweet Jesus, yes," McAfee blurted out, the weight of the can of pop he'd downed earlier pushing on his bladder.

"If you need to go to the washroom, there's a coffee shop right over there." Ron nodded towards a hole-in-the-wall place with the familiarity of a street cop who knew his beat. "They're usually pretty good to us, so I don't suppose they'll mind if you use the facilities."

McAfee began to walk in that direction.

"Wait, Preston," Ron sighed, putting an arm out to stop the young man while reminding himself that, for better or worse, this kid would likely be a star witness if and when this matter ever got to court. "Make sure someone is here to take over for you before you leave. And if you need something to eat, get someone to pick it up for you and eat it away from the body. I don't want your chicken sandwich wrapper turning up in any scene photos, right?"

"Right." The young officer nodded, pulling himself back to his post. "Sir?"

"Preston?"

"I need to take a piss, sir."

"Of course, you do. Call for relief. Like I told you. Want to grab another coffee, Mike?" Ron asked, dismissing McAfee from his mind. "It's going to be a long night. Going to need something to keep me going."

"Okay. Just don't get too excited on me," Mike grumbled. The heat, the long day, and the late-night whiskey were taking an increasing toll on him.

"I'll try to keep it down."

* * *

"What do you want?" Ron asked as they approached the glistening glass counter that revealed croissants and vegan snacks below.

"Just a coffee. A good coffee. None of that flavoured shit," Mike replied, turning his back on the intimidating coffee menu on the wall.

This place was not like the one across from the crime scene. The washrooms here were clean, gender-neutral, and sure to have plenty of soap in the dispensers. Looking around, Mike saw that most of the patrons sat alone, mesmerized by their computer screens. Even those sitting in couples looked as if they were more engrossed in their individual electronic devices than with each other.

"Suit yourself. I'm having a vanilla soy latte, half-sweet, to stay," Ron announced to Mike and the aproned server behind the counter.

"I'll have coffee. Regular coffee. No vanilla. No soy. No half-sweet. Just a coffee. To drink. Here," Mike said.

The server looked blankly back at him, paper cup in one hand, black marker in his other, frozen.

"You *do* serve that here, don't you?" Mike asked.

"My treat," Ron advised, handing the young man a twenty. "Grab us a seat, Mike. I'll bring your coffee over."

Mike found a circular high-top table with two tiny chairs that, apparently, could support the weight of an average-sized adult. He already missed the familiarity of the cookie-cutter coffee shops he was used to.

Ron set both cups down and settled himself on the chair across from Mike.

"Before we get started," Ron said, removing his fedora, looking for a place on the table to put it before giving up and hanging it on the back of his chair, "I think we need to let each other know where we stand."

Mike sighed. "Look, if it's about—"

"I was given a medal for one, cleared of the other. That's all you have to know about that," Ron interrupted, snapping the lid off his latte.

"You ever…?" Mike began, looking down and pulling his coffee towards him before looking across at Ron.

"No. I don't. And, as far as I'm concerned—"

"So why didn't they catch the guy? Malcom?" There it was. Point blank. Just like the shot.

"I don't know," Ron replied, taking a sip before pulling his bottom lip up to clear any soy foam that may have gathered on his top lip. "I did my part. You did yours. It's not up to us any more."

"But Homicide hasn't—" Mike pressed.

"I thought we agreed not to talk about this."

"Yeah." Mike nodded. Nothing to talk about.

The two men sat in silence, waiting for the moment to pass.

"What I wanted to say," Ron began again, taking another sip of his latte, "was that we both have a history. A known history. And people think things about both of us, whether those things are true or not."

Mike looked away. They both knew that they were tied together for life. They were the only two men who knew the truth. Who believed the truth. Who had lived the truth.

"And here we are," he finally said.

"And here we are," Ron agreed, raising his cup to Mike as he shifted gears. "Just so you know, I like to do things right the first time, and that ticks a few people off. So be it. I'd rather get the job done right than hurry through things. Traffic investigations taught me that."

Ron wasn't exaggerating. Everyone knew he fastidiously adhered to the rules, and he liked it that way. The light was red, or it was green. Easy.

But for his brief foray into Mike's world more than a decade ago, Ron Roberts was as straightforward as his name. He didn't socialize with the platoon, and he was definitely not one of the boys. As the memory of what had happened faded, Ron was blending back into his comfort zone of relative obscurity, where all anyone could say of him was that he was dependable and that his conviction rate was high. After thirty-six years on the job, Ron was more than content to leave it at that.

"Suits me fine," said Mike with a shrug. *New partner. New rules. New rhythm. Pain in the ass.*

"Fair enough." Ron looked intensely at Mike, sizing him up. "So I'll do this call, you do the next. That's how I work. Unless you really want this one?"

"Sure. Sounds great." *Pain. In. The. Ass.*

"Good. Now," Ron looked down at his steno pad, "there's always scuttlebutt going around, but is there anything I need to know about you right now?"

"My wife is likely in the midst of leaving me, and I don't like dead bodies."

Ron looked askance at Mike and raised an eyebrow.

"Bodies," Mike repeated, taking the first sip of his coffee, hoping that Ron didn't pay too much for this dog piss. "I don't like them. They creep me out. I can deliver compassionate messages, bash in heads as required, and wrestle drug dealers to the ground, but I do not touch bodies. I'm assuming you got the part about my wife leaving me."

"Yes. I got that part. Okay, this may work out well. The bodies part, I mean. Not your wife leaving," Ron stammered. "I'm not very good with compassion, or people, for that matter. And while I can certainly hold my own, violence is not my go-to. And the addicts can overdose for all I care. I'll handle the bodies."

"And I like going to court.," Mike said, leaning back, careful not to fall off the awkward chair.

"Fine with me. My wife and I just bought a cottage, and I need my days off to get things done. Looking to retire there in a couple of years."

"Looks like a match made in heaven then," Mike said, taking another sip of coffee, the muscles in his shoulders beginning to relax. Rolling his neck, he heard some cracking noises.

Now he looked—really looked—at Ron for the first time. When did the man get so old? Hair turned grey. Eyes still sharp—piercing, really. A few wrinkles around the eyes. Certainly no laugh lines. White shirt likely as starched as the uniform one he wore back then.

As for himself? Well, if he looked the way he felt, Ron might as well be sitting across from a bag of hammers. Mike took another sip of coffee. Not bad, he had to admit.

"So now that we've got that out of the way," his partner said before taking another sip of his latte, "what do you make of our one-legged man?"

"Head whacked to rat shit. Throat split open. No blood. Killed somewhere else and dumped," Mike said between his own sips, glad to be back on familiar ground. "Our fellow is too big to have been carried, with or without both legs. Someone must have seen a car. Pretty brazen, though, a mid-afternoon dump."

"You don't mean to tell me anything still surprises you?" Ron laughed. "Damned shame the scene was such a mess. Not McAfee's fault, though. Good kid, but—"

"What's his deal?"

"Legacy hire. You don't have family on the job, do you?"

Mike shook his head.

"Good. Never agreed with that. McAfee's dad was on the job. Dad's dad was on the job. First one was a good cop, apparently. Second was okay. Third generation, by all accounts, has been too distilled. Probably work out okay in the end, but he's *that* kind of guy." Ron somehow managed to lean back easily in his chair, latte in hand. "You know,: the kind who *would* get written up for not wearing his hat?"

Mike nodded. *That* guy was everywhere. Never really did anything wrong, but wasn't smart enough to keep himself out of trouble.

"You okay with him being point?" Mike asked.

"Not my choice, but he's first on scene. With our help, I suspect he'll be fine. Before body removal takes it away, we'll have to remind him to seal the body bag and the drawer it goes into at the morgue."

Mike rolled his eyes.

"Yep. That's the sort of thing I'm talking about."

"Gotcha." Mike looked down at his watch. "Shall we go back to the scene or to the station to interview those hipsters with their mongrel? She seemed like a total space cadet, and he didn't seem fazed by any of it at all. You'd think finding a dead guy would be a bit—"

"Off-putting?" Ron offered, sipping the last of his latte.

"One would think." Mike felt his cell phone vibrate and reached into his coat pocket, checking the screen as he pulled out the phone. "Gotta take this. Yeah. I'm at work… Great. No, I don't think Carmen will be coming with me. Or Lucas… No. Everything is fine. I'll tell you about it later… Okay. Bye."

Mike looked across at Ron before self-consciously stuffing the cell phone back into his pocket. "Sorry. Just confirming dinner. The whole family goes home for dinner every Sunday, and my mom phones every Thursday to remind us all."

"*Every* Sunday?" Ron queried.

"*Every* Sunday. Unless you're dead. Or close to. Mom's rules. For all of us. Me, my sisters, husband, wives, partners, kids, grandkids, friends of grandkids… No exceptions. Which reminds me, I'll be ducking out for Mom's dinner for an hour or so on the Sundays that we're working. You're more than welcome to join. In fact, Mom will be expecting you."

"We'll see about that."

"Suit yourself."

"I think we should see what's happening back at the scene. While I don't like to make people wait around, the witnesses can sit. Likely don't have anything to tell us that we don't already know. Homicide might want to talk to them first anyway."

Mike nodded as they both stood up, empty cups in hand, scanning for the garbage bin. Mike adjusted the suit he'd been wearing since before 7:00 a.m., now quite aware that cheap-shit cologne was a poor shower substitute.

Chapter Ten

Thursday, August 23, 2018 - 7:00 p.m.

Mike pulled in behind Preston McAfee's cruiser, wondering if its roof lights had stopped flashing because they had been turned off or because the car battery had died. The sun still hung heavy above the horizon, and just as Ron had predicted, it was unseasonably warm for so late in the day. A newer looking car parked across the road led Mike to guess that Homicide had arrived.

A woman approached the two detectives as they walked along the now clearly defined access/egress route.

"Is that…?" Mike began, looking the newcomer up and down, his own fatigue and the seclusion of the alleyway overriding his sense of professionalism.

"Yep. Amanda Black. *Detective Sergeant* Amanda Black now. Apparently, she's our lead from Homicide."

"Really? When did she get promoted? Again." Mike's curiosity was piqued. He knew there was only one female detective sergeant in Homicide and that her caseload put her colleagues to shame, but he did not know that it was Amanda Black, and he certainly was not expecting her to look like *this*.

"A few years ago, maybe? Used to work in this district after getting promoted out of Morality. Married to a plumber. Second husband. First husband was Larry Marcovic."

"I know who she is, but I didn't know she was married to that idiot. Wow.

She's held up well over the years, all things considered…." Mike let the words trail off as he instinctively sucked in his gut and straightened his tie. "Didn't Marcovic get suspended for knocking out another copper in the parking lot after a fucking game of shinny?"

"Yep. Thick as horseshit. Worked with him once, many years ago. That was enough. And don't waste your time," Ron advised as he saw his partner preening like a peacock. "You clearly don't know Ms. Black."

"I actually do, but—" Mike smiled.

"I'm serious. Watch your step around her, partner. She knows her stuff, and she doesn't suffer fools."

"Hi, boys." D/S Amanda Black smiled as if at a cocktail party, somehow able to maneuver around the dead body and into the personal space of both men without a misstep in her tight black dress and three-inch stilettos. "Nice of you to stick around until I got here."

"Sorry, Amanda," Ron crisply apologized as Mike was all but stumbling over his own feet. "My new partner and I had a bit of follow-up to do and wanted to catch up on our notes before things got going here."

"No doubt," Amanda said, her lips tightening into that forced smile Mike knew well as she looked him up and down in a very different way than he had just assessed her. "Been a long time, eh, Mike?"

"Like Old Home Week," Mike nodded.

"Don't believe anything they've told you, Mike," Amanda advised with a smile. "But then again, you'd know all about that, wouldn't you?"

"I suppose we all would." Mike smiled back. She was the one they talked about, testifying in court in her black power suit covering a crisp white blouse cut just low enough for interest but not enough for gawking. She was the one they referred to as the pit bull, the one who always looked like a corporate lawyer going in for the kill, whether the call-out was at two in the morning or 1:30 in the afternoon. She was the one whom most of the women on the job hated, and all of the men were afraid of because of her competence. This was what had become of Amanda Black, Morality-Squad-Trixie-turned-Homicide-Investigator-Extraordinaire.

"So," Amanda looked over at Ron, dismissing what she sensed Mike was thinking with a nod, "what can you tell me?"

"Not much more than Constable McAfee can, to be honest. We've got a one-legged dead man who is," Ron's eyes twinkled, "dead, and since he has only one leg, I can conclude that he didn't walk here."

"Ron, I just finished a brutal three-month jury trial yesterday. We got the conviction, with no hope of an appeal. Thank you." Amanda smiled briefly before continuing, her words coming at them like a volley of bullets from a machine gun. "Today I got to have breakfast with my husband and children for the first time in twelve weeks. I then got to go for a 10K run and have a glorious shower."

Mike wasn't sure whether she looked at him or not, but he could feel the greasiness of this past day on his body.

"In fact, I was just on my way out to buy a pair of shoes because that's what I do when I win a case, but my phone rang because I'm on call and somebody was murdered. I've been feeling very good all day, Ron. Great, even. And I still feel great. But not *that* great."

The two men looked more like a couple of delinquent schoolboys than seasoned detectives as they stood silently before the detective sergeant.

"Maybe instead of going for coffee with your new buddy, Mikey, here—oh, and by the way," Amanda gave Mike an icy look, "women aren't meat, so try keeping your eyes in your head, Detective—the two of you could be a little more familiar with your call. Now, Ron, you're going to do some groundwork for me to make my life easier. Sound reasonable?"

"We are at your disposal," Ron replied, feeling as overwhelmed by Amanda Black, a woman he knew well, as Preston McAfee had felt by him an hour earlier.

"Good. Find out who this dead guy is. Maybe do a press release asking for the public's assistance in identifying a suspicious death, blah blah blah. I saw that you had the officers do a two-block canvas. I shudder to think of what their canvas was like. In any event, get them back. I want a five-block canvas. Wait a minute. That's not your job. Who is the road boss on this one?"

Amanda looked around for the uniform sergeant.

"Spackman." Ron waited for the fireworks to begin.

"Shit. Okay. Well, you can't pick your road sergeants. *'There's our first obstacle, Your Honour,'*" Amanda's eyes rolled back in her head as she mimicked her testimony on the stand. "Sorry. Did I tell you that this is my first day off in three months? Anyway, Ron, I know it's not your job, but fucking Spackman? Never mind. Let's just dig in and fix what we can."

"No problem, Amanda," Ron said.

"Oh, and Mike?" Amanda glanced over at him. "Get that suit into the drycleaners. It looks like you've slept in it. Or worse."

Mike shook his head, exhausted, as Amanda walked to her unmarked car. "Plumber, huh? Wouldn't want to be that guy."

"I don't imagine that she'd want you to be, either," Ron smiled.

Chapter Eleven

Thursday, August 23, 2018 - 7:25 p.m.

"What time do you want me to have you back at the scene, Detective Roberts?" McAfee asked, memo book in hand, his bear forearms glistening with sweat.

"You never have us leaving until we actually head in for shift or I tell you differently. Otherwise, you spend the shift recording Detective O'Shea and myself walking in and out of your scene."

"But Detective Sergeant Black said—"

"Don't let her get to you," Mike said as he walked over to join Ron who was leaning over the body. "She's no different from you and me. Just a city copper. She may have a higher rank and," he looked down at McAfee's shoes, "higher heels, but she's still just a copper."

He grimaced as his partner poked and prodded at the body, now beginning to give off that sicky sweet smell of decomposing flesh as it continued to rot in the evening heat.

"Just confirming that there are no bullet holes and that he's not lying on a knife," Ron said, flicking a bug from the deceased's chest with his pen, which he then casually placed back in the inside breast pocket of his suit jacket.

Mike turned away in disgust.

"Is your Sergeant Spackman around?" Ron asked McAfee, disregarding Mike.

"He's over there, sir. Want me to call him on the radio for you?"

"No, that's okay. We'll walk over. I'm sure some of the neighbours have come out to have a look. Did you get their names?"

"Yes, sir." McAfee fumbled for his memo book.

"That's okay, Preston. I don't need them now. Someone will talk to them later. But tell the guys to let us know if anyone saw or heard anything of importance. If that's the case, my partner and I will interview them ASAP. Got it?"

"Got it, sir."

"And don't forget to seal the bag before body removal takes him away."

"I won't, sir."

"And you will be following them to the morgue. For continuity of evidence."

"Right, sir."

With a sharp nod, Ron left McAfee with the body, and he and Mike made their way back up the alleyway. A uniformed officer stood at the top just behind the police tape, politely answering questions from passersby while being captured in the media shots of the scene. The access/egress route was working well, and Ron was pleased. Mike was considering their next move when they were approached by the uniformed sergeant.

"Joe Spackman," the portly man announced, extending his hand to Mike.

"Mike O'Shea. Just transferred from C Platoon." Mike shook the sergeant's hand.

"I know who you are. Welcome aboard. I think you'll like the shift. A good bunch of guys. The D is a plug, but I'm sure you'll get around him." Spackman smiled at Ron, who did not smile back.

"Hello, Joseph. I've got a five-block radius for your officers to canvas and some potential witnesses McAfee may have for you to look at."

"All business, eh, Ron?" Joe smiled broadly. "We already did a two-block canvas, just like you asked, and I've cleared my men."

"Yes, and now Detective Sergeant Black would like a five-block canvas."

"Sorry. Can't be done. I've only got a couple of cars here now, and there's no way they can do five blocks."

"Perhaps you can call other cars then." Ron looked pointedly at the stripes on Spackman's uniform as a reminder to the sergeant of his authority.

"Unless we get authorization for overtime, which we won't, I can't get that canvas done even if I did have the whole platoon on scene."

"Well, that's not my problem today, Joseph. I've got enough on my hands right now."

"Well, I'm just telling you, Ron—"

"And I'm telling you, *Sergeant*, that *Detective Sergeant* Amanda Black wants a five-block radius, and she's going to get her five-block radius."

The two men stared at each other. Mike's gaze bounced back and forth between them as he wondered who would win this pissing contest.

"If Black wants it done, she can fucking well do it herself," Spackman said, breaking the standoff.

"I've got her number here," Ron replied, not missing a beat as he opened his steno pad. "Do you want to call her and tell her, or shall I?"

Spackman looked at Ron, then over to Mike, who looked back towards the crime scene, shaking his head.

"I'll do the best I can with what I have." Had Spackman been a dog, Mike was sure that his ears would have flopped in submission.

"That's all I'm asking, Joe. No one expects miracles. Just do what you can." Ron turned on his heel, leaving Mike to follow.

"Anything I need to know?" Mike asked as he caught up with his partner.

"I just don't have the time of day for him. He's a lazy bugger who is creating a platoon of lazy buggers, and I don't like it. He was probably a lazy constable and should never have become a sergeant."

Mike nodded as he and Ron hustled towards their car.

"And," Ron continued, "he hates Amanda Black. There was some story going around at some point that they dated or lived together or something like that, and it ended badly."

"For him?"

"I would imagine, although I doubt it's even true, to be perfectly honest. Look at her. She's a D/S in Homicide, and he's a lazy uniform sergeant. She's also a helluva lot smarter than he is, but that's beside the point. Judging by her track record, it would appear that she doesn't go for the smart ones.

Anyway…"

Ron stopped abruptly and waited for Mike to unlock the car doors.

"So is he going to be a problem?" Mike asked over the roof of the car.

"No. He's in a bit of shit himself right now and won't rock the boat."

"Shit?"

"Personal stuff. Domestic."

"Good call on Amanda's part dropping him then," Mike mused, unlocking the doors.

"None of my business, really. All just rumours."

The two detectives got into the car, which would be their on-site office for the next couple of hours. Ron began making some notes, while Mike turned on the ignition to get the air conditioning going, then stared straight ahead through the windshield. It was starting to get dark, and people were out walking their dogs, asking the uniformed officers what had happened, who it was, and if they were safe in their homes.

He glanced over at Ron scribbling away. It was going to be a long first shift together.

Chapter Twelve

Thursday, August 23, 2018 - 9:30 p.m.

After too many roadside interviews of potential witnesses generated from the door-to-door canvassing, Ron and Mike finally left the scene and went back to the station. Even though it was mid-shift, the back lot was overflowing with marked and unmarked cars. Back in the day, that meant that everyone was in at the station with their arrests. These days, it was just another sign of the times: not enough officers to fill the cars. Sooner or later, something had to give.

"Thoughts?"

"Whoever dumped our body had to know the area," Mike said, squeezing their car between the gas pump and another unmarked car. "Easily accessible, yet not busy."

"Or it was a lucky guess?" Ron offered, opening the door before the car was properly parked.

"There's no luck in homicide," Mike said, turning off the ignition. "Especially for the victim."

"Got a call for you, Detective," Cathy, the civilian station operator, said as they entered the station. Both men looked over at her. Calling 'Detective' in a police station was like calling 'Dad' in a hardware store. "Oh, sorry. Detective Roberts. Not you, Mike."

"I'll take it in the back, thanks. Give me a minute to get to my desk," Ron called out as he rushed towards the half-lit hallway that led to the dingy detective office. Mike followed at a much slower pace.

"We've got a couple coming in half an hour to give us a statement," Ron said, eyes on the computer screen as one finger on each hand danced madly over the keyboard. "They were watching the news and heard about a one-legged man being murdered. They called to say they may know who he is."

"I don't recall a press release saying anything about our victim having only one leg, do you?" Mike sank into his chair at the desk directly across from Ron, being careful not to knock his knee on the overflowing banker's box underneath.

"No." Ron stopped typing. "I don't believe it did."

"So where is this information coming from? Let's see what they're saying." Mike reached over to another cluster of desks and grabbed the greasy remote for the TV.

"Make sure you wash your hands after touching that thing. Who knows where it's been," Ron warned.

This from the man who flicks bugs off stiffs with his pen, Mike thought with a shudder, clicking on the TV that was perched on a filing cabinet surrounded by boxes.

"I'm just running a few checks on some of the addresses near the alley to see if we can identify our victim before our witnesses arrive," Ron continued as the illegally wired cable connection took a moment to kick in. "He might have lived in one of the houses, and we've dealt with him before, or maybe he's known in the area—"

"*...Police are tight-lipped about the investigation at this point, except to say that the victim, according to the officer at the scene, had only one leg...,*" Janelle Austin, this station's resident crime reporter, was saying as the camera panned carefully over her shoulder to show Police Constable Preston McAfee pacing around an orange blanket, underneath which, by implication, lay the victim's corpse.

"You put a pretty girl in front of a tired copper, and this is what you get," Ron said, not bothering to look at the screen behind him, shaking his head in disgust. "McAfee probably didn't even notice the microphone and cameraman."

Mike clicked off the TV. "Might not be all bad. Let's see what these folks coming in have to say."

* * *

Mike met Mr. and Mrs. Majewski at what smelled and looked more like a dirty fish tank than the front counter of a police station. The two witnesses were compact, barely a head taller than the worn grey countertop that should have been replaced a decade ago.

"What a shithole," Mike said to no one in particular as he walked towards the couple, almost tripping on the chipped and cracked floor tiles that had lost their lustre years ago.

While Mrs. Majewski's black sweater coat was more subdued, Mr. Majewski's Osh Kosh-type overalls and bright cowboy-checkered shirt created a marked contrast to the filthy bile-coloured walls around them. It was dark outside now, but the large front windows had no blinds or curtains to cover them. Whatever window covering had existed had been damaged beyond repair and removed long before Mike's time. The windows themselves had been replaced as regularly as they had been smashed by angry protesters over the years, but they seemed to have a permanent haze on them that obscured any chance of sunlight or streetlights shining through.

This shabby glass box that was the entrance to the oldest station in the city was also where bereaved family members came to collect the belongings of their next-of-kin who had died alone, perhaps in some hole somewhere, or in a midnight car crash fuelled by alcohol, speed, or rage. It was where walk-in victims of assaults and robberies sat with blood still running down their faces, waiting to speak with investigators. It was where young kids were passed between parents whose relationship had shifted from soulmates to names on restraining orders. And it was where witnesses like the diminutive Mr. and Mrs. Majewski arrived to speak to detectives like Mike, volunteering their time and energy to help solve a crime in their community.

Since there was nowhere for them to sit, Mike hustled the couple into the musty basement tof the station's outdated interview room. It was the only part of the basement that did not flood every time there was even a moderate rainfall. The rooms originally dedicated to Major Crime Unit, disclosure storage, and Wellness were not as fortunate, however, and consequently, the MCU guys periodically relocated, bankers' boxes were kept in the D office, and Wellness was left, for the most part, under water.

Mike motioned to both the husband and wife to sit down on one of the four metal chairs around a table in the middle of the room. There was a blue couch along the far wall, but it was reserved for the so-called soft interviews—typically, incidents involving sex and/or children. Ron, meanwhile, fiddled with the camera on a tripod that was facing the table before placing his tape recorder in front of the Majewskis.

"Really?" Mike questioned, eying the antiquated device.

"Video is unpredictable," Ron stated. "I haven't lost an audio interview yet."

Mike returned his attention to the Majewskis. "Can I get you a cup of coffee or a glass of water?" he offered.

"I am sorry." Mr. Majewski began. "My English is not so good, and my wife is worse."

The man helped his wife move her chair in towards the table before settling in himself. They both had their arms out in front of them, staring expectantly at Mike and then Ron, who had returned to fidgeting with the camera.

"Something to drink?" Mike said, making a drinking motion with his hand.

"No. We are fine."

"So," Ron sat down, glancing between the husband and wife, and then at the camera behind him, "you know you're both under oath and that this interview is being videotaped?"

"I'm sorry?" the little man looked over at Mike. His wife looked down at her hands.

"Thank you for coming in, Mr. and Mrs. Majewski. My partner here is just letting you know that you cannot lie and that we're taping the interview," Mike said, holding one hand in front of his face to mimic a lens while the other hand rotated around his ear like an old-time movie camera.

"We should have an interpreter," Ron suggested.

"Video. Yes. I understand. Okay." The man's face brightened.

"And you can't lie," Mike repeated, this time much more sternly, as he glanced at his partner.

"I think there is a language barrier here," Ron continued. "We should have an interpreter."

"No lying!" the man repeated. "You, too," he said, patting his wife on the hands, his stubby fingers fumbling on the enormous costume ring she was wearing on her left ring finger, a playfully stern look on his face. Her eyes bulged as she looked at him, lips pursed. He withdrew his hand, smiling timidly at Mike.

"Great," Mike smiled as much at the Majewskis as at Ron. "Let's get started."

Ron let out a heavy sigh.

After writing down their names, getting their dates of birth, and other formalities, Mike began. Open-ended interview. Let them speak.

"So you told my partner here, Detective Roberts, that you have some information that might be able to help us. Is that correct?"

"Yes, yes. I want to tell you about man with one leg. I know him. He is tenant. He live in house me and my wife rent. Mostly students, but this guy, he come and he want to rent so we rent. He pay on time, every month. Cash. No problems. No drink, no drugs, no smoke. Just play cards with friends."

"What is this man's name, your tenant with one leg?" Mike asked, looking at both the husband and wife.

"I know him as Sergei. My wife, Yolanda, say others who rent call him Sam."

The little man and both detectives looked over at the woman. She was nodding emphatically, her jowls taking on a life of their own.

"Did he get any mail there?"

The little man looked at his wife, who looked blankly back at him.

"Here we go," Ron muttered knowingly as he jotted down what little conversation was occurring on the steno pad in front of him.

"Mail. You know, letters? Bills?" Mike grabbed the pad of paper from Ron, dramatically flipping the pages.

"Ah, bills," the little man laughed and nodded. "No. No bills. I never see anything, just cash on first day of month."

"Did he have any friends?" Mike passed the pad back to Ron, who looked incredulously at him. Mike just shrugged and Ron resumed his scribing.

"No friends. Just men who come over to play cards. Always playing cards. I tell him no gambling. He say no gambling, but these men, I know them. They gamble."

"How do you know?"

"Sometimes, when I go by house—"

"You mean you don't live there?" Ron interrupted.

"No," the man abruptly pushed his body back from the table as if it held an electrical charge. "We have our house outside of city. These three houses, we rent out. Just rooms. She cleans once a week. I keep fixed up and collect rent."

Mike and Ron looked at each other, trying to conceal their surprise from the camera.

"Okay, so you go over to the house, and what happens?" Mike continued.

"I see Sergei. He looks worried. He tells me, 'Jorge, I owe lots of money.' He always owes lots of money, but he says not to worry. He will have rent. And he always does."

"When was this?"

"Lots of times. He always owes money. And then he don't."

"What do you mean 'then he *doesn't*'?" Ron asked, intentionally emphasizing the last word.

"He leave twenty dollars for Yolanda when she come to clean. She tells him she no take, but he says it is good money, a tip for hard-working lady. He always good with my wife."

There was a pause. The little man looked over at his wife, who smiled warmly back. Apparently, all had been forgiven.

"So no hanky-panky?" Ron asked, looking at the woman.

"Hanky?" she looked at Ron, uttering the first word she had spoken since the interview began.

"Panky. You know," Ron rubbed his chest with his left hand, pen on paper with his right. "Touching you."

"Ack!" Mrs. Majewski's voice became high-pitched as a string of Polish words erupted, her body shuddering as she pushed herself away from the table.

There was another pause, but only in the interview. A heated exchange in Polish, which neither Mike nor Ron could understand, erupted between Mr. and Mrs. Majewski. Then another pause.

"*We* will not speak to your friend again," Mr. Majewski spat at Mike, his face turning a shade of purple, then simmering down to a heated red. "*We* are hard-working. *We* come to this country, and *we* do work no one else want. My wife scrub *your* shit out of toilet in *your* country. My wife raise four boys here. *All* my boys go to university. *All* my boys have jobs now. Good jobs. Because of my wife. My wife, she is not," he hissed, "a *whore*."

"I'm sorry," Mike said, nodding like a bobble-head on the dash of a car, his hands raised defensively in front of himself. *Fucking Roberts. He should know better. No wonder no one wants to work with him. Fucking idiot.* "My friend is sorry. He was worried for Mrs. Majewski. We don't know what kind of a man this Sergei is. We want to make sure your wife is safe."

Ron looked at his partner, but knew better than to contradict him, especially on camera.

Mr. Majewksi spoke to his wife in Polish under his breath. She nodded, smiled warmly at Mike, then gave Ron an angry scowl.

"Now," Mike continued, giving his partner an equally angry side-glance, "What about this Sergei or Sam character. He always owed money?"

"Always," Mrs. Majewski piped up. "He tell me he not lucky in love *or* in cards."

"Do you know who he played with?"

"I do not know his friends," Mr. Majewski said flatly. "My wife and I are *not* like those people."

"But he was a nice man?" Mike suggested, hoping to remind them of how much they liked the now-deceased to bring them back onside.

"Yes," the old man agreed, "but he have bad friends."

Ron stopped scribbling. He reached around and clicked off the camera behind him, then looked at Mike.

"May I speak to you outside for a moment, Detective?"

Puzzled, Mike looked over at his partner.

"Now?" The metal chair scraped loudly on the floor as Ron stood up.

"Excuse us a moment," Mike said as he followed Ron out of the room, gently closing the door behind him.

"I've seen these kinds of people before. Probably gypsies. Probably as dirty as their one-legged tenant, just different. If you're buying this crap—"

"You fucking called me out of an interview to tell me this?" *In like the vacuum. Out like the wind.*

"If you're buying this crap," Ron repeated, "go ahead, but it sounds like a lot of hooey to me."

"You called me out—"

"And I want an interpreter."

"Do not *ever* call me out of an interview again unless you are fucking dying or the building is on fire. Got it?"

Mike swung open the door, a smile fixed to his face. Mr. and Mrs. Majewski jumped in their seats.

"My apologies. Camera on, partner?"

Ron snapped the toggle up and slumped down into his chair. "It was never like this in Traffic," he muttered balefully.

"You were saying something about friends. What friends?" Mike continued with the interview, ignoring Ron and hoping the mic didn't pick up his comment. *In like the vacuum. Out like the wind.*

"Mostly guy he call Cockeye."

"Do you know him by any other name?"

"No," Mr. Majewski replied definitely.

"Do you know *why* they call him Cockeye?" *Guys like this are a gold mine,* Mike thought. *Just gotta keep fucking Traffic Man Ron away from him.*

"His eyes," the little man began, shaking his head spastically while he wiggled his stubby fingers in front of his face, "they go like this."

"For the record," Mike looked down at Ron's antiquated tape recorder and then back to the Majewskis, "his eyes don't look straight ahead?"

"No. They look everywhere else," the little man nodded heartily.

"All the time?" Ron pressed in moderate disbelief, trying hard not to roll his own eyes.

Of course. Our victim has one leg. Our suspect can't see straight. Our star witness here looks like a garden gnome. Why am I not surprised? Mike thought.

"Enough of the time," the little man huffed, sensing that Ron was mocking him.

"So you have seen him?" Mike asked, trying to maintain control of the interview.

"*I* have seen him," Mrs. Majewski jumped in. "Lots of times. Since three times ago, every time."

"What do you mean, Mrs. Majewski: 'since three times ago'?" Mike was pretty sure he knew what she was talking about, but a judge wouldn't give a shit about what Mike *thought* the witness meant.

Mr. Majewski looked over at Mrs. Majewski, biting the left side of his lower lip. She said something to him in hushed Polish.

"In English, please?" Ron looked back at the camera, and then to the Majewskis. "For the video?"

"She say Cockeye there lots of times before when she there to clean, but he been there now every time for past three weeks," Mr. Majewski enunciated clearly, staring right at the camera.

"Is that what she says?" Ron huffed, looking at the little man. "Since you're now the interpreter, then let me ask this: Would she recognize him again?

The old woman gave Ron a nasty scowl.

"Mrs. Majewski," Mike offered softly, "would you know Cockeye if you saw him again?"

The woman suddenly sat upright, her eyes beginning to bulge, and she began violently shaking her head 'no'. The colour disappeared from her cheeks, further emphasizing the liberal application of blush she had applied to her pale skin. She again said something under her breath to her husband.

"What is it, Mrs. Majewski?" Mike finally asked.

"My wife is afraid of this man. She said she thinks he killed Sergei."

"You are afraid of him, Mrs. Majewski? Why is that?" Mike asked.

The couple spoke rapidly to each other in Polish.

"I really think we should have an interpreter in for this," Ron finally said. He stood up, getting ready to shut the camera down again.

"No! No interpreter!" the woman almost shrieked, a far contrast to her quiet demeanour when they first began the interview.

"Mrs. Majewski, what is it you would like to say?" Mike looked directly at her while motioning with his right hand for Ron to sit down.

"I hear them fight. A lot. I hear Sergei crying to man. I cannot understand what he say, but I hear him. And I see man—" The woman was becoming increasingly agitated and her hands gesturing wildly.

"You saw Cockeye?" Mike interjected.

"Yes. Cockeye, he slam door…" The woman mimicked the motion of a hand slamming a door, almost taking her husband's ear off in the process, "…and walk out as I am cleaning hallway outside. He look at me and he scare me with his eyes. I call Jorge to come get me. Sergei open door when he hear me on phone. He has been crying…"

"How do you know Sergei has been crying?" Mike needed it all laid out for any future court disclosure. Gone were the days of a couple of lines scratched in a memo book. It was all about the video now.

Mrs. Majewski sat back in her chair, frowning. The look on her face told Mike she was probably wondering why she had to explain what was so obvious in her mind.

"His eyes, they are red and swollen," she slowly began. "His face is wet. He is scared, not sad. He ask me if I am okay. He offer me to come into his room. I don't go. I don't feel safe. I wait out front for my husband."

"And when was that?"

The woman looked over at her husband.

"What day?" Mike gently repeated.

"Not this morning. Two morning ago," the woman said, pointing first in front of her, then beside her.

"Like when?" Mike said, scrambling for the calendar in his cell phone and holding it out to her.

"Here," Mrs. Majewski said, pointing to the previous day.

Mike held the cell phone to the video camera over his shoulder to show where the woman had pointed.

"So not today, but yesterday? Wednesday?" Mike confirmed, glancing quickly over at Ron, who was writing as the woman spoke.

"Yes. Wed-nes-day," Mrs. Majewski repeated, pronouncing each syllable carefully. "Before lunch. I hear them as I clean other rooms, but Cockeye leave early in morning."

"Have you been to the house today?" Mike asked the woman.

"We no clean today, and it not end of month for rent," Mr. Majewski answered for her.

"So the only people who have been in the house since yesterday are the tenants?"

The little man looked quizzically at Mike, then over to his wife, who looked as confused as he did, and then back again at Mike.

"No one but the people who live there have been in the house since you picked your wife up yesterday," Mike tried to clarify.

"No one." The little man nodded his head in approval.

"And how would you know?" Ron sighed, a slightly sarcastic edge to his voice. "What about any friends or visitors?"

Mike's eyes narrowed. The question was bang on, but the tone was definitely off-putting.

"They have no friends," the little man said flatly.

"So none of your tenants have friends? Except, of course, for this Cock-eye fellow?" Ron shot back.

"I clean rooms. I know what goes on in those rooms. They have no friends," the wife replied, her chin extended almost pugnaciously.

"Great. Okay, while the investigation is ongoing, would you mind staying away from that room until we tell you?" Mike broke in, trying again to reclaim his interview.

The couple looked at each other.

"We need to do some checking, but if you're right, we're going to need to search the house," Mike continued. Both Majewskis stared blankly across at him.

"If our dead guy and your tenant are the same person," Mike began, speaking very slowly and clearly, "then we are going to have to go into his room and have a look around."

Both old people nodded, although Mike wasn't sure whether the nod meant they understood or they were giving him permission to search.

"We may need to take some things from the room, in which case we'll need to get a warrant," he went on.

"You cannot take house!" The little man's eyes were starting to bug out of his head.

"No, no. We aren't going to take your house. We just want to look inside," Mike calmly replied.

"I clean first," the little woman said.

"No! Leave it! That's why I don't want you going into the house. I want you to leave it the way it was yesterday afternoon." Despite his best efforts to speak calmly, Mike found that he was practically shouting at these people.

The two looked at each other, then nodded to one another.

"You are going to do search warrant, like on TV!" the old man said. The old woman was beaming.

"Yes. Search warrant. Like on TV." Mike sighed heavily, looking over at Ron, who was now rolling his eyes.

"Okay. I know search warrant. We stay out. You need keys?"

"That would be great," Mike said.

"Here. I give you keys. No kick in doors." The little man reached into the pocket of his overalls and pulled out a ring of keys. "This one for front door. This for Sergei's room. These for all other rooms. You want I kick tenants out?"

"No. I don't think that will be neces—"

"Might not hurt," Ron interjected.

"How about we send a police car to the house and ask the tenants to stay away from the area around Sergei's room?" Mike suggested to the couple and his partner.

"Suit yourself. I'd just as soon have everyone leave. Makes it easier if there's DNA all over the place," Ron said.

"And if they have nowhere to go?" Mike turned to him.

"Not my problem."

"Let's see if we can accommodate them. Right now, we don't have enough for a search warrant anyway. I think this will be more of a 'check address' kind of call."

Ron glanced over his shoulder at the TV screen. "Still running," he reminded Mike.

"Do you have any concern for your tenant, Sergei?" Mike asked the couple, not missing a beat, but glad of the prompt.

"Yes, I have concern! That is why we are here!" the man said, looking at both Mike and Ron as if they were idiots.

"So you would like us to go over there to see if he's okay, then?"

"Yes. That is why I give you keys. Go. Go now."

"Okay. That's great. We'll let you know how it goes," Mike said, preparing to wind down the interview.

The couple looked at each other.

"We will phone you after." Mike motioned as if he were dialling an old dial phone with one hand, holding his other hand up to his face like a receiver. The couple smiled and nodded.

"With an interpreter," Mike added, looking over at Ron, who was reaching over to turn off the video camera.

Chapter Thirteen

Thursday, August 23, 2018 - 11:45 p.m.

"What the fuck, Ron?" Detective Dave Rumble exclaimed as he hustled past the detective's desk towards his own in the quadrant behind Mike, holding a cardboard tray with two coffees in one hand and a briefcase in the other. "You trying to win the award for the most overtime by a single D, or what?"

"Homicide," Ron sniffed, his index fingers feverishly tapping away on the keyboard in front of him. "Amanda Black is lead on this one."

"Really? Wow, I remember her from back in the Morality days. Wonder who she blew to get into Homicide. Need any help?" Dave set the tray down on his desk, then did a quick scan of the surfaces beside him for food, crack cocaine, or any of the other detritus the investigators who worked in this office were accustomed to finding before tossing his trench coat down beside him.

"No, thanks. I've got my new partner over here, and I think we're good," Ron replied, motioning to Mike with his chin, his fingers not missing a beat, his eyes never moving from the computer screen in front of him.

"Sorry for your luck, Mike." Dave glanced over at Mike before logging himself into his own computer. His boyish face and youthful energy were a marked contrast to Ron's deepening wrinkles and stiffening stride, even though the two detectives were only a couple of years apart in age. "Heard you were being transferred over but didn't know when. Hope you know what you're getting yourself into! What happened to your old partner, Ron? Wear him out?"

"Parental leave," Ron answered, flipping back a page on his steno pad as he scanned the screen in front of him. "Where's your other half?"

"At the front talking to Staff," Dave answered, popping one of the coffees out of the tray. "If I knew you were working tonight, Mike, I would have brought you one. I guess you know your partner doesn't drink coffee."

"Not true," Ron corrected, his two fingers resuming their attack on the keyboard. "Just not this late at night. Unless I'm going to get caught up in some overtime. Which I will be."

Mike caught Ron glancing over Mike's shoulder at Dave, who was carefully snapping the lid off his coffee and inhaling its aroma with appreciation.

"One of the simple pleasures of police work," Mike said.

"Watch out, Mike. He's a slave driver. You actually did wear out your last partner, didn't you, Ron?" Dave playfully suggested.

"Also not true." Ron stopped typing for a moment, taking the bait. "I told you already. He went on *parental leave*."

"Ryan's a bit old for that, isn't he?"

"One would think," Ron gave in to the other detective's insistence on making conversation. "Despite my best attempts to wear him out, as you so coyly put it, he apparently had enough energy for *that*, didn't he?"

"For what?" Julia Vendramini made her entrance into the office with a grace and aplomb very seldom seen in a police station, let alone among its denizens.

"*Fucking*," Dave said cheerfully, taking great pleasure in trying to shock his partner, even thought he knew that she was as familiar, if not more so, with vulgarity as he was.

"Mikey!" Julia exclaimed, arms outstretched, ignoring Dave as she rushed over to her old JPTF colleague.

Mike quickly jumped up in anticipation of the prodigious embrace and Nonna-like kisses on both cheeks that he had come to expect from her.

"Do you two need a room, or—?" Dave inquired, moderately embarrassed by this public display of affection.

"You know Mikey and I go back. I cannot tell you how many times this man has made me laugh when I wanted to cry," Julia kissed Mike again before wiping away the red marks her lipstick had left on his cheeks. "How is Max? He must be…what? Fourteen or fifteen by now? Still living with you, or did *she* come back? How is your mother? Still doing Sunday dinners? Have you been yet, Ron? God, that was the best corned beef—it *was* corned beef, wasn't it—and cabbage that I've ever had. Those were the days, weren't they, Mikey?"

"Max is seventeen now," Mike began. "He's good. And still with me. And Mom is still doing dinners on Sunday. You?"

"Same old, same old. Just me, Keith, and the dogs. No kids. Not in God's plan, I guess." Julia sighed, her left hand caressing the gold cross that she always wore around her neck as she hung the black overcoat she had been holding on the coatrack hook beside Mike's. "But life is good. Here," she reached out towards Dave, wiggling her fingers at him, "give me your coat. You don't want to leave it there. You never know what's been on that table. Disgusting. Grab me some wipes while you're at it. You still play the piano, Mikey? Ron, did you know he plays the piano? Like Mozart practically. Last time I heard you play—"

"No. I don't play any more," Mike said. "Not since—"

"Excuse me, partner?" Ron interrupted. "Sorry to cut in, but do you have the time our interview with the Majewskis ended? Just finishing up this supp—"

"Oh, I am so sorry, Mikey. I thought… Never mind. We'll talk later. I see you're busy." Julia looked past Mike over at Ron, the only D in the station she would have had to admit to disliking if it had been in her nature to dislike anyone. Then she smiled back at Mike. "God, it's good to see you again, Mikey. I now have a reason to want to come in to work every day."

"I don't know what you've got, buddy, but she never says that to me, and I'm her fucking partner," Dave groused. The monitor on the screen lit up his face as he returned to his work and scrolled through an endless list of his outstanding cases, stopping at a Break & Enter occurrence with a red exclamation mark beside it indicating that it required immediate action.

"This man saved my life more times than I can remember," Julia replied, putting her oversized purse in the bottom drawer of the desk across from her partner's before leaning back and running both of her hands through her long hair. "Good," she said to no one in particular, picking a strand of hair from her black turtleneck and examining it. "It's one of the grey ones. Not that they're not all grey under this dye job. Okay, Mikey, what do we have going on here?"

"Thanks, Julia, but I think it was *you* who saved my life," Mike softly replied.

The phone on his desk rang.

A woman's voice slurred a few lines of "Happy Birthday," then, "Still chasin' bad guys, Detective?"

"How are you, Brenda?"

"A little drunk right now," the caller said, giving a self-deprecating chuckle, "but otherwise good. You?"

"I'm doing well. Thanks for asking." Mike couldn't recall Brenda ever having called and not being 'a little drunk.' Who could blame her? Certainly not him.

"Still nothing?"

"Still nothing. I'm sorry."

"I know, Detective O'Shea. We're all sorry."

The hallway outside the office was floodinged with noisy uniformed officers heading out to the back parking lot in preparation for their midnight shift.

"Guys? Please?" Julia called out, her voice cutting through the low, exclusively male hum that was echoing off the hallway walls. "We're trying to work in here."

A few comments about the job being fucked and that a trained squirrel could manage this shitshow better than their sergeant were the last of it before the noise subsided. Both Dave and Ron gave Julia a nod of thanks.

"Please, Lord, give me the strength that I need to face today," Julia whispered, eyes closed, head bowed, right hand grasping her cross. "I don't have to worry about tomorrow. If You just give me the strength that I need today, that is all I need. You know the rest. Amen."

"If this so-called God of yours exists, tell Him to pull up His socks. He's slacking," Ron huffed, annoyed at his relief's pre-shift ritual.

"Oh, and God?" Julia added, bowing her head as she pulled her coffee from the tray. "Be kind to Ron. Even if he isn't kind to anyone else. I'm sure he tries in his own special way. Amen."

She lifted the plastic top off and savoured the smell before taking what would be, as usual, the only sip of hot coffee she would have time for during her shift.

* * *

Mike was only half-listening to Brenda. In fact, he could hardly hear her voice over the racket that had been just outside the doorway prior to Julia's intervention, not that he couldn't have practically scripted this conversation by heart. The calls during the first five years or so had been a little more hopeful. Now they were just annual calls.

"I think about my baby every day, you know?" Brenda's voice broke as she began to whimper.

"So do I." And he did.

Julia turned her head slightly, her ear closer to Mike. Even though it had been years since that night, and it could have been anyone on the other end of the line now, she had a good idea of who the caller was. While it wasn't quite the same, she had a few callers like that herself. Everyone who had been in the Juvenile Prostitution Task Force did: usually a mother or sister of one of the girls who didn't make it out. Some called on an anniversary of something, while others just called when they were lonely. Or drunk. Julia had one mother whom she met every December 15th in a little bistro around the corner from where her daughter was killed. That one was easier, if there was even such a thing as easy in these cases. They had caught the guy who killed her little girl. And the girl was dead. Closure, or so they said. By the slump in Mike's shoulders, Julia figured that his caller hadn't been so lucky.

"She's twenty-seven years old today, you know?" Brenda's voice broke as she struggled to continue. "If she's still alive."

"I know." Mike remembered her birthday. And the last time he saw her as Malcom was plucking her out of the group of frightened girls to be his hostage, leaving them—including Mike and Ron—to die in the burning factory. Chelsea Hendricks was fourteen then. Had been on the stroll ever since she was twelve. Because there was a demand for sex with twelve-year-olds.

The muscles in his neck tightened.

"Thanks for remembering. So," Brenda took a deep breath, "tell me about your life, Detective O'Shea. You get married again? And your boy?"

"Yeah," he sighed. They weren't supposed to talk about their personal lives. It had been one of the few explicit rules of the JPTF, but it was impossible not to give something back to these mothers who had lost everything. "And my son is doing well, thanks for asking."

"I'm so sorry for calling…." She began to cry again.

"No. It's okay. I'm glad you did. That you do," Mike said, vividly recalling that little girl standing on the corner, caught up in a grown-up world, becoming increasingly unrecognizable as the addictions consumed her child's body and undeveloped brain. "It's been thirteen years now, hasn't it?"

Julia rose from her chair, her eyes welling up as she looked at Mike. She knew whom he was talking to. She wanted to hug him and remind him that he had done everything he could—that they all had—but things just didn't work out. That's what he had always told her when a case went south.

But this wasn't just a case, though. And it wasn't just about the girl.

"Yeah. Hard to believe, eh?" Brenda said, fighting back her tears. "I still remember that night you came to our door, you and that girl cop. Some days—most days—it feels like it was yesterday. You were so handsome back then. Are you still handsome, Detective O'Shea?"

"Depends who you ask," Mike glanced around the room, noticing Julia moving from behind her desk, walking towards him. He waved her back, embarrassed. This wasn't the old JPTF office. No hugging here.

"Still funny, too." He could hear the woman on the other end of the line pausing to take a long sip of whatever the hell her anesthetic- of- choice was tonight. "No leads on where my baby is?"

"No leads." *Not a fucking break in thirteen years.*

"She was a good girl, you know?" Mike was sure the glass Brenda was drinking from was emptying quickly now.

"I know." *They all were good girls...once. Fuck.*

"Just got in with the wrong crowd. That happens, right? I mean, it's not like her father and I didn't love her. Did you know we broke up, me and Jeff?"

Gin, Mike recalled. Brenda always drank gin. He could hear the cap on the bottle being unscrewed as she prepared to pour herself another ounce. Or two. Or three.

"Yeah, I remember you telling me that." Mike looked out into the hallway just outside the D office, noticing the uniforms still filtering towards the back door that would lead them into the night as the parading sergeant, clipboard in hand, passed out keys for the cars.

"Such a shame, you know? Good man, Jeff. It's just… well, after Chelsea, it was too hard, you know? The drinking didn't help, mind you. Happens a lot, apparently. The counsellor that we went to—thanks for setting all that up for us, by the way—said that having a child go missing like that is worse than a death. Funny thing to say, eh? Anyway, said it was one of the hardest things on a marriage. I guess he was right."

"I guess."

"Jeff was the only one strong enough to sober up." Mike heard Brenda take a gulp of gin before returning to her usual-suspect theory. "I still think it was that guy she met at the mall. You checked him out, right?"

"Yes. Many times." If he had been talking to anyone but Brenda, Mike would have lost his patience by now. But he wasn't. It was Brenda, and he had all the time in the world for her. It was the least he could do.

"And it wasn't him?"

"No," Mike replied gently, knowing that he was breaking her heart all over again. "It wasn't him."

"I mean, maybe not *him* him, but somebody he knew? Before that, she was such a good girl: no drugs, no boys, no sex. And then she met him. Jeff said

I overreacted, that I pushed her to him. The counsellor said blaming didn't help, but I know Jeff blamed—no, still blames me. If anyone's to blame, it's Jeff. He didn't say anything when he had the chance."

"I'm sorry."

"It's not your fault, Detective O'Shea. None of it—"

"Sure." Mike watched the parading sergeant rubbing out something on his clipboard with the eraser on his pencil as he detailed the last of his officers.

"I know the papers were pretty hard on you. About your partner getting shot like that. And you not even pulling your gun, but I know you would have—"

"Yeah."

"When the two of you came to the door that first time and told me and Jeff that you knew where Chelsea was and that she was a hooker, I wanted to kill both of you, you know?" Mike heard the metal cap working its way off the bottle again, then the gin gurgling into the waiting glass. "I honestly wanted to gouge your eyes out. Like it was your fault. And then, after everything, when you came to our door the last time, just you by yourself, I kind of felt like it was my fault, you know? That if I hadn't have wanted to kill you both, your partner would still be alive. How's that for fucked-up thinking, eh?"

Mike watched as the parading sergeant turned around to walk back up to the front of the station, all of his charges accounted for. Then he looked at Ron reading over what he had been so feverishly typing, his brow furrowing occasionally as, Mike assumed, he was reconsidering his choice of words. As if it mattered.

"It's okay, Brenda," he said, hearing the glass click on her teeth as she took a big gulp and began to cry.

"Is it really? Honestly? I hope so, because I feel anything but normal now. With Chelsea and Jeff both gone…" Mike heard her finishing off her drink. "I think he's remarried, you know. A girl from work, I think. Like it never happened. How do people do that, Detective? Just pick up and move on?"

"I dunno."

"You haven't moved on, have you?"

Mike took a deep breath.

"You okay?" Ron's voice brought Mike back to the present. Mike nodded yes at his partner.

"You were right there when your pretty- boy partner got shot, weren't you, Detective?" Brenda's words got slower as the alcohol held her closer and closer. "The papers said you were right behind him. That the guy tried to kill you, too, but the gun jammed. That you didn't even have a chance to get your gun out before—"

"Yeah. That's what they say."

"Must have been hard for you. For his mother. He had a mother, right?" Again the sound of the cap being twisted off the bottle.

"Yeah. He had a mother."

Mike had not known Sal's mother before the funeral. Before he held out the pillow with her son's forage cap on it. Before she took the cap, cried quietly for a moment, wiped her tears, and hugged him.

"You ever have nightmares about that?"

"No."

"Going for coffee. Anyone want one?" Dave jumped up from his seat, reaching for the coat that was no longer on the desk beside him before smiling over at Julia.

"You just came in with one!" Ron objected.

"You never know what's been on that desk, Dave," Julia cautioned, passing him his coat from the rack. "I once got home and found a mouse in my purse. Seriously. That's why I keep it in the drawer now. This place is disgusting."

"You're never going to find her, are you, Detective?" The voice in Mike's ear repeated what the voice in his head told him whenever it could. "My Chelsea?"

"We're doing our best, Brenda."

"But no one is actually out there looking any more, are they?"

"Not from the JPTF, no, but—"

"This is the only chance I'll have tonight," Dave hollered by way of an explanation as he hustled out the door. "Last call!"

"Shit, I'm out of fucking gin!" Brenda screamed to no one in particular, and then without missing a beat, continued talking to Mike, her voice much softer. "*You're* still looking, though, aren't you?"

"I look every day."

"I have to hang up now, Detective," she concluded abruptly, as she did every year when the booze ran out. "Same time next year?"

"Same time next year."

"Unless you find her?"

"Unless I find her."

"Goodnight, Detective." Her voice broke as she began to weep.

"Goodnight, Brenda."

"Oh, and Detective?"

"Yes?"

"I include you in my prayers every night."

"Thank you, Brenda. If I prayed, I would do the same for you. Goodnight."

Chapter Fourteen

Friday, August 24, 2018 - 2:30 a.m.

"Are you going to join us for our debrief or do you need an invitation?" Amanda Black inquired, seeing Ron sitting at his desk as she poked her head into the D office.

"Sorry. I didn't realize that you were here," Ron replied, looking over his shoulder as he began to get up.

"Where the hell else would I be, Sunshine?" Amanda's words lingered behind her as she made her way down the dimly lit hall towards the inspector's office. Sadly, this was the only half-decent place in the building that she could find to use, outside of the unit commander's office.

Mike looked at Amanda over his computer monitor, his fingers frozen on the keyboard.

"I guess we'd better go," Ron said, gathering his suit jacket off the back of his chair.

"Formal event?" Mike stood up, pushing his shoulders back to stretch his back.

"Jacket not required, but highly recommended." Ron adjusted the cuffs of his sleeves and straightened his tie before reaching for his steno pad.

"Gotcha." Mike sighed, grabbing his own jacket and shrugging into it as he followed after Ron.

* * *

"Thank you all for being here," Amanda began, looking around at the mix of officers in uniforms, suits, and old clothes as the two latecomers entered. "I'm not going to go around the room having us all introduce ourselves because, bluntly put, I'm exhausted, I really don't care what your name is, and I want to get this investigation going. Instead, when we go around, please tell me how you fit into my case and what you know."

And so began a typical Amanda Black debriefing. Efficient. Effective. Informative. Not warm. Not fuzzy. No hugs here.

"I'll start," a huge heavy-set man sitting beside Amanda began. "Detective Hank Moreaux, Homicide. I'm Detective Sergeant Black's partner. At this point, we have positively identified the deceased as one Sergei 'Sam' Kuzminov. He was fifty-three years of age and resided in Room 8 at 147 Loxitor Avenue, which is a rooming house of sorts. He was unemployed and was receiving a monthly disability cheque from the government that was directly deposited into his bank account. He has no known next-of-kin."

"Well, at least we know our witnesses are solid," Mike whispered, leaning over to Ron.

"Pardon?" Ron asked a bit louder than Mike thought necessary.

"Excuse me?" the huge man said, looking around the room at everyone but Ron.

"Sorry," Ron replied. As well as having a slight hearing loss, Ron occasionally was unaware of how loud he was speaking.

"Yes. Just to advise, during my briefings, all questions and comments are to be held until the end." Unlike her subordinate, Amanda did look directly at Ron. "Carry on, Hank."

"Right." Hank paused for a moment. "Mr. Kuzminov came to this country on his own in 1998 as a refugee claimant. Clearly, his claim was accepted—"

"Of course, it was," Ron rolled his eyes.

"And he has remained here ever since," Hank snapped. "At the time of his arrival, he was listed as a construction general labourer. He had his left leg amputated in 2005 as a result of a work-related accident, which resulted in a hefty insurance claim being awarded to him in its entirety, but that was subsequently spent within the year. By the end of 2006, he qualified and began receiving government assistance."

"Of course, he did," Ron whispered to Mike and inadvertently to the rest of the room.

"As mentioned earlier," Detective Moreaux fired a look for support over to his superior, who was busy studying the ragtag team of investigators that she had been given, "Mr. Kuzminov has no known relatives in this country, and Immigration has indicated that they are unable to locate any next-of-kin from their files. We are in the process of locating friends or anyone who can provide us with a more fulsome understanding of who the deceased was."

"Might want to try the landlords," Ron commented, this time intentionally out loud.

Moreaux sighed dramatically, dropping his chin to his chest to accentuate his exasperation as the room erupted in guffaws.

"Detective Roberts, do you have something that cannot wait until we get to you," Amanda let the iciness in her voice sober the atmosphere before continuing, "or is what you have to bring to the table so important that it merits our immediate attention?"

"I'm just saying," Ron responded, "that I suspect the landlords would be able to provide your man with an overview of the deceased in terms of his daily life."

"Hank, make a note of that," Amanda directed her partner. "In the meantime, Ron, try to keep your thoughts until the end. We have a lot of ground to cover."

"Sorry, just sharing."

"Save it," Amanda shot Ron a plastic smile and then nodded to Detective Moreaux to continue.

"She was much nicer when she was in Morality," Mike muttered as he shifted uncomfortably in his chair.

"I don't get paid to be nice in Homicide, Detective. I get paid to solve murders here. Anything else?"

"That's all I've got, Amanda," Hank replied, forgoing her formal title, a common practice by officers when it involved women who outranked them. "I'll check out the landlords, like the officer suggested, once we're done."

"You might want to take along an interpreter," Ron offered.

"After the briefing, gentlemen?" Amanda suggested, eyebrows raised, glancing over at an officer who looked more homeless man than cop. "Next."

"Detective Constable Bloom. Major Crime. Been doing a work-up on some possible suspects. We got a guy in the mix that kinda looks good. Real name is Mark Johnstone. Has the fucking weirdest eyes…" tThe officer glanced quickly over at the detective sergeant. "Sorry there, Amanda. Forgot you were in the room—"

"I dunno, boys," Amanda looked around the room with a half-smile, "It's my case, my briefing, I'm the only woman in the room, and he forgets I'm here. Does that disturb anyone but me?"

An uncomfortable chuckle ran around the office before Amanda continued. "For future reference, never forget that I'm here, but don't apologize for using foul language, either. I've pretty much heard it all during my rookie years when I resided in the glamorous world of Morality as a trixie looking for a couple of bucks for blowjobs. Maybe some of you are too young to remember me when I was here as a D. Enhanced my linguistic education a bit further. All that is to say, I've heard a few things in my time. Don't think you can shock me, but don't go out of your way to try, either. Carry on."

"This guy, Mark Johnstone," the officer continued, looking sheepishly at Amanda, "is known as Cockeye because of the googly-eye thing he has going on. He's into a little bit of everything. Mostly street robberies and shit like that. We've had him up on some pretty vicious assault charges in the past. Nothing sticks. Victims are always fucking criminals themselves. Never show up in court. Anyway, he's been investigated in the area where the one-legged guy lived as recently as two weeks ago for checking door handles at 3 a.m. We also got a partial plate from a couple of witnesses and are doing a batch run now to track down the suspect vehicle. That should be finished within the hour, and then we can do some obs on a few places."

"Excellent, Detective Constable. Thank you for that. First officer on scene?"

"I am Constable Preston McAfee," the young uniformed officer said as he hastily stood up. "I was the first officer on scene."

There was a pause.

"Wonderful. And what do you have to tell us, Constable?" Amanda prompted.

"Nothing much," McAfee began, his voice quivering until he found his stride. "Just that a couple found the body and came to the station for an interview. I don't know what happened with that. I stood by until the coroner came and then sealed the bag and went to the morgue with the body."

McAfee was visibly sweating. Well into hour four of overtime, he, like Mike and likely most of the other officers in the room, had been in court all day prior to starting his shift the day before. The inadequate ventilation in the room, the weight of his uniform, and the stress of speaking in front of the guys he so desperately wanted to impress only exacerbated his fatigue and nervousness.

"That's great, Constable. I'm assuming you've done your report?"

"Yes, ma'am."

"Very good. Why don't you sign your book off and go on home. Unless there's anything else?" Amanda suggested in what appeared to be a flash of compassion.

"No, ma'am." The look of gratitude was palpable on the young officer's face as he sprang to the door. "Oh, uh, goodnight, everyone."

"Cute kid," Amanda mused aloud once McAfee had closed the door behind him. "Clearly gone as far as he's going to go in his career. First investigators on scene?"

"Detective Ron Roberts," Ron began, then looked at Mike. "Or do you want to take this?"

"Go ahead, Ron. I'm good," Mike replied, too tired to care.

"Ron Roberts, District Detective. My partner, Mike O'Shea, and I got the call at…" Ron fumbled through his steno pad.

"I don't think we need such detail, Detective. We're good. We all kind of know what time everything took place, I'm suggesting," Amanda interrupted.

Ron looked at her, motionless.

"Go ahead," Amanda prompted.

"Well, do you want my update or don't you? I mean, if you just want me to say that my partner and I were the first Ds on scene, then that's what I'll say. And if you just want me to say that my partner and I interviewed the landlords, which," he looked over at Detective Moreaux, "you've already heard me say, then I will. And if you want me to talk about our ensuring that the scene was properly maintained—"

"Yes," Amanda directed, nodding vigorously. "That's what I want you to say. And I don't need my senior investigator behaving like a sulky teenager. I just left my own sulky teenagers at home. I don't need one here, too, thank you very much."

"It was not like this in Traffic," Ron muttered under his breath.

"Road sergeant on scene?" Amanda looked directly at Joe Spackman and had to consciously not cringe.

A baby cop, a sulky teenager, and now this. Can it get any worse? she wondered.

"I think you all know who I am," Spackman began, chest puffing out as he glanced at Amanda. "Sergeant Joseph Spackman, District Road Sergeant."

A whistle came from someone in the room, followed by a soft chanting of "Jo-ey, Jo-ey."

"Gentlemen…?" Amanda called out.

"Yeah. C'mon, guys. Show the girl some respect," Spackman declared.

"Thank you for *that*," Amanda commented, sure that a wad of phlegm was rising in her throat as she rammed the thought of her and Joe Spackman together back into the realm of station gossip where it belonged. "Continue."

"I was the road boss when the call came over. I detailed officers to conduct a canvas for the area five blocks from the scene," Spackman shot a dirty look at Ron and then looked back at Amanda, "and had the officers submit their reports before signing off for shift."

And so it went for more than an hour, officer after officer detailing what he knew, how he knew it, and when he knew it. Amanda took some notes, but mostly listened. Anything that was said in this room would likely appear on paper somewhere down the line.

"Thank all of you, gentlemen," she stated after the final officer had provided the room with his information. "My team will take over the investigation from here."

"Homicide has stepped in and stepped on—" someone muttered.

"We will call on investigators from Major Crime," Amanda continued, ignoring the comment she had heard many times in the past, "to follow up on this Mark Johnstone character, and we might even get you to set up obs on him for a bit."

"Sure," a scruffy old-clothes officer said, absently pulling up his ratty T-shirt to scratch his hairy beer gut.

"I'm going to ask you, Detectives," Amanda shuddered in spite of herself before looking over at Ron and Mike, "to make yourselves available to assist with the search warrant if I don't have enough people, okay?"

"Do you mean write it or…?" Ron asked, beginning to mentally catalogue the hours of work of his own that would have to be set aside to accommodate her request.

"No. I've got my own people to write the warrant. I'm just going to need a couple of guys to run with it. You and Mike might be my go-tos."

Ron huffed loudly.

"I'll see to it that you don't have anything else going on, Detective," Amanda assured him, fully aware of the imposition a homicide could make on a district detective's workload.

"Well, at least she's not as arrogant as most of them," Ron muttered, again a little too loudly.

Amanda ignored his comment. "Stop," she called out, holding her hand to her ear. "Is that rain I hear? Please tell me that it is not rain."

"Afraid it will ruin your hair?" someone shouted, not even attempting to be discreet.

"No, asshole. Afraid it will ruin my scene." Amanda shot the remark into the room without missing a beat or caring where it landed. "Even faster than a defence lawyer working off a huge retainer. Who's my Forensics on this one?"

"Amy," Hank Moreaux advised, flipping through his steno pad.

"Good. She's good. She'll look after things. Thank God, it's not that knuckle-dragger I had on my last case. My husband could have taken better photos." Amanda sighed. "Any of you boys have any other comments to make about my hair? Or the way I dress? Or how I speak to people?" She looked over at Mike, who was half-asleep in the corner of the room. "Excuse me, Detective O'Shea?"

"Hmmm?" Mike looked up.

"Is the investigation of a murder too exhausting for you, or just too far beneath your interest level to keep you awake?"

"Sorry, boss. Court all day."

"Look around the room, Crumply-pants. I don't suppose anyone here was having a lie-in this morning. Or will be going home any time soon tonight. So," Amanda addressed the entire crew, "that's it for now. I'm going for an hour and a shower, and I'll see everyone afterwards."

The mixed bag of law enforcement personnel groaned as they began to shuffle out of the office, some stretching, some reaching for their smokes, all of them eager to do their part in putting this investigation to bed so that they could do the same, sooner than later.

"I've been up for a long time, too, and I wouldn't mind an hour and a shower on company time," Mike commented to Ron as they left the room.

"Be my guest," Amanda called after him. "If you think one shower and a little nap will sustain you for the next seventy-two hours that you'll be working on this before you sign off for shift, please feel free. I'll even fluff the towels and adjust your pillow for you."

"Are you always like this?" Mike muttered, too tired to care about his insubordination.

"I think we should get back to work," Ron advised, hustling Mike into their grimy office and away from Amanda Black. "You do not want to piss off *this* detective sergeant."

Chapter Fifteen

Friday, August 24, 2018 - 5:17 a.m.

The torrential rain that had begun around 4 a.m. was just beginning to slow down. Having been up since 9:30 the previous morning, first testifying in court and then investigating the murder of one-legged Sergei Kuzminov, Mike was beyond punchy. Even Ron, who had started his shift several hours later, had commented that the sight of the dayshift crew would most certainly be a welcome one.

"Christ," Mike yawned, "is this what it's going to be like with you? First shift together is supposed to be easy. A couple of Fail to Complies, get to know each other a bit, grab a coffee or two—"

"Heard you boys had a fucking busy night," Russ McLean, the old D who was their relief, interrupted. He was wearing a suit that looked even worse for wear than Mike's. "What are you doing here, Mikey? Callback, you money-grubber?"

"Nope. New platoon," Mike replied.

"Well," the old detective snorted, looking Ron up and down. "Good luck to you, I suppose. So what's up with this fucking homicide that the staff sergeant at the front was telling me about? Didn't even let me get in the goddamned door before he's on about some dead gimp in an alley or some other bullshit?"

"Don't know yet, Russ. Just doing what we can," Ron said, continuing to organize his papers. He knew himself well enough to avoid engaging at this late hour with a man whom he so disrespected. Even the marginal professional courtesy that Ron might normally muster was nonexistent.

"Well, if there's anything you need done…." McLean let the words dangle as he took off his weathered trench coat, fully revealing his disgrace of a suit, which included some of his dinner from the previous night, or maybe the night before that.

"Uh, you're not quite who we'd hoped for," Mike commented, having forgotten that McLean was going to relieve them.

"What the fuck is that supposed to mean? Come on, Mikey, you know how it is," McLean grumbled, plunking himself down at his desk, his head already buried in the day's newspaper, or more specifically, the daily pinup girl's picture. "I got a shitload of fucking shit to get through since my days off, but I'm here if you need me."

Mike and Ron continued with their work in silence for several minutes, their relief making no attempt to actually assist them

"All right, enough of this excitement. I'm going for a coffee. I'll be back in about half an hour." McLean sighed loudly as he grabbed his stained trench coat from the desk where he had tossed it and walked towards the door. "I've got today's paper here if you want it. I'll just leave it on the desk for you."

"We're kind of busy," Ron replied.

"Just offering. Today's chick is kind of cute. A bit on the chunky side, but she's got nice jugs." McLean looked again at the picture, leaving the paper open to the page as he left the office.

Mike rolled his eyes and tried not to shake his head. "Thank Christ I didn't end up with *that* fucking gem," he said as he watched McLean walk out the door. "There'd probably be two homicides on the go by now if I had been."

"I briefed the dayshift staff sergeant, who probably wanted him to actually help us."

"Sounds like he did by going for coffee and keeping his fingers out of it," Mike suggested.

"They say he was a good copper in his day, but he's a lazy, cantankerous pain in the butt now."

Mike's eyebrows shot up. But for the lazy part, many people would use exactly the same words to describe Ron Roberts.

"Lives above a bar, they say," Ron continued. "Likely lives *in* the bar and rents a room above it. In any event, more overtime for us. And besides, I have to be downtown today for ten."

"You got court, too?"

"No. Doctor's appointment. Nothing serious…" Ron said, letting the words hang.

Mike knew Ron wanted him to ask about it, but all he said was, "Okay." He didn't really want to play along.

"Yes. Well, you know," Ron sighed, "it's for my wife. Woman thing. Just routine checkup. With a specialist."

Mike definitely did not want to know any more.

"So it should only be for an hour or so," Ron continued. "Routine, they tell me."

"Great. Yeah. Good luck."

"I don't think it will make any difference in terms of my coming back for two this afternoon," Ron added, nervously shuffling papers that had already been sorted.

"Okay. I might be a bit late, too," Mike reminded him, ignoring his partner's unspoken need to talk about what Mike was sure was anything but a routine checkup. "Depends how long I'm in the box today."

"Oh, well, in that case," Ron stated, frowning at the confusion he'd created before he began re-sorting his papers, "I'll be sure to be in on time. It's just a routine checkup. With a specialist."

"Uh huh," Mike said absently. He knew nothing about Ron Roberts's personal life and was glad of it, wondering instead whether or not he would have time to drop in at home and grab something to eat between work and court later this morning.

"I've just got a few more things to sort out before I go," Ron offered, banging the bottom of his newly arranged stack of papers on the desk, resigning himself to the fact that Mike was not going to ask anything about his wife's appointment. "Why don't you head out now? Maybe grab a paper and have a coffee?"

"Maybe." Actually, no, Mike realized. He, too, had a few loose ends to tie up first. He could pick up a fried egg sandwich from the coffee shop across from the courthouse or maybe a Danish from the bakery just down the street here.

"Do you read much, Mike?" Ron asked, and then, without waiting for an answer, continued. "I can't say that I do. Marie, my wife, reads quite a bit, but I'm kind of a hands-on type of guy, which is good when you own a house. You have a house, don't you?"

"Yeah," Mike absently responded, considering what else had to be done before he left for the day.

"Downtown, isn't it? Can't say I'd live there. Too busy," Ron continued, still banging hais stack of papers on the desk. "And dirty. No lawns. No driveways."

"Nope." Mike clicked on an icon that pulled up a new report template onto his computer screen and began filling in the blanks.

"Don't know why you'd want to live there. Regardless," Ron's clipped words were picking up speed like a car going down a steep hill with a driver too nervous to stop it, "there's always something to do a when you own a house, isn't there? I remember when Marie and I were first married, and we lived in an apartment. Not too far from here, actually...."

Mike leaned back in his chair and stretched, hearing something inside him crack just at the moment when his body felt better than it had all night. He hunched again over the keyboard to continue with his report, the rat-a-tat-tat of the keys reminding him that Ron was talking to him.

"I guess we always liked this area of the city. Funny to think that this is where I'll be finishing up." Ron opened the top right drawer of his desk and pulled out a stapler. He examined his sheaf of papers again before inserting it into the stapler, slamming down the handle with a bit more vigour than was necessary,

"Huh?" Mike grunted, becoming increasingly aware that he could not hold off his partner's concerns much longer.

"You know. Retiring. After that, we'll go on a couple of cruises. Not too many, though." Ron examined the staple that had just been shot into the papers with annoyance before addressing it with an *oh-bugger-you* under his breath and scrambling for his staple remover.

"You're pretty scared about this checkup, eh?" Mike interrupted.

"Huh? Me? No. She'll be fine. And if she's not, she's got the best specialist in the country looking after it. No, I'm not scared. It's this damned stapler that's getting my dander up."

"If there's anything you need to talk about—"

"Oh, no. I'm fine. In fact, Marie and I were just talking about maybe going on one of those trans-Atlantic cruises and then touring Europe, maybe even before I retire." Ron tore out the staple and replaced it with a large paperclip, studiously avoiding making eye contact with Mike.

"Assuming that all goes well today?" Mike persisted, keeping his eyes on his computer monitor as he continued with his work, needing a distraction from the can of worms he feared he may have opened.

"It will. Just routine. Nothing to worry about." Ron quickly jotted down something in his memo book. "Marie suggested the trans-Atlantic cruise. Said it would give her time to rest up and read while I wander about the ship."

"I'm thinking *Titanic* here."

"Pardon?" Ron asked.

"I was kidding."

"We're looking at the *Queen Mary 2* or something like that," Ron said. "Totally different cruise line."

"Well then," Mike chuckled, "that changes everything. I hope the two of you get to go."

"Why wouldn't we?" Ron stopped what he was doing for the first time since this conversation began and stared across at Mike. His face had that look of disbelief usually reserved for children on the cusp of discovering that not all dreams come true.

The two men held each other's gaze like a couple of cats looking across a laneway at one another. They both knew that there was no such thing as a routine visit to a specialist, and being cops, they also both knew that there was no such thing as justice in life. Or death.

The silent standoff finally ended when Ron cleared his throat and turned his attention back to his work.

Chapter Sixteen

Friday, August 24, 2018 - 6:03 a.m.

Amanda absently poured her protein shake into a travel mug while she checked her Blackberry.

"No one uses those any more, Mom," Amanda's fifteen-year-old daughter groaned from the doorway.

"Well, good morning, Nickie-doodle," Amanda smiled as she turned around to face the disheveled figure stumbling towards her. "How come you're up so early, my little ray of sunshine?"

"I dunno. Maybe the less-than-dulcet roar of the blender?" Nicole deadpanned, making her way to her mother. "And don't call me Nickie-doodle. Ever. Please?"

"Sorry, sweetie," Amanda kissed her younger daughter on the cheek. "I saw your light on when I came home. What's up?"

"Nuthin'," Nicole said with a heavy sigh, slumping over the counter beside her mother as if the weight of the world was resting on her young shoulders.

"Oh, honey." Amanda instinctively opened her arms, pulling her daughter into that familiar sanctuary. Holding her baby tightly, she silently acknowledged that her ability to provide asylum from the hurts of the world had an all-too-real, albeit still looming, expiry date. "Anything I need to know?"

"No. Just stuff." Nicole sniffled, reaching to rub her nose before disentangling herself.

"Listen, it's game time, so I have to get back to work," Amanda began, turning away to pick up the mug from the counter.

"I know," Nicole sighed again, all too familiar with the routine of no family dinners, no home-and-school meetings, and no family-emergencies-that-only-Mom-could-handle for the first three days of a new case.

Amanda took a sip of her shake. "Oh my, that is *good!*"

"Gruesome?" Nicole's teenaged angst temporarily dissipated, as the possibility that she might find out something that no one else knew hit her.

"The shake?" Amanda smiled.

"No, Mom," Nicole heaved a big sigh at her mother's pretend- stupidity. "You know what I mean: the case."

"Not overly." Amanda continued to look at the messages that were rolling in on her Blackberry.

"In your world or the real world?" Nicole asked, claiming the cup from her mother's hand to take a quick sip, earnestly hoping for anything she could use as currency to gain entry into the cool kids club, and wishing that her mother could understand just how ugly, stupid, lost, and alone her little girl felt.

"What are you? Some kinda cop asking so many questions already?" Amanda feigned her best Bronx accent as she playfully snatched the cup back from her daughter.

"Any left in the blender?" Amanda's older daughter, Kristie, asked as she waltzed into the kitchen.

"Hi, baby. No. I didn't think—"

"That I, your number one, absolute *favourite* daughter, would need a protein shake before morning practice? Thanks, Mother Dearest. How am I going to be the greatest runner on the planet without the proper diet?" Kristie only half-joked as she reached around her mother for the bottle of protein powder on the counter.

"As if," Nicole mocked, sensing that her moment in the spotlight had been usurped by her much more gregarious older sister.

"Shut up, Nickie-doodle," Kristie shot back.

"It's not the running that you need protein for, is it, Kristie Pits?"

"Mom!" Kristie howled in objection.

"Girls! Come on, get it together," Amanda said, crouching down to reach into the cupboards below the counter. "Where are the coffee beans?"

"Is this a ladies-only event, or can I join in?" Tony asked, making his way to his wife. "Bag is right there. Where your hand is."

"Ugh. Trained observer. Thank God, I'm at home," Amanda responded without turning, standing up with the bag of beans.

"I'll say." Tony leaned in, placed his hands gently on Amanda's shoulders, and planted a brief kiss on the side of her head.

"Good morning, lover," Amanda smiled, setting the bag down before turning to take Tony's face in both of her hands, giving him an exaggeratedly passionate kiss.

"Really, Mother?" Nicole winced. "Was that necessary?"

"Grow up, Doodle. That's what adults *do*," Kristie snarked.

"You should know," Nichole shot back.

"Shut. Up." Kristie shot an icy scowl at her little sister. While there were only two years chronologically between them, a world of differing interests and maturity divided them.

"Ladies, please." Tony turned from Amanda to caution his step-daughters. "Your mother has to get back to work. She deals with enough conflict without you two adding to it."

"It's *her* fault," Nicole insisted, nodding towards her sister.

"Why don't you shut your big stupid mouth, you frigging space oddity," Kristie shot back.

"Kristie!" Amanda chastised. "Do not call your sister names. I'm sure she gets enough of that at school."

"Really, Mom?" Nicole squawked. "I'm right here."

"Well, she's right. Everyone knows you're a weirdo."

"Mom!"

"Girls. Please," Amanda said, shaking her head. She looked at Tony. "You're up awfully early, my darling husband. What's up?"

"Got a cleanup I have to do before my scheduled jobs. Client called last night. Said her water wasn't flowing properly."

"Oh?" Amanda's eyebrow rose in feigned interest as she checked her Blackberry again.

"Yeah. Got that new apprentice working with me," Tony remarked, scooping coffee beans into the grinder. "Likely just a messy soldering job. No big deal, but I said I'd be there first thing in the morning to take a look and clean her pipes or do whatever has to be done."

Amanda glanced at her watch. "Shit! I have to go. Love you all. Nicole, happy up. Kristie, be nice to your little sister. And you, Mister, it's just lucky you're a plumber. Otherwise, I wouldn't be too happy to hear that you'll be spending your morning cleaning some other woman's pipes!"

Tony smiled as he raised the bag of beans in salute to his wife, knowing that it would likely be days before he saw her again.

Amanda hurriedly kissed her children and her husband and dashed down the hall, travel mug in one hand, Blackberry in the other, to be tossed into her purse waiting by the front door. Looking more like a whirling dervish than a homicide investigator, she was out the door, down the walkway, into the unmarked car, and disappearing down the street she had just driven home on no more than ninety minutes earlier.

Chapter Seventeen

Friday, August 24, 2018 - 6:43 a.m.

"Looks like this Cockeye Johnstone character could be our man," Detective Hank Moreaux began, waving the papers in his hand and all but tackling Amanda as she walked through the door of the inspector's office, which they had commandeered for the duration of their on-scene investigation.

"Occam's razor?" Amanda asked, stepping behind the desk before turning her back on her partner to unbutton her coat and straighten her dress. She stared at the wall in front of her as her mind focused on the case.

"Huh?" Moreaux grunted.

"Never mind. Talk to me."

"I read the notes those two Ds left for that video statement they did with the landlords. Looks like we can place Cockeye at the rooming house where the deceased lived around the time of the murder."

"Do they reference him by name?" Amanda asked, turning to face Hank as she hoisted her litigation bag onto the desk that separated the two investigators.

She noticed her partner's questioning look. "This was given to me after my accused was convicted of that mass shooting we had a couple of summers ago. I've never taken anything from anyone after a conviction, but it was from a group of local businesses near where it happened. Pretty nice, eh?"

"Yeah. Sure," Hank agreed. "But with regards to Johnstone, no, they don't give a name, but they refer to a guy with funky eyes, so the description—"

"So what I'm hearing is that you're good to arrest a guy for murder because he may or may not have the same eye disorder as a guy who visited our now-deceased a number of times?" Amanda's head tilted from side to side in harmony with her singsong tone. "That's it then? We're done?"

"Well—"

"Have we established time of death yet?"

"Not yet," Hank said, his body seeming to shrink with each question Amanda fired at him.

"So we've got a googly-eyed guy who knew our deceased before he died. That's it? Great work, Detective. Maybe a good person of interest," Amanda suggested as she continued to pull file folders from the litigation bag. "Certainly worth taking a second look at, but I sure as hell wouldn't be arresting him at this point."

"I dunno. I'm thinking this *is* the guy," Hank pushed, undeterred by her sharp words.

"Well," Amanda continued, sitting down behind the desk, pulling out her newly-acquired reading glasses before looking down to organize the files in front of her, "you get me a line-up with another eleven funky-eyed guys. We'll show the landlords so that we can at least confirm that we're all talking about the same guy, and then we'll go from there. Now what else?"

"The autopsy is scheduled for first thing this morning. Do you want to go, or do you want me to go?"

"Why don't you go, Hank?" Amanda replied as she popped her head up from her files, pulling off her glasses. "You haven't had a break yet, and it'll give you a chance to get away from this circus for a couple of hours. Any word on my warrant?"

"All good. JP signed it without question. But speaking of circus, Janelle Austin is at the front desk. Wants to speak to you."

"I know," Amanda sighed. "I saw her when I stepped out to speak to the unit commander. She can wait for the media scrum. Have we notified next-of- kin?"

"Not yet. Can't find any."

"Press release through Corp Comm. That always shakes someone out of the trees," Amanda suggested. "And O'Shea? Is he going to do my warrant?"

"Why? We've got Griffiths and his team."

"Yeah, I know, but I want O'Shea to go, too," she said, logging into the computer in front of her. "Another set of eyes that isn't Forensics."

"I suppose, but that'll have to be arranged between you and him."

Amanda stopped what she was doing. She slowly removed the glasses as she looked incredulously over at her subordinate.

"I made sure we had Griffiths," Hank cautiously added, realizing that he had likely overstepped his place.

Amanda continued to stare.

"That's what I was asked to do, and that's what I did."

"Is it too much to ask that you speak to O'Shea?"

"I'd rather not."

"Because?"

"Because I think they should have fired him after he let his partner get shot—"

"Stay in your lane, Detective," Amanda cautioned with a sharp tilt of her head, her eyes getting colder. "I would suggest that you know nothing of what actually happened that afternoon and that you ought to keep your ill-informed opinions to yourself."

"Yes, Detective Sergeant," Hank acquiesced with a slight nod.

"We have a lot of work ahead of us," Amanda continued, her voice warmer but her clear blue eyes still icy, "and I believe that my time is better served forging ahead than coordinating our officers, don't you?"

"The district Major Crime Unit guys all came in after you left," Hank continued, eager to get himself back into her good graces. "They've been shaking some of their regulars down. They've been kind of focusing in on this Cockeye character—"

"Too early to focus.," Amanda repeated, eyes back scanning the screen in front of her.

"They don't seem to think so," Hank persisted.

Amanda looked over at Hank, a slight frown on her face. "Listen,

Detective," she stated, pulling off her glasses and stabbing the air in front of her with them to accentuate her words, "you go and tell those MCU knuckle-draggers to hold off."

Hank felt his blood pressure rising.

"We will wait until we get the victim's DNA from the lab and the suspect's DNA from the scene, along with a positive ID from the landlords, before we go talking to anyone."

"But—"

"No buts. Right now, we don't even know definitively if this guy knew our deceased. Given our victim's lifestyle, we probably have a lot of other people to rule out before we go hog-wild on your Mr. Johnstone."

"We both know that that's not exactly true," Hank corrected.

"We both also know that too many good investigations go horribly wrong because of tunnel vision. Is *that* not *exactly* true?"

"Yes, but—" the investigator sputtered.

"Right now, we've got nothing on this Johnstone character. Even if he *is* our guy, if we start messing with him at this point, he'll run. You know that as well as I do."

"Okay, so—"

"And I don't have anything to support a warrant for his arrest. Do you?"

"No, but—"

"Now let's turn this around," Amanda continued, deciding to take the time to explain what Moreaux ought to have known. "If he's *not* our guy, then we need to rule him out sooner rather than later because otherwise, we're wasting our time."

"I get what you're saying, Amanda, but—"

"Either way, I don't want this investigation fucked up by some cowboy bringing anyone in prematurely."

Amanda put her glasses back on and looked down at her files, indicating that the conversation was ended and Hank was dismissed.

Hank, however, was oblivious. "How about a spin team?" he offered, "Maybe follow him for a bit? Grab a discard so we can compare DNA?"

"Last time I checked, the lab was two weeks delayed. Give them a call. Get on the list. But that's it. If things change, we'll discuss. For now, let's get boots on the ground and start rustling up names."

"Why not just put one of the MCU guys on him?" Hank persisted.

"Absolutely not. I know their hearts are in the right place, God love them, but one of them is liable to jump the gun and pinch this guy before we have our ducks in a row, and then he'll be lost in the wind forever."

Hank stood silently over his boss.

"Have I been clear enough?" Amanda asked, not looking up as she scribbled madly on the steno pad in front of her.

"Very," Hank replied, backing away from her to return to the little table by the door that had become his desk, finally willing to admit that her approach was the best course of action.

"Fine. Just give me a couple of minutes to catch up on my notes, and we'll get our game plan together for today. I've got…" Amanda glanced at her watch, "about twenty minutes before the early half of dayshift parades. I want to make sure everyone is on the same page."

"Right."

"And Hank?" Amanda lowered her chin to look over her glasses at the big man sitting at the tiny desk. "Do not—I repeat, *do not*—let anyone so much as lay a hand on Mr. Johnstone until I have enough to make the charge stick. Unless the Homicide gods smile down on us and allow the perfect witness or the perfect accused to fall from the sky, we have a fuck-ton of work to do before we are anywhere near considering an arrest. Got it?"

"Yes, ma'am."

Chapter Eighteen

Friday, August 24, 2018 - 6:46 a.m.

"Would one of you dicks mind talking to this chick at the front desk?" the uniformed station operator asked from the doorway of the D office before turning around to waddle back up the hall, not waiting for an answer.

"Detective Sergeant Black is lead on this. Get her to do it," Mike yelled after the officer. "And that's *Detective* to you!"

"Tried," the officer hollered back from halfway up the hall, almost directly in front of the open door of the office Amanda Black and her partner now occupied. "She ain't gonna do it."

Mike glanced guardedly over to Ron.

"I'll go," Ron offered, pulling his suit jacket from the back of his chair as he stood up. "I know how to deal with these people."

"The media or the front-desk personnel?" Mike chuckled.

"Both."

It was shift change again. Ron took a deep breath before attempting to weave his way between one group of officers picking up their memo books from the side counter and another other group, weary from a long night shift, dropping theirs off. He was appalled at the carelessness with which shotguns were being loaded by several adventurous officers amid their more casual peers who were too busy signing hand-held radios and car keys in and out to realize that a slip of a finger could result in someone's head being blown off.

He cleared his throat enough times for the sea of blue uniforms to part enough for him to squeeze through and make his way towards the woman at the front desk. There was no mistaking who she was as she stood on the other side of the counter that divided the community from the police, her cameraman already pulling up his camera.

"Thank you so much for speaking with me, Inspector," Janelle Austin said, using her tried-and-true trick of referring to cops by at least one rank above what she knew them to be. She reached across the counter to shake Ron's hand.

"That's 'Detective,'" Ron corrected as he pulled down the front of his suit jacket, insulted that this woman thought he would fall for that old chestnut. "And please tell your cameraman that he cannot film on police property."

"Of course, Detective," Janelle smiled as she motioned to her partner.

Turning off the camera as he lowered it to his side, the cameraman was not surprised that *his* tried-and-true trick hadn't worked. Cops were used to cameras, and having one shoved in their face rarely pushed them into giving that jaw-dropping comment that his livelihood depended on. Still, it had been worth a try.

"There isn't much I can say, Ms. Austin," Ron stated, touching the knot of his tie to be sure that it was straight. Camera or no camera, looking professional was half the battle. "Detective Sergeant Black is the Homicide lead on this. I am assuming, of course, that you're here for the homicide?"

"Yes. And I've been told that Detective Sergeant Black is quite busy right now. Perhaps you can help me?" Janelle tilted her head slightly to one side.

"I'm sorry, but—" Ron began, preparing to end this tête-à-tête before it began.

"Have you been on the case all night, Detective?" Janelle, for her part fully aware of police tricks to avoid interviews, interrupted.

"Yes. My partner and I were the first investigators on the scene," Ron stated. "There will be a media scrum shortly where Detective Sergeant Black—"

"And you were the ones who found the body?" Janelle continued.

"No. We were called out by the uniforms," Ron answered, tapping the fingers of both hands impatiently on the counter between them. While it had been a few years since he'd done an interview with the likes of Janelle Austin, he knew what she was up to. There were only two kinds of reporters who would show up at the station so late at night: the old warhorses hoping to get some inside scoop by relying on their name or collecting on some unclaimed debt, and the newbies who thought they could leverage their youth in exchange for information that was not supposed to be released. Both banked on inexperienced—or lonely—cops. Ron knew that Janelle Austin was not a newbie, and he expected her to appreciate that he was no Preston McAfee. Nor was he lonely in a way that she could work to her advantage.

"So they found the body on routine patrol," Janelle pressed on.

"No." Ron's lips tightened, his eyes looking over the reporter's shoulder at the cars rushing along the narrow street out front, splashing the night's rainwater onto the sidewalk.

"I understand that the victim had only one leg. How do you suppose he ended up in such an unusual place?"

"I really can't—"

"And there were no crutches or a prosthetic around?" Janelle shook her head in mock astonishment.

"That's correct." Ron's tired gaze settled on the soggy lawn across the street from the station.

"So he was likely dumped." Ron found his attention focused on the eyes of Janelle's made-for-TV face.

"I don't know," he answered, thinking how old his eyes must look in comparison.

"Do you think maybe he was robbed and someone took his crutches or prosthetic?"

"*Highly* unlikely, Ms. Austin."

"So he must have been dumped. I understand the victim was a gambler. Do you think this has anything to do with a bad debt?"

"I have no idea." Ron looked over at the clock to his right. Almost 6:50 a.m.

Marie would be getting up, likely just getting into the shower. He should have been home hours ago, but she was used to that. He wondered if she had been up all night, worrying about her day today. He wondered if he would have been if it had been him instead.

"What? That he was a gambler or that this was a drug-related homicide?"

"Who said anything about drugs?" Ron's attention snapped back to his non-interview with Janelle Austin.

"So the murder is not drug-related? Just a gambling debt, or is there a significant public safety element here? I mean, he was found in a residential laneway."

"I don't think there's any real public safety concern."

"So this was targeted." Janelle was relentless.

"I really can't say."

"Just to get up to speed here: A one-legged man was murdered somewhere else, dumped in a residential laneway, and then…?" Janelle was determined to walk out of this station with something for her two-minute spot on the 7 a.m. news. She reminded herself that she refused to stand out in the pouring rain for most of the night and then drag her tired ass out of bed and pile on all this makeup just to let some crotchety old bastard like this cop waste her time. No, she was damn well going to get a story.

"I never said any of that." Time to shut down this charade. Ron had not spent his entire shift, and then some, digging and documenting every lead he could think of to have this washed-up talking head jeopardize the investigation. *He* was going to control the message…and the investigation.

"I've spoken to a few of the neighbours and they don't recall anyone in the area with one leg. Where do you think the victim was murdered?" Janelle was relentless, determined to find the spin that would not only give this story a life of its own but also the chance of more than one round of repeats before the media scrum took its place on the TV station's news segments.

"I have no idea," Ron answered, also having decided on a course of action: short, closed answers. "This is not my investigation to discuss."

"So he was dumped. Do you have a suspect vehicle yet?"

"I never said he was dumped."

"People are saying," Janelle leafed through some pages in the steno pad she had pulled from her purse and set down on the counter, trusting that this cop would not notice that the pad's contents had nothing to do with her question, "that they saw an old car in the laneway around the time the victim's body would have been dumped. Do you have any information on that vehicle, Detective?"

"I'm sure there were many old cars in the laneway that day."

"So you've followed up on all of the plates of the cars that passed by? You'd be getting that info from the security cam on the garage right beside where the body was found, wouldn't you?"

This was news to Ron. He didn't recall seeing any cameras on any garages in that laneway.

Janelle didn't know of any cameras back there, either. It was a shot in the dark that she thought was worth taking.

"I'm sure we would, but—"

"And you would know, then, that there would have been at least two suspects involved, is that correct, Detective?" she continued with renewed vigour, having caught Ron in a lie and now holding the upper hand in their cat-and-mouse game.

"Not necessari—"

"I mean, it's highly unlikely that the murderer would park the car, get out, and pull out the body of the guy he'd just beaten to death. The victim *was* beaten to death, wasn't he, Detective?"

"The coroner is going to determine the cause of death at the autopsy later this morning," Ron replied, thankful for the opportunity to throw out an indisputable truth.

"So the autopsy is this morning?" Janelle reached into her purse and pulled out a pen, appearing to jot this information down on the pad on the counter between them before looking back to Ron. "But seriously, Detective, you have to admit it is highly unlikely that someone would drive to a rather public laneway, park the car, and then drag a body out of the car after driving it from…where? Where would the body have been?"

"This is not my investi—"

"I understand, and I really do appreciate your time. I know this is a busy place." Janelle looked behind Ron, giving him a moment to breathe, sensing that she had pulled the line that held them together as tight as it would go without snapping. "Wow. Was that a shotgun I just saw?"

Ron nonchalantly looked over his shoulder, nodding as he returned his attention to the reporter.

"The officer on the scene…" Janelle continued.

"Yes," Ron sighed.

"…seemed to think that you had a suspect in mind, likely with some distinguishing physical features. What do you say to that, Detective?"

The night had been busy, and Ron was tired. Struggling to recall whether or not Cockeye Johnstone's name had been mentioned and if it had, whether it was before or after the victim's body went to the morgue, he suggested that it could be so, but then recalled that she would have no way of knowing that.

Dammit, dammit, dammit! He had been duped again.

"There are some pretty tough neighbourhoods in this district," Janelle commented, as she looked over at two more officers loading shotguns. "There are probably enough places to dump a body where it wouldn't be found for a few days around these streets. Why do you suppose our victim was dumped where he was?"

"I have no idea," Ron replied. If he could not utter an entire sentence, the least he could do was stick to short, closed answers going forward.

"Do you think the murderer or murderers intended to dump the body there, or do you think something or someone spooked them before they got to their intended location?"

"I really can't say."

Despite her youthful appearance, courtesy of good genes and the strategic application of MAC products, Janelle had been around the block enough to know when it was time to shift gears to keep an interview rolling. "Word on the street is that our victim was a boxer. Did you know that, Detective?"

"Yes, I figured that out." Ron couldn't help giving himself a bit of credit for his clever deduction.

"So you saw the body. Must have been horrible." Janelle closed her eyes as she shook her head, trying to conjure the illusion that she was actually envisioning that horrible sight.

"I've seen worse." Ron's years in Traffic had exposed him to more gory deaths than all the scenes that these well-dressed Homicide investigators put together would ever see.

"I bet you have. So tell me," Janelle began again, glancing over at the clock to her left; the 7 a.m. deadline was looming. Taking a deep breath and one last stab at getting a definitive scoop, she continued, "We have a murdered one-legged former boxer who was beaten to death over some gambling debt by someone who would stand out from the crowd, is from this district, and would have access to a car and knowledge of the area. Who is it we're looking for, Detective?"

Ron stared at the expectant reporter.

"In approximately six minutes, people all over the city are going to be watching my live broadcast while they drink their morning coffee and get their kids ready for school." Time to pull out all the stops. "They are going to hear me tell them that someone was beaten to death, right here in this city. This community. They are going to hear that there is a suspect on the loose—a homicidal suspect who would think nothing of beating a disabled man to death. Likely in his own home. That's scary stuff, Detective. I mean, if our vulnerable populations aren't safe, then who is? I'm feeling a bit scared, aren't you?"

Ron coughed.

"Oh, right. You're a cop, and cops don't get scared," Janelle said with a slight self-deprecating laugh. "But the rest of us do. What can I tell that frightened mother who is getting her kids ready for school? Or the disabled man watching this, wondering whether or not he'll be the next victim? Or the murderer himself? Do we have a picture of him that we can use? We will be live in…" she looked pointedly at the clock, "four minutes. What can I tell our viewers, Detective, or is there something you'd like to say directly to the murderer now?"

On cue, the cameraman turned on his camera, ready to hoist it up to his shoulder onat a moment's notice.

"Nothing. I've got nothing," Ron replied.

"Roberts, is it? Usual spelling?" Janelle jotted something on the notepad on the counter before replacing it in her bag. "Thank you so much, Detective Roberts. I really appreciate you giving me so much of your time this morning."

Ron grimaced and returned to the D office, where Mike had turned on the TV to catch the interview.

* * *

"And now over to 6th District police station for an update. Good morning, Janelle. What do you have for us?" the dark-suited news anchor asked the still-dark screen at the far edge of his desk.

Within a second, the screen lit up with Janelle Austin's face. "Good morning, Richard. As you can imagine, the investigation is still pretty fresh, but I did manage to speak to Detective Sergeant Ronald Roberts…"

"*Detective Sergeant*? Look at you!" Mike chuckled as he glanced over at Ron, who was settling in at his desk, adjusting his chair to see the TV behind him.

"…who told me that while they didn't have much on the murderer, he is likely known to police and has a distinct physical deformity of some sort."

"I *never* said that," Ron objected, turning back to the computer monitor in front of him.

"According to Detective Sergeant Roberts, the suspect is likely from right here in Toronto and was either a gambler himself, as was the victim, or was the muscle for a gambler."

"I never said *that*, either," Ron huffed, looking for some papers to shuffle.

"Detective Sergeant Roberts did not provide me with the name of the victim when we spoke a few moments ago," Janelle advised as she looked down at her steno pad, the mud on her bright yellow rainboots suggesting that she, too, had been slogging through the crime scene, "which suggests, of course, that they are still looking for next-of-kin. Detective Sergeant

Roberts did, however, confirm that the victim was disabled."

"I see." The camera cut back to the anchor as he shook his head. "Tragic, Janelle, when members of our vulnerable communities are targeted."

"My thoughts exactly, as were those of Detective Sergeant Roberts."

"I'm sure!" Mike chortled. Ron was not amused.

"Well, thanks for that informative update, Janelle. I imagine that you'll be reporting live all morning?"

"Quite likely, yes, Richard. The officers here at," she turned to showcase the building, "6th District are just starting their morning shift, and as I have just seen during my conversation with Detective Sergeant Roberts, they are working hard to solve this murder."

"Very good. In the meantime, anyone with information is, I'm sure, encouraged to call."

"I cannot *believe*," Ron said, jumping up to manually turn the TV off, "that they allow this type of crap to pass itself off as news."

"I cannot believe," Mike countered, "that you let that pretty young woman think you were a detective sergeant. Amanda is going to be *so* pissed!"

Outside in front of the station, the camera's red light went off, Janelle lowered her microphone, and then she and the cameraman were in the truck in a flash and on their way to a bakery for a bite before filming their next segment.

Chapter Nineteen

Friday, August 24, 2018 - 7:20 a.m.

"Well, look at you two! Still at it!" Amanda Black said, returning to the D office. "I knew I had at least half of a good team when I saw you last night, Ron. Oh, and thanks for talking to Austin, by the way. She annoys the shit out of me. You certainly saved me a lot of grief."

"I should think so!" Ron looked up from the files he had been sorting through in the bankers' box underneath his desk.

"Here we go," Mike muttered from behind his desk, rubbing his face with both hands before stretching his arms out in front of himself.

"I never said *any* of those things she said I did," Ron stated emphatically, flipping the lid down on the box before shoving it back into place with the others under his desk with his foot.

"Nobody cares," Mike sighed, dropping his head into his hands.

"A little sleepy, are we, Crumply-pants? Well, hold on to your hats, both of you, because I've got a detail for you."

"I thought it was the job of your subordinate to hand out details to us peons," Mike mumbled a little louder than he had intended.

"There is no rank in Homicide," Amanda shot back. "And you should be thanking me."

"Well, I'm busy," Ron announced.

"I know you are, Sunshine. We all are. But you and your partner over here are going to be executing my search warrant in an hour."

"I can't. I have to be downtown," Ron said bluntly.

"Whatever you have going on downtown can take a back seat to my investigation."

"He has an appointment with a proctologist," Mike said, glancing playfully at Ron and then to Amanda.

"Oh?"

"I don't have a proctologist appointment. It's an appointment with a specialist for my wife," Ron clarified.

"In which case, Mr. Crumply-pants," Amanda said as she looked at Mike, knowing Ron well enough not to ask any further questions, "looks like you're my man. I have a search warrant to execute, and no one to do it. Except you, apparently."

"I've got Court at ten. Gotta see the crown before that. What about Russ McLean?"

"The guy who is your relief and left to get coffee about an hour ago instead of jumping in? Let me think about that for a moment. No." Amanda glanced towards McLean's desk, where the picture of the day's pinup girl was visible. "Absolutely not."

"I'm on the stand for a big case—"

"There are no small cases, only detectives with small parts. Regardless, I've got a one-legged dead guy who was thankfully filed safely away at the morgue before enough water rained down over the past three hours to wash away whatever DNA evidence the tarps didn't cover. I also have a possible known suspect who actually resides in your district, and finally, I need someone to be the investigators' eyes when the warrant is executed."

"Isn't that what Forensics is for?" Mike asked.

"Walk with me."

Mike fell in beside the detective sergeant as she strode along the tiled floor of the hallway towards the front desk. The clicking of her high heels seemed so out of place here. Mike was more used to hearing that sound in the upscale restaurants he had learned to enjoy with Carmen, not between these grimy walls. He wondered if his wife—soon to be ex-wife, he was sure—had been to any of those restaurants on those nights when she said she was working late. Probably. Hopefully, it was on his dime, whoever he was….. Unlikely.

"I want you to stand by my search team. The warrant has already been written and will probably be sworn to within the hour."

"And you need me to do what?"

"You know Griffiths? Good guy. He's the D running the team that'll be handling the entry."

"I've got a key," Mike recalled, fumbling in his pocket to find it among the loose change that made its rounds from one pair of pants to another as the days passed. "I meant to put it in Property last night after the landlord gave it to me, but—"

"Well, a little disappointing for Griffith's guys. I'm sure they'd enjoy a good door-kicking, but this will definitely make things easier."

"So I'll be doing—?" Mike asked again, holding out the key to Amanda.

"No, don't give it to me. Take it with you. Forensics will seize everything. Don't know who it'll be." Amanda stopped at the open door of her impromptu office and gave Hank a thumbs-up. "Amy is still at my scene. God, I love that girl. Give her a bone, and she'll find the whole dinosaur. Anyway, I want you there. Whole thing should be done by nine, which will give you plenty of time to get to court."

"Sounds like you've got everything covered." Mike put the key back in his pocket as the pair walked on.

"I do," Amanda stated with the certainty that came with knowing that she was one of the best, if not *the* best, homicide investigator in the city. She slowed her stride as she scrolled through the myriad messages that were coming through on her Blackberry.

"So why am I going?"

"I want you to be the eyes. *My* eyes," she advised, not looking up at Mike as she stopped to respond to one of the messages. "Sorry. It's the chief. He wants an update. Can't make him wait. Anyway, photos are great, but I want a *real* detective's perspective on the scene to give me a better sense of it."

"Why me?"

"Because you're good. Really good. I remember you from that afternoon on the corner. Me a million years younger, and you…"

"And look how that turned out."

"There's nothing you could have done differently."

"Yeah. I know that, but—"

"You're a good cop, Mike. A clever investigator. A c—"

"Coward?"

"No. The only guys who would say that are the guys who have never been where you've been."

"I know. Every unit commander I've ever worked under after Sal fucked it all up has told me that. To my face. But I know what they're saying behind my back."

"Listen, are you going to help a girl out here, or are you going to stand around feeling sorry for yourself?" Amanda said, looking at her watch and taking a couple of strides towards the glass doors that would lead her upstairs. "Look, I've got to deal with the chief and get this warrant done."

"What about Ron?" Mike replied, taking one long step to catch up before reaching to open the door for her.

"I've known that man for years…" Amanda nodded her thanks, stepping in front of Mike and heading up the stairs. "And if he's taking time off from work to go with his wife to see a doctor, then she's really sick. She can't be any older than me. Not good. So you're my man. Call me once everything is done."

She stopped short on the landing to pull a business card from the binder she was carrying, causing Mike to almost run over her. While he was not a big man, he was almost twice her weight.

"Sorry, boss," he apologized, rubbing his scruffy face as he moved back down a couple of steps.

"You know, I like my men close, but not this close. Anyway, here's my cell number." She handed Mike a business card with a phone number written on the back of it. "Oh, and would you mind dragging a razor over your face? Doesn't look good when the district D looks worse than the hounds that live in the house where we're seizing shit, you know?"

"Sure. I'll get right on that."

"If you want, I've got a razor that I use to shave my legs in my gym bag in the back of my car," Amanda offered.

"No, I'm good."

"We need to look the part. We are living pretty much everyone else's dream, you know. Top TV shows are about cops like us, and people have expectations. Remember to call me when you're done."

Before Mike could offer any further objections, she was through the door and inside the parade room, ready to update the dayshift uniform platoon. He was left wondering whether or not he had a razor in his locker. And whether or not she was hitting on him. He allowed himself to believe she was.

Chapter Twenty

Friday, August 24, 2018 - 8:05 a.m.

"Do we get to kick in the door, Mike?" the long-limbed young man in uniform asked, almost salivating as he considered the prospect. "Sorry, Big Nick," Mike replied as he took a sip from his fourth shitty coffee since 3 a.m. He pulled the key from his pocket. "I got a key."

The young officer's shoulders slumped. His partner—all five-foot-three of him—maintained a dispassionate million-mile stare in the direction of the house directly across from the porch of the rooming house where the two had been detailed to stand guard.

"You wouldn't be doing it anyway. It would be the old clothes guys," Mike offered by way of consolation, looking up at the six-foot-five officer who came by his Big Nick name honestly.

"They usually get me to help out," Big Nick smiled wistfully.

Mike nodded and looked away, squinting in the sunshine. He'd been up since 8 a.m. the day before. Well, really, since 3 a.m. or so. He glanced down at his watch. 8:07.

On hour thirty now. Shit. Get this done by nine and then off to court. Bright-eyed and bushy-tailed. He rubbed his eyes, and his hand instinctively fell to his cheek. *Shit. Forgot to shave. Gotta do that before I get in the box.* He took another sip of the crayon water that passed itself off as coffee as he continued to rub his stubbly face and took stock of the house. Typical for the neighbourhood. Solid brick, probably double- or triple-bricked, three storeys, shared drive, wooden garage in the back. Mike counted nine separate mailboxes and buzzers by the front door. Plus, there was a basement side entrance with its own buzzer, too.

That little bastard Majewski must be making a killing. Hold on to the place for a few years, let it pay for itself, and then sell for as much as some hipster is willing to pay. And they have three of these places? Good for them.

An old Chev pulled up on the wrong side of the street.

"You Griffiths?" Mike called out as he made his way across the tiny front yard to the car.

"That'd be me. You O'Shea?" the ratty-looking driver said, reaching his right arm out the open window, revealing a sleeve of tattoos.

"Yep," Mike replied, shaking the old clothes man's hand through the window.

"I've heard about you," Griffiths said, eyeing Mike as he pulled his arm back into the car and grabbed a pack of smokes from the dash.

"Uh huh," Mike mumbled, withdrawing his hand. *Here we go.*

"You're kind of a legend in the world of juvie prostitution. Surprised to see you in this monkey suit."

"Well, I guess that's what happens when your partner gets capped," Mike replied.

"Or you get too into the booze and broads. Wouldn't be the first guy to get punted for either." Griffiths winked, casually flipping open an old-school zippo lighter and lighting up his cigarette. "Anyway, Amanda Black said you'd be running the uni end of the show. I'll run our end."

"I'm not running any end," Mike stated. "And it wasn't like that."

"That's not what I was told, but whatever. Now that you've gone all vanilla with your expensive haircut and designer suit, don't forget how real police work is done, eh? Make sure your guys keep the shit rats out down here at the door while my guys go up and do the warrant. You said something about a key?"

"Nope, I didn't, but I've got one. And I'll just hold on to it until we all go in."

"Really?" Griffiths blew a lungful of smoke Mike's way.

"Look, I'm not in the mood to play Silly Bugger," Mike snapped, disliking Griffiths more than was probably reasonable. "I don't know what you were told about how this is going to go, but it sounds like you got it all wrong."

"Landlord on his way?" Griffiths asked, casually dismissing Mike's objections and taking another drag from the cigarette.

"No. Don't need him. I have the key," Mike repeated.

"We prefer to have the landlord present," Griffiths said, now giving Mike the once-over.

"I doubt that, but regardless, *we* prefer to get the warrant done. I have the key, and I have to be in court for ten, so let's go."

"Ten? Shit. Might as well kiss that appearance goodbye," Griffiths all but guffawed, making no attempt to get out of the car. "No way in hell we're gonna be done here by ten, even if we did use your key."

"You can sit in your car all day if you want," Mike spat out his words, trying not to grind his teeth. His stomach was churning. "But I got the key, you got the warrant, landlord knows we're coming in, so it looks an awful lot like we're ready to go."

"I'm callin' Amanda," Griffiths declared after a few more seconds of deliberation and another drag on his cigarette.

"Great idea," Mike said aloud, and then added under his breath, "and she'll tell you exactly the same thing, you fucking cowboy."

He stepped back from the car and watched Griffiths pull out an old flip-up cell phone and begin punching at some numbers. *Shit, I hope I wasn't such a prick when I wore old Ts and tight jeans to work every day.*

"Amanda? Griffiths. O'Shea has the key but no holder. Says he's comin' in with us. That's not what we agreed to…. Uh -huh…. Well, I got my way to roll, and I don't know this guy from…. Of course. Everybody knows he was, but…. You know I do everything above board…. Yeah, but that's not what I'm sayin'…. So what do you want me to do?…. Uh-huh…. Right…Yeah….Okay, I'll tell him….Thanks." Griffiths flipped the phone closed, took a deep drag on his cigarette, and slowly exhaled the smoke towards Mike before saying, "The D/S says wait. She's having the landlord attend."

"Is that all she said?"

"And that you're comin' in with us."

Mike just shook his head. He turned and took a couple of steps towards the target house across the street.

"Listen, I know what you're thinkin'," Griffiths called after him. "But I gotta cover my ass."

Mike stopped and spun around to see Griffith's tattooed arm dangling casually out the window, his cigarette pinched between his fingers.

"I thought I heard you say that you do everything above board," Mike said.

"I do, but it's about street cred with your guys. You know how it is, man. They expect us to lead. They don't want to listen to a suit—"

"Another D, you mean?" Mike corrected.

"Whatever. You've walked the walk. You know what I mean." Griffiths seemed to be almost pleading for Mike's understanding.

Mike did know what Griffiths meant. The squad guys were able to do what they did because they believed they could. Part of that was believing that they were better than the uniforms and cut from a different cloth than the suits. Mike remembered that feeling of invincibility, and he was reminded every day since Sal was shot that he was wrong.

"Whatever you say," he replied. "At least, you can blame Amanda Black for this one."

"Don't worry. I will be," Griffiths chuckled. "But don't tell her that. She's one broad I'd never want to cross. Tough as nails, and she'd have your balls on a platter for breakfast if you did."

"What part of that do you not want me to tell the D/S?"

"Hey, wanna hop in the car and wait with me?" Griffiths offered, trying to create a common ground between the two detectives.

"No. No, I don't."

"Suit yourself," Griffiths nodded, his gaze scanning the streetscape in front of him. He stopped for a moment, nodded again as if acknowledging something, and then glanced back at Mike. "I'll have my guys wait in the parking lot around the corner until I hear from you. Call me on the air when the landlord gets here."

Griffiths abruptly tossed his cigarette butt at Mike's feet and spun the car around, leaving Mike to wander back to the group of uniformed officers that had arrived and were now all waiting on the front porch of the rooming house.

* * *

But for the crispness of their uniforms, the men waiting on the front porch gave off a very casual vibe—too casual for Mike's liking. The initial buzz of excitement had become a murmur of different conversations about baseball standings mixed in with ongoing commentaries assessing the women passing by on their way to the bus or school with their little ones. Hats were off, and some officers were leaning against the porch railing, while others were sitting on the front steps.

"Mister Mike? Where is Mister Mike?" a little man dressed more like a circus clown than a landlord called out as he wormed his way through the officers on the stairs towards the front door, a ring of keys jangling authoritatively in his hand.

"Step back from the doorway, sir," Big Nick barked, springing to life. His partner popped up beside him.

"But I own here!" Jorge Majewski said with great indignation, hoisting up his aqua green pants to meet an orange shirt with embroidery on the collar and cuffs.

"It's okay, Big Nick. He's the landlord," Mike interrupted, motioning to the man to join him at the side of the house. "Thanks for coming by on such short notice."

"Sorry, sir. I didn't know," Big Nick called to Mike.

"Is okay." Mr. Majewski grasped the tall officer's limp hand and shook it vigorously, assuming that the officer was apologizing to him. "You do good job, but I go talk to Mister Mike. The police lady who call says to talk to Mister Mike."

Once he had adequately forgiven the officer for his faux pas, Mr. Majewski scrambled down the stairs. Mike took a step back; this new burst of energy was a bit jarring at this late hour of his day. The officers on the porch seemed to perk up as well, replacing hats, extricating themselves from the comfort of the stairs, stepping away from the railing, and casual conversation.

"Give me a second, Mr. Majewski, while I call in the other team," Mike said, stepping back from both Mr. Majewski and the expectant gaze of the uniforms. By adding a foot of distance, Mike felt that he had lifted the weight of several men off his back. *I'm getting too old for this shit.* He rubbed his eye as he felt the sun assault his face anew. *And I think I'm gonna be fucked for court.*

"No need for team. I let you in," the little man said, his eyes dancing as he jingled his keys above his head towards Mike's face.

"I have a key, too, remember? We just want you here because..." Mike's voice trickled off as he lost his train of thought. He waited a moment until he could refocus. "We just want to show you the search warrant. Remember how we talked about that?"

"No need search warrant if I am here. I see that on TV. You can look anywhere. Is my house. I say yes."

"It doesn't quite work that way. Just hang on a minute." Mike called Griffiths on the police radio that was tucked in his jacket pocket. Everything had to be above board. Everything had to be recorded.

Within seconds of the call, three unmarked cars carrying a total of six scruffy-looking guys squealed around the corner, each car almost slamming into the next as they all came to a stop in front of the house. The fourth car, Griffiths's, glided up to the address like a land shark, stopping a respectable distance away.

The officers from the first three cars piled out of their vehicles. Each over-sized officer in his under-sized jeans and T-shirt lumbered up the stairs to the front door, elbowing aside their uniformed counterparts and taking up an equally vacant stare as they waited, looking ominously across the street at nothing in particular.

Between the six old clothes officers, Big Nick, his little sidekick partner, and four other uniformed officers, the load-bearing capacity of the old wooden porch had to be pretty close to maxed out. Mike was waiting down below on the walkway with the landlord, more than a little hesitant to join the dozen men on what he was sure was an accident waiting to happen. No doubt the neighbours would now be peering out at the scene from behind living room curtains.

"I got what you want here," Griffiths said, pulling some papers out of his back pants pocket as he butted out his cigarette on the walkway of the rooming house with his boot. Mike chuckled as he got a good look at the old, faded grey T-shirt and baggy jeans Griffiths was wearing. It was a look that only guys their age thought was hip, unless, of course, they had teenaged kids to tell them otherwise. And the scuffed-up cowboy boots on Griffith's wide feet might actually be the pair that Mike had worn twenty years ago and had just tossed in the Goodwill bin last month when he cleaned out the basement.

"Signed, sealed, and now," Griffiths grunted, handing them to Mike, "delivered."

The grungy old clothes cop elbowed his way past Mike up the stairs to the porch and stood by his men. He shook hands with each of them, pointedly ignoring the uniformed officers.

Mike took a deep breath before pulling the cuffs of his shirt down under his suit jacket.

Mr. Majewski's eyes, meanwhile, had grown increasingly large as he watched the group of old clothes officers converge upon his property. Mike was pretty sure that, in all likelihood, if the little man had not known that they were cops, he would never have allowed them near the house. In fact, when juxtaposed against the clean-cut uniform officers, these men looked like goons, and had they not found their niche within the old clothes branch of policing, Mike was willing to bet that most of these guys probably would have ended up being goons.

He had never been like that when he was an old clothes guy. Neither had Julia or Hoagy. Or Sal.

"Here is the search warrant," Mike advised Mr. Majewski, clearing his throat. "This is what I have to show you to get into the building legally. I'll leave a copy of it for you to hold on to."

"Is okay, Mister Mike," the landlord said as he watched the detective pull the staple from the top corner of the document and hand him the page underneath. "I let you in now."

"Let's get this party started then," Mike sighed, handing the paper over as he climbed the six steps onto the overflowing porch.

He looked down at his watch to record the time of entry and saw that it was already 9:22.

Shit. There is no way in hell that I'm going to be in court before ten. Shit. Might as well call Amanda. She can tell the Crown why I'm not there.

Mike went back down the stairs to make his quick call, and then, key in hand, marched back up to the porch where the sea of sworn officers parted to let him open the door.

* * *

"No kicking doors," Mr. Majewski pleaded from the ground below the porch, shaking his ring of keys.

"Don't worry, Mr. Majewski. No one will damage your place. You have my word," Mike said over his shoulder, hearing an ominous crack coming from his back as he did so.

He checked his watch again to get the exact time of entry: 9:37. *Fuck.* He was beyond tired. Beyond jittery from all the shitty coffee. Beyond annoyed that he'd gotten caught up with this fucking old-clothes cowboy and his fucking cowboy junkies when he ought to be on the stand giving testimony to put that asshole Sanderson away.

In like the vacuum. Out like the wind. Forensics will be here soon. Just stand by. In like the vacuum. Out like the wind. And look engaged.

The mantra wasn't helping, and his eyelids were getting heavy. He felt a vibration in his chest.

Great. I'm having the Big One.

The vibration stopped. And then started again.

No. Cell phone. He reached into his jacket pocket and pulled out the phone. It was a text message from Amanda: **Excused from court. Crown is passed. Poached. Pinched. Pissed. Fuck I hate spell check!!!**

"You Detective O'Shea?" A man in a suit called up to him from the bottom step.

"Yep. You Forensics?" Mike said, replacing the phone in his pocket and pulling out a piece of paper.

"Uh -huh. Got the warrant?"

"I hope you have lots of bags," Mike warned, passing the warrant over.

The officer nodded as he glanced at the warrant, then pulled a white paper jumpsuit over his suit without taking off the jacket. To Mike, the guy looked more like the Michelin Man and the Pillsbury Doughboy's ugly lovechild than the expert witness he would become.

Chapter Twenty-One

Friday, August 24, 2018 - 10:01 a.m.

After so many years of doing this kind of thing, Mike found that buildings fell into categories. This one, at least from the outside, was clearly a typical rooming house: three stories, maybe a dozen eight- by- ten foot rooms rented to one or two people per room plus their 'guests.' Shared kitchen, a couple of shared bathrooms with toilets that might or might not overflow, sinks that might or might not have running hot water, and bathtubs that were definitely beyond use.

As he unlocked the door, Mike had to admit that he was pleasantly surprised. No rotting odours assaulting his nostrils. No dried blood or unidentifiable body matter staining the walls. No voices screaming or music blasting from behind the rows of the plywood doors. As he looked down the hall to the shared kitchen, he noticed that the worn-beyond-repair parquet flooring was more or less clean. Not bad for a downtown rooming house.

"Warrant is good for up here, boys," Griffiths said, pushing past Mike to take the lead, his cowboy boots stomping their way up the stairs.

"I have keys. No kick in doors!" Mr. Majewski called out as he pushed his way through the officers until he was right behind the cowboy.

"Yeah, yeah. Don't worry. Nobody's gonna kick in any doors," Griffiths snapped as he reached the door to be breached.

Mike stood back and let the perverse little conga line head up the narrow stairs ahead of him. A cowboy, a little Polish clown, a man in a bunny suit with a briefcase full of cameras and bags and dust, a hoard of scruffy men with guns, and a handful of uniforms, and Mike bringing up the rear. All making their way to a narrow landing that would lead to a narrow door.

"Key?" the cowboy said, reaching his hand behind his body without looking back, reminding Mike of a surgeon requesting a scalpel.

"Hey, Griffiths!" Mike hollered up the stairway, mimicking taking a picture to remind his colleague that a photo would have to be taken of the stairwell, the landing, and the door before anyone entered Sergei's room.

"Shit. Right. Thanks," the cowboy said, stopping himself from turning the key in the lock. "Okay. Everyone, back up. Down the stairs. Outside. Fuck. Yeah, thanks, O'Shea."

For a moment, the two men were actually colleagues.

"That's why I'm here," Mike said, pivoting on the stair to lead the entourage in their retreat.

"Amanda said you had a nice ass. I don't see it," Griffiths called down from the landing above.

"Fuck off," Mike called back, a slight smile crossing his face.

Once everyone had reached the main floor, they regrouped, and the team started up the stairs again. This time, the forensics officer was in the lead, taking pictures as he went. He was followed by the landlord, then the cowboy and his minions, and then Mike and Big Nick and his partner. The remaining uniforms had been told to wait outside. No need to have everyone involved if they didn't have to be. While the six old clothes goons and the cowboy should be able to handle themselves, Mike was of the opinion that a uniformed presence never hurt. Big Nick and his partner would certainly be enough. The cowboy did not object.

"Keys, sir?" Forensics asked, turning to Mr. Majewski, who passed him a keychain full of keys.

If this room turned out to be the location of the murder, the forensics officer knew that the scene was likely to be a sight that the landlord would be ill -equipped to deal with, so he suggested strongly that Mr. Majewski wait outside. Having been exposed to the occasional dead tenant over the years, Mr. Majewski did not object. He squeezed past the numerous participants in the warrant and hustled down the stairs out onto the porch.

"Bingo," Forensics said as he swung the door open. The other officers shuffled back down the tiny hallway. No matter how many times they saw violent death and what precipitated it, there was still that moment when the gag- reflex kicked in. Some officers got over it, s. Some did not.

Big Nick fell into the latter group. As the rest of the officers stood outside of the room, careful not to touch or disturb anything or get in the way of the rapid-fire photos being shot, Mike looked over and saw the colour leave Big Nick's face. Pushing past everyone, Big Nick then scurried down the stairs, hand clamped over his mouth, trying to stifle what Mike assumed were the chunks of vomit that were undoubtedly pushing their way up his throat with each loud heave. Big Nick's partner dutifully followed, albeit at a much slower pace.

"Maybe we shoulda picked a different uniform," Mike mused.

"Yeah. Or maybe he shoulda picked a different line of work," Griffiths suggested, pushing past Mike to poke his head inside the room, being mindful to remain behind the forensics officer.

Whether or not Big Nick was the uniform for the job, there was no doubt that the one-legged man had come to a very violent end, more than likely in this room. Judging by the amount of blood splattered all over, both Mike and Griffiths concluded that if he wasn't murdered here, then somebody else was, and they had another body to find.

'Scene shock' was what the psychologists called it. 'A day in the life' was what coppers called it. Regardless of the terminology, this bloody mess was quite a vision to behold.

The room itself was fairly large, as far as rooming house rooms went. It had probably been rented furnished, judging by the four matching wooden chairs that were strewn about and the table resting on its side. The bed and dresser looked as if they had been a set, too. There was a small TV in the corner and a large window with heavy floral drapes. All things considered, this room was a fairly decent place. It could likely have been a lot of things for someone, although it clearly hadn't been for this particular tenant.

Taking a deep breath, Mike elbowed Griffiths back and peered around the room, taking in the scene. Had Mike not known any differently, he could easily have concluded that someone had swung an open sack of blood around the place. The drapes covering the window weren't floral-patterned at all, he realized; they were splattered was blood. Lots of it. The matching chairs were covered in blood. Streams of blood had made their way from the top of the cheap plywood door into the room down to the bottom and had pooled on the floor. Even the ceiling did not get away unscathed. The only thing that didn't have any blood on it was the TV.

The bed looked as if it bore the brunt of the now-brown dried blood. Mike took a closer look at it. There were no sheets under the blood-soaked blanket.

It wasn't uncommon for down-and-outers to have no sheets, a bourgeois luxury. But the blood-soaked pillowcase on what looked like a reasonably good pillow suggested that there should have been sheets to match.

Body wrapped in the sheets and dragged out?

Mike peeked around the flimsy door into the hallway. No obvious bloodstains.

Had the deceased bled out entirely in the room before being moved? Would have taken some time if he had. Would the killer have sat by watching his victim die?

Mike recalled the condition of the body in the alleyway and looked around the room again.

Or had the killer left and come back again to dispose of the body?

With all of this blood, it wouldn't take long for a pretty good stench to take hold. Luckily, it wasn't too bad now. If Big Nick puked at this, Mike could only imagine how he'd deal with the smell of a *real* sudden death.

Mike took one more look at the nightmare scene, trying to lock in as many details as he could without potentially fucking up any prospects of sleep he was hoping to catch later. Then he stepped out of the room. There was nothing more for him to do now. It was up to Forensics to work their magic, and to the old clothes guys to dig around for witnesses.

"I'm done," Mike called out. "I got you guys in, you guys have your scene, and you can knock on doors to see if anyone heard anything. I'm out."

Mike wove his way past the scruffy men in the room and slowly walked down the stairs and out into the sunlight.

It would be days—maybe even a week or so—before Forensics got through this mess. Mike would advise the staff sergeant to maintain the perimeter, and he would give Amanda Black her update. Beyond that, whatever he could offer would have to wait until he got back in to work in—he looked at his watch—only four hours. *Shit!*

The sunlight assaulted his eyes. Even after only twenty minutes or so spent in the darkness of the house, the contrast with this light was too much, and his eyes were burning and watering. He rubbed them, squinting as he told the uniform officers on the porch to make sure no one entered while Forensics was there. He interrupted Mr. Majewski, who was flailing his arms while talking on his cell phone, to let him know that they had a homicide scene inside and that different officers would be doing the updates now.

Finally, he looked over at Big Nick standing in the garden beside the house, shadowed by his little partner, looking down at a pool of his own vomit.

Just another day, Mike thought, making his way to his car. *Just another fucking day.*

Chapter Twenty-Two

Friday, August 24, 2018 - 12:35 p.m.

As he stumbled through his back door into the kitchen, Mike heard someone upstairs. Max should have been at school, so either Carmen had come home, or he had an unexpected houseguest. The note on the table offered no further clue: **Dad. I need $40 for the baseball game tomorrow. Love you. Max.**

"Mom?" Mike looked up as a familiar figure came into the room. "What are you doing here?"

"Well," his mother began, her brogue likely thicker than when she had left Ireland almost fifty years earlier." I've been helpin' Maeve at the pub for the past couple of days. Poor wee Nolan had his tonsils out and—"

"Mom!" Mike cut in, annoyed with himself at having asked such an open-ended question of such a long-winded woman.

"And she's been at her wit's end," Mary-Margaret continued, "what with tryin' to look after him and keep up with the cookin'."

"Uh -huh."

"Johnny's brother sent a batch of real Guinness over from home, and I used some of that for the stew that will be the special tonight, but—"

"So what you're saying is that you dropped by to give me some stew?"

"Well, that's only the half of it…" Mary-Margaret's voice dropped as her eyes shifted from side to side.

"Mom," Mike whispered with an equally lowered voice, "unless there are burglars upstairs, you and I are the only ones here."

"Well, there might as well be, let me tell ye." She looked knowingly at her son. "When I let meself in, Carmen and a young lad were just lettin' themselves out. And she was carryin' more than a handbag, *if* ye know what I mean?"

"I see," Mike said through gritted teeth, annoyed at being forced to see this whole fuckup as more than just a bad dream.

"Michael," his mother cautiously began, pulling him in to her as only a mother would, "I'd be lyin' to ye now if I said I was sorry. I do believe that this is a blessing."

"I'm sure it is, Mom," Mike sighed, extricating himself from his mother's arms. "So are you just on your way out or…?"

"In fact, I am," she said, straightening her back and lifting her head to achieve the totality of her five-foot-two height. "The stew is in the fridge."

Mike removed a couple of twenties from his wallet, placed them beside Max's note, and turned to leave the kitchen without acknowledging his mother's answer.

"Michael," she called after him. Recognizing *that* tone, he instinctively stopped and looked back at her. "I have loved ye since before ye were born, and I will love ye until I take me last mortal breath on this earth."

"At least, somebody will," Mike muttered.

"Ye've not been lucky in love, I'll give ye that, my son. But ye have so much else to be thankful for."

"I'm sure I do. Like a bed with my name on it."

"I'm serious, Michael. We all know that God works in mysterious ways. There's somethin' waitin' out there for ye that is more important and much bigger than ye can even imagine."

"Mom, I'm not your wee lad any more," Mike softened. "I know your heart is in it, and I *do* appreciate you stopping by like this, but I'm bone-tired, and I'm supposed to be back at work in less than an hour."

"Well, I'll just call and tell them you'll not be in this evening, then."

"Really, Mrs. O'Shea? And what will you say? 'Hello, this is Michael's mother—'"

"As a matter of fact, I just might at that." Without waiting for a response, Mary-Margaret hustled past Mike, stretching up to give him a peck on the cheek as she went. "I'm off now. We'll see ye Sunday for dinner, then."

And with that, she was out the front door, locking it behind her.

Mike made his way up the stairs to his bedroom, any ounce of energy he had in reserve sucked from him by the interaction with his mom. He removed his pants and was about to toss them over the chair when he remembered Amanda Black's comment. He smiled as he walked over to his closet and hung the pants up before crawling into bed and almost immediately falling asleep.

Disjointed images and sounds swirled through his mind before his alarm went off. The two little girls in the photo he found in the wallet of the man who died in the coffee shop. His mother's voice telling him that she was going to wait until the other wee ones had finished their snacks before telling them that their Da was dead. The weight of Sal falling on him, the gooshy chunks of Sal's splattered brains in his hand.

And then the alarm sounded. Reaching over and turning it off, he opened his eyes, and it all went away.

* * *

"Well, did they find anything up your ass?" Mike called out to Ron as he waltzed into the D office, which was dingy as ever and empty except for Ron.

"It was an appointment for my *wife*," Ron corrected unsmilingly, swivelling his chair around to face Mike as he looked at his watch, noting that his partner was not as late for evening shift as Ron had anticipated he would have been.

"I know. I was kidding."

"Hrmph," Ron snorted, returning to the pile of papers he had laid out on the empty desk beside his. "How was court?"

"Didn't make it. Didn't get home until 12:30 this afternoon."

"Calloway is going to be pissed at you."

"Black called."

"Oh, that must have been wonderful," Ron commented, looking up from one of the piles of papers that he was busy stapling together. "As rumour has it, they can't stand each other."

"So this impacts me how?"

"Not at all, I suppose."

Mike walked over to the old coat rack in the corner and hung his coat up. He then undid the top button of his shirt and loosened his tie as he made his way back to his desk.

"We have to go back for more tests," Ron said cautiously as he leaned across his desk towards Mike.

"Oh," Mike said, logging into his computer, hoping to hear no more.

"You have no idea how difficult it is to find parking around Mount Sinai at 9:30 in the morning," Ron sighed, leaning back, attempting to fill his voice with exasperation to mask the fear that he felt swelling up again inside him.

"I live downtown, Ron. I get it. Yes, parking is a hassle. Luckily, it's not winter. Otherwise, you'd freeze your nuts off walking around Hospital Alley. It's a fucking wind tunnel at the best of times," Mike said, referring to that relatively short stretch on University Avenue where four major hospitals and a huge rehabilitation facility were. "It sounds like a tough day. You could've taken this evening off. Why didn't you?"

"Same reason you didn't, partner," Ron replied, without missing a beat. "Likely due more to curiosity than dedication, though."

"Curious about what?" Mike squinted as he watched the icons on his computer screen come to life.

"Whether or not tonight will be the night they catch him." Ron moved forward in his chair to look directly at Mike.

"Catch who? The guy who offed our one-legged man? Come on, tell me that doesn't keep you up at night." Mike laughed and reached into the desk drawer to pull out a steno pad.

"No. Not him. You know who I'm talking about. You can't tell me that you don't think about him? Sal's shooter?"

"Fuck." Mike's body slumped.

"Kind of an obvious-looking guy," Ron began. "High-profile murder, shooting a cop like that. You were right there. Excellent witness. I'm sure I'm not the only one who finds it curious that they never caught him."

Mike took a deep breath, placed his fingers on the keyboard in front of him, then let his shoulders slump. The back hallway was surprisingly quiet.

"I thought we weren't going to talk about this."

"We weren't. But we are."

There was no way of avoiding Ron's direct gaze.

"Okay. Wanna know what I think?" Mike acquiesced. "I think someone dropped the ball. I think someone knows exactly where the shooter is, and he could have been arrested in a heartbeat. I think he's still out there, and I think someone knows where he is."

Ron sat back to consider for a moment.

"Is that what you wanted to know?" Mike asked.

"Doesn't that bother you?"

"Every. Fucking. Day." Mike replied, feeling the muscles in his already-tired back begin to spasm.

"And so?"

"And so I keep my eyes open, my ears to the ground, and—"

"A lot of good that's done you," Ron said, looking around his desk for a pen that he had misplaced.

"Yeah. A lot of good. Listen," Mike huffed, "I'm not interested in getting into it with you now, but let's just say that I haven't given up."

"Fair enough. Do you think this Cockeye fellow is our man?" Ron knew when to stop pushing. They had a long night ahead of them.

"Not a clue. Out of our hands now. Homicide has taken over." The first wave of fatigue was just starting to roll over Mike. He arched his back in the hope of undoing some of the knots, but released a tremendous yawn instead. Between the Sanderson shitshow, his home life, and now this fucking reminder of what was always at the forefront of his mind, this homicide investigation was the last thing he wanted to think about. In fact, he was looking forward to something new for them to investigate sooner rather than later, just to get back into his comfort zone.

"And what about our victim? What do we know? Staff says uniforms are still at the scene. There must be a fair bit for Forensics to do. Did Amanda want us to do anything else?" Ron could feel his thoughts spinning, but knew that as long as he could focus on work, he, too, could block out everything else. *Likely nothing to it. Just wanting to err on the side of caution. That's what the doctor said. That's all the next appointment is about. That's all.*

"Dunno. I was gonna give her a quick call this morning just before I got into bed, but my head hit the pillow, and I was gone. I imagine she's got her guys running around chasing down leads. I'm thinking we're done. Cut out of the picture."

"Wouldn't be the first time," Ron sighed, returning to the piles of papers that seemed to be growing in complexity with every reshuffle, rather than becoming more orderly.

"Nope." Mike starred blankly at the computer screen, which stared back at him. Running his hand through his still-thick hair, he added, "I wouldn't mind going out to grab a coffee. You want one?"

"No, thanks. I've got plenty of paperwork to do here. If it's quiet, though, I might take off a couple of hours early tonight, if you don't mind. Marie's a little… you know."

"No problem." Still uncomfortable, Mike stood up and stretched.

It didn't seem to do much good.

Chapter Twenty-Three

Friday, August 24, 2018 - 4:20 p.m.

"Who wants him?"

Mike put down the keys that he had just picked up from the desk where they'd been left by the previous shift.

"What have you got?" Ron asked, looking up from his papers at the new arrival.

"Only the murderer," Detective Constable Ricky Jergensen said smugly as he emerged from the hallway that led from the booking hall into the back of the D office, the grin on his face making him look like the boy who'd caught the Big One.

"Say what?" Mike said, moving towards the district old clothes officer. His coffee would have to wait.

"I got Cockeye."

"How do we know he's the murderer?" Ron asked, standing up but not moving from behind his desk. Mike shot a skeptical glance at his partner.

"It's been all over the news." Jergensen smiled confidently at Ron. "They had a press conference about an hour ago, and the D/S says this is our man. Hey, Sarge! How ya doin'?" Jergensen walked over to Mike, hand outstretched.

"Been better, been worse, Ricky," Mike replied, shaking the young man's hand, recalling how this kid had started his policing career on Mike's old shift just a couple of years earlier. "Last time I saw you, you were a clean-cut recruit. What the fuck have you done to yourself?"

"Grew my hair. Got a couple of tatts and some piercings. Doing real police work now, boss, just like you used to. Done with shaving every day, wearing the monkey suit, and writing traffic tickets for a living." Jergensen gave Ron a condescending glance.

"And now you're bringing in murderers, eh?" Mike smiled at Jergensen and then looked back at Ron. "You'd think the D/S over at Homicide might have dropped a dime and let us know that we had a named suspect, eh, Ron?"

"One would think." Ron looked down again at the paperwork on his desk. As a Rules & Regs copper, the world of old clothes and the type of officers it attracted generally rubbed Ron the wrong way. He also very much disliked Ricky Jergensen personally.

"So what do you want me to do with this guy, Mike?" Jergensen asked.

"Where is he now?"

"In the holding room over there." Jergensen pointed toward the long, narrow hallway where prisoners were held pending further investigation when they weren't in the cells. As he did so, the sleeve of his tattered jean jacket rode up to reveal the series of recently acquired tattoos.

"Well," Ron began, taking a deep breath in an attempt to suppress his immediate distaste for what he was sure would follow, "I suppose we ought to call Detective Sergeant Black to see what she wants with this fellow and then go from there."

"Cool. I'll start writing up my notes," Jergensen replied, plunking himself down at the empty desk behind Mike, absently grabbing Russ McLean's morning newspaper, which was still open to the page with the girl on it. "Wow. Wouldn't mind a motorboat ride with those."

Ron stopped what he was doing and looked up at the young officer, who had moved on from the photo and was now firing up the computer in front of him. He could feel himself becoming increasingly annoyed, his face reddening against the collar of his crisp white shirt. On the best of days, Ron had little time for guys who thought ogling pictures of women on company time was acceptable. Now, after spending a difficult morning at the hospital with his wife, hearing this particular little shit make flippant comments about some woman's breasts was almost more than Ron could stand.

"I suspect she'll want to seize his clothing, officer," Ron prompted curtly, trying to rein himself in by finding comfort in procedures.

"Oh. Right."

Jergensen's flippant tone made Ron even angrier. Procedures were clear. Collecting evidence. Accused's clothing as evidence. Seizing said clothing. A fairly common practice that any half-decent investigator would have known to follow. That Ricky Jergensen didn't appear to have even considered it was no surprise to Ron.

"How about you make sure we have a bunny suit for your prisoner, and I'll call Forensics to see if they want to do the seizing or if they'll let you do it," Ron suggested to Jergensen before looking over at Mike and adding, "This is not going to go well."

"Sounds good to me, boss," Jergensen said, seemingly oblivious to Ron's discomfort as he hopped out of the chair and walked briskly back towards the booking hall, albeit not before taking another look down at the girl in the newspaper.

"I don't like it," Ron said after a long pause, leaning over closer to Mike.

"What?"

"This. Why didn't Amanda at least give us a head's-up, and what are the chances that this guy would be caught within hours of her press conference?"

"Well, we don't catch the smart ones, do we?" Mike replied as the eager young officer returned with a sealed plastic bag containing a white one-piece paper jumpsuit. "But you may be right. There may be more to this than meets the eye."

"I still don't like it," Ron repeated.

"Don't like what?" Jergensen asked, removing the paper coverall from its packaging. "The suit? It's the only size they had in the booking hall. Are we seizing, or is Forensics?"

"I haven't had a chance to call. Where did you find him?" Ron asked.

"What do you mean?"

"Where was Cockeye arrested?" Mike said, hearing the combination of disbelief and confrontation in Ron's voice. *Clearly, more to this than meets the eye.*

"At Soupy's," the young officer replied. Mike knew the place well from his old-clothes days: a local watering hole where every known criminal and the woman who loved him could be found on any given day.

"Just sitting there?" Ron's lips were tightening.

"Yeah."

"So you mean to tell me that this man killed another man yesterday, was awfully sloppy about it all, and was sitting in the most obvious bar in the city having a drink when you found him?"

"Yeah. Like Mikey said, we don't catch the smart ones." Jergensen's jaw was starting to protrude as he tried to dismiss Ron's comments.

"Do you have witnesses?"

"Say what?" Jergensen's eyes narrowed as he looked at Ron.

"Witnesses. Because I find your story highly unlikely." Ron puffed his chest out, squaring off for a fight. "And that's *Detective* O'Shea to you, officer."

Mike could feel his hair practically starting to stand on end from the tension in the room.

It was a given that just as the homicide Ds operated a little differently from their district counterparts, the old clothes and squad guys marched to the beat of a different drummer than the uniforms did.

"Suit yourself, but I'm just saying that I got your murderer sitting in your interview room. If you don't want him, I'll do up the fucking paperwork myself." Jergensen's jaw was now so tight that Mike almost expected his teeth to pop out of his mouth from the pressure.

It was the younger man's clenched fists, however, that concerned Mike more.

"How about we leave Cockeye on ice for a few while you start up the record of arrest and fill in what you can? My partner and I will make a few phone calls and see how Homicide wants to play this, okay?" Mike suggested in the hope of defusing a potentially ugly situation.

"Yeah. How about I do that?" Jergensen snarled, tossing the bunny suit down on the desk beside him and sulking.

"And how about you and I step out in the hall here for a second and get our game plan together?" Mike said to Ron, leading the way out of the D office. To his surprise and relief, Ron followed.

"What the hell is going on, Ron?" Mike asked, maneuvering his partner out of the main thoroughfare into the tiny photocopy room across the hall.

"He didn't arrest that guy at Soupy's. He grabbed him, probably from his bed in his house or wherever he's flopping these days," Ron announced, shaking his head in disgust. "I know Jergensen. He's a dirty cop."

"Oh?" Mike raised his eyebrows. "That wasn't my experience with the kid when he was a rookie, but a lot can happen between uniform and old clothes."

"Yes. I can't get into it now, except to say that he's being sued for a couple of million bucks as a result of a false arrest on a case I ended up running, and he almost dragged me down with him. Let me tell you, Mike, if I have anything to do with it, the complainant will get that money and more. And then there are the near misses, where all I've lost are the cases. That kid has messed up searches and flat-out lied about them on the stand. *And* been called out. I don't want his name anywhere near mine on anything I'm involved in, especially a homicide case."

"Well, okay, then," Mike nodded. "This is Amanda Black's case. She's the one who's going to come down here and process the body. And she's the one who is going to run this through court. But before that, I suspect, she's going to make damned sure that this charge is going to stick. And if she thinks there's a problem with the arrest at this stage of the game, I imagine that she'll deal with our Officer Jergensen accordingly. I don't imagine she's got to where she is by being anybody's fool."

"Well, I have to tell her what I know," Ron said.

"Sure. She'll hear the details of the arrest, then we can tell her our concerns, and then she can deal with the arresting officer. Or not. In any event, we have our suspect here. We can't really let him walk out the door scot-free, can we?"

"If we have nothing, we have to," Ron replied, disgust heavy in his voice. "And that will open up a whole can of worms."

"You know, though, if this Cockeye guy is as much of a rounder as we know he is, I'm sure we can find something else on him to keep him for a while." Mike turned to walk back into the D office, wishing that he'd made the decision earlier to go for coffee and perhaps missed dealing with this mess altogether. "In the meantime, you continue on with your paperwork, and I'll get young Richard going and give Amanda a call to let her know what we have."

"This is going to go very badly," Ron muttered.

"I'm too old for this shit," Mike muttered at the same time, preparing himself for a situation that he, too, was beginning to suspect would go very badly, indeed.

Chapter Twenty-Four

Friday, August 24, 2018 - 5:51 p.m.

"What the fuck do you mean,: 'We have your man'?" Amanda Black's bellow could be heard in the room as Mike pulled the receiver away from his ear.

"I have an old clothes guy here who says that you did a press conference about an hour ago identifying Mark Johnstone as your murder suspect, and he's arrested him and brought him here."

"I don't know what fucking channel your boy is watching, but I *did not* say that. At. All."

"Well, Mr. Johnstone is in our interview room right now. I've got a copper here in ratty jeans who's trying to look like he hasn't seen a bar of soap in a week who arrested him, and I'm looking for a little direction," Mike replied, deliberately slowing his speech as Amanda's usual quick phrasing accelerated to prestissimo.

"I am just around the corner at the scene where they found the body. Do *not* have anyone so much as *look* at Johnstone until I get there," Amanda demanded. "And tell that fucking little asshole of a copper that he'll need a better story than that when I talk to him, or I'll be ripping him a new one."

"I shall pass on the message," Mike replied, turning around to look at Jergensen, who was sitting back at McLean's desk with the newspaper open to the picture of the woman, nonchalantly chewing on one of the fingernails.

The line was dead before Mike could get the words out.

"So she coming here?" The young officer spat a nail onto the floor, not turning to look at Mike.

"Yes. Detective Sergeant Black is on her way," Mike replied. His head was starting to ache from fatigue, or maybe caffeine withdrawal.

"I can't wait to see this one," Ron said, not quite under his breath.

Jergensen turned his chair around to shoot a glance at Ron over Mike's shoulder. Taking another nibble at his fingernail, he looked at Mike.

"Everything's cool, right, Mikey?"

"'Cool' is not quite the world I would use," Mike cautioned, eyes still on Ron. "Homicide is adamant that they never identified Johnstone as the killer, and the D/S is wondering where you got that intel from."

The words hung in the air for a few seconds.

"What do you mean?" Jergensen spat another piece of his mangled fingernail on to the floor.

"Detective Sergeant Amanda Black is on her way here. You'll need a better story, my friend." Mike stood up and arched his back, wincing a little as he did so. Then swivelling his chair around, he bent forward to lean against the back of it and looked directly at Jergensen.

"Are you saying I'm fucking lying?" Jergensen's left temple was visibly starting to pulsate, his jaw was tightening, and he had squared off at the shoulders.

Fight or flight.

"Listen," Mike offered. "I'm just saying that the D/S isn't happy, and I've heard that she can be rather... clear... when she's annoyed, you know?" He suddenly realized that he'd been squaring himself up as well.

Ron had tried to remain distanced from this interaction, but now he slowly pushed himself back from his desk, at the same time glancing up at Jergensen from behind his computer screen.

"Fuck you!" the young officer said, leaping to his feet, almost knocking Mike's chair back. "I'll just let the fucker go then, and you fucking assholes can find him later!"

He spun around and stomped the few feet it took him to get out of the office and down the short hallway to the holding room, where he grabbed the latch on the door of the closet-sized space.

"Hey, Cockeye. Get your shit!" he yelled through the door, struggling to undo the latch.

"What?" came a muffled response.

"Hold up. What are you doing?" Mike demanded as he made his way down the hallway and yanked Jergensen away from the door.

"Getting ready to release him. You guys obviously don't know your fucking heads from your fucking assholes, and I've got bigger fucking shitheads to deal with than you today."

Mike stopped. Maybe it was because he was tired. Maybe it was because Jergensen's story didn't hold water. Maybe it was because Jergensen just had that same fucking look in his eye that Sanderson had had when he leaned over to talk to his lawyer the other day.

Or maybe it was because he knew now that he wasn't the only one who thought they had fucked up Sal's murder investigation.

Whatever it was, Mike took a breath to give himself a moment to 'consider his options'. The company therapist loved that phrase.

In like the vacuum. Out like the wind.

It didn't help.

Again.

In like the vacuum. Out like the wind.

Nope.

Mike took another breath.

Then as Jergensen stepped in to push past him, Mike took one final breath and, without saying a word, pulled back his fist and punched the scraggly young officer in the head as hard as he could, knocking the young man out cold.

That helped.

A lot.

"What the—" Ron came running over, having seen the punch connect before hearing the sound of Jergensen's head hitting the ground.

"It's all right, Ron. I think we'd both agree that our friend here had a little attitude adjustment coming to him," Mike said, calmly straightening his tie.

"Fuck you!" Jergensen slurred, shaking off the effects of the blow and attempting to take a run at his opponent as he regained both his consciousness and his footing, without considering that Mike was his superior. Or perhaps not caring.

"Hold your fucking horses, dickweed," Mike said, easily sidestepping the young officer's attack and pinning the still-stunned man face -first against the door to the interview room.

"This is not at all like Traffic," Ron said, not getting any closer to the two men. "I'll call Staff at the front—"

"No. I think we can handle Young Blood here on our own."

Jergensen's face was crimson. Luckily, his head had not split, but Mike could see a goose egg forming above his left eye, even with his face pushed up against the door.

"Hello? Hello?" a voice from behind the door called sadly. "Can I get out of here?"

"You're okay, fella," Mike replied. "You, on the other hand," he said to Jergensen, turning his subordinate around by the collar of his jean jacket, pinning the younger man's shoulders to the door, "are so fucked. First off, that goose egg will probably give you a shiner with bragging rights by tomorrow morning—"

"And I'll charge you with assault, you fucking asshole." Ricky Jergensen tried to sound indignant, but the words came out more like a high-pitched whimper. Mike was not even remotely intimidated, but he managed to refrain from laughing.

"Fair enough. And I'll charge you with insubordination, discreditable conduct, perjury, and a few other cool little things that I'm sure Internal Affairs will tack on to the file they probably already have on you. Oh, and wait until I tell them how you tried to let a prisoner go free, which, by the way," Mike was on a roll, "gives me carte blanche to use as much force as necessary to prevent it from happening. And then you can explain *that* to the detective sergeant—"

"What the *fuck* is going on here?" D/S Amanda Black's voice pierced the air as she came to a stop beside Ron and addressed the two erstwhile combatants in front of her.

"Can I get out?" The voice from behind the holding room door almost snivelled.

"Boys, I don't have time for this. If you want to do a little dick waving, I suggest you do it outside on your own time. Now I repeat: What the *fuck* is going on here?"

"This officer just tripped and... uh, hit the door, wasn't it, Ricky? I believe he was on his way to get a glass of water for *his* prisoner," Mike offered, adjusting Jergensen's collar and lining up the shoulder seams of the younger man's jean jacket before turning to address Amanda.

"I don't want any glass of water. I want to get outta here," the voice called out again, gaining strength from hearing the confusion on the other side of the door.

Amanda looked at Mike, then at the old clothes officer, her eyes burning holes through both of them. Ron stood motionless beside her. Everyone ignored the prisoner.

"Do you want me to get Staff?" Ron finally offered, breaking the unbearably painful silence.

"I don't think that's necessary. How about you, Rick?" Mike asked, looking pointedly at the younger officer.

Jergensen tenderly touched the area around his eye with his right hand, then checked his nose to see if it was broken or bleeding. After thoroughly examining his hand for any sign of blood but seeing none, he submitted to the older man, giving Mike the same look a son gives his father when he knows that he has pushed the envelope too far and has been called out on it. "I, uh, fell. Against the door. Like the D...Detective O'Shea...said. I'm good."

"All right, then." Mike stepped back and took a deep breath. "I'm going to go get a coffee while you advise the D/S of your arrest. Make sure you get some ice for that, or else have a really good story ready for tomorrow morning because you're gonna look like hell once that thing finishes swelling."

Amanda shot a look at Mike that would have dropped a lesser man.

"With due respect, Detective Sargent," Mike countered her look, "I believe that this is your case, and this will be your body. This is Ricky Jergensen, your arresting officer, and I don't really have anything else to offer." Mike brushed past Ron, picking up the car keys he had left on the table as he made his way to the doorway out of the D office, passing Amanda as he walked away.

"Don't. Anyone. Move." Amanda snapped, causing Mike to freeze in his tracks. "I don't know what happened here, but I'm not dealing with this right now. You," she pointed to the young old clothes officer in front of her, "come sit over here and tell me why Mark Johnstone is on the other side of that door. And you," Amanda swung around, directing her attention to Mike, "get yourself a goddamned coffee or whatever it is that makes you human as fast as you can. I need you to cool down and then tell me what the fuck just happened. And you," she pivoted to finally look at Ron, "tell the staff sergeant that I'm here and I want to talk to him when I'm finished talking to this officer."

"What about me?" the voice behind the door asked.

"*You* shut the fuck up," Amanda barked.

Chapter Twenty-Five

Friday, August 24, 2018 - 7:02 p.m.

Mike's phone vibrated in his suit coat pocket as he got back in the car, coffee in hand.

Sorry to bother. Might be going over to Kyle Sampson's after game. Pick me up after work? the text from Max read.

Mike sighed. His heart tightened every time Max started a text with 'sorry to bother.' This was his flesh and blood, his world, his true responsibility. But he had a job to do, and Max had grown up knowing it. One day, Mike wouldn't be chasing down criminals. One day, he would catch the one that he was really after. And then….

Sure. Will let you know if on overtime. Mike texted his son back.

Overtime. Always overtime. Investigations that took on a life of their own, victims who needed more support. His JPTF days had been the worst: Mike was victim liaison, which meant carrying the company cell 24/7. And answering it 24/7. Sometimes, one of the girls would just be drunk or high and want to talk. Other times, a girl needed a safe house now because her pimp was going to kill her for going to the cops. Every call came in on that phone, every call was answered 24/7.

But that was a long time ago. Being a district D was supposed to be different. Easier, less demanding. Or so they said. Mike still ended up with a lot of overtime. All part of the job, but the thrill was gone, and it was becoming more of a grind.

Leaning back in his seat, Mike set his steaming coffee in the holder. He stared absently out the windshield into the coffee shop where he and Ron had done CPR on that guy yesterday.

Just a regular family man. Same age as me. I doubt he survived.

Thx. Be safe. Max responded.

You too. Mike texted back, his lip creeping into a half-smile.

At this stage of the game, it was hard to say whether it was Max or Mike who was more likely to have a dangerous night.

"Any unit to attend for a male threatening suicide," the dispatcher's voice came through the car speaker. "Neighbour calling in. Says there's a man on the balcony next door. Say's he's threatening to jump. Says the neighbour is a retired police officer. No further description at this time. Anyone available. 14:47."

Mike rubbed his forehead with the fingers of his right hand before dropping the car into drive and reaching for the mic under the dashboard.

"IV2. Where is it, Dispatch," he said, assuming but not positive that he was the only investigative unit out and about. "I can swing by. And is it the caller or the guy on the balcony who is supposed to be the retired copper?"

"I think it's the man on the balcony, IV2." The dispatcher's voice warmed up, knowing that she had a unit to respond to this priority call.

"Okay. Put me on it. Address?"

"24 High Park Avenue; complainant is in apartment 1201. Says neighbour is in apartment 1203, overlooks visitor parking. You solo?"

"Yes, I am, Dispatch. I'll head over. Send another unit when one is available. No rush. I'll advise." Mike took a sip of his coffee and put it back in the holder before taking his foot off the brake pedal.

"Thanks muchly. Can I just get your badge and call signs again, IV unit responding to the male threatening suicide at 24 High Park Avenue?"

"Badge is 32833. Detective O'Shea. IV2."

"Thanks, Detective. I'll have another unit head over when one clears," the dispatcher advised.

"2201 call." What sounded to Mike like a very young voice called out over the airwaves. "We're just around the corner. We can back up the D if you'd like."

"Great. Thank you, 2201. And there are two of you on board? I'll mark you on the call with IV2," the dispatcher said, the sound of her fingers tapping on the keyboard audible through the cars' speakers as she updated everyone's status.

Recognizing the address as one of the nicer buildings in the area, Mike found himself rolling up in front of the high-rise within minutes of taking the call. "I'm on scene, Dispatch. I'll advise once I get upstairs."

"Great. What's your portable there, Detective?" The dispatcher was downright conversational as she asked for the item number of the hand-held radio she expected Mike would have.

"I don't have one, Dispatch. I'll give you a call on my cell once I get up to the apartment if anything changes."

"Please stand by until the other unit arrives, Detective," the dispatcher advised. Her cautionary tone reminded Mike of Rose, one of the best dispatchers he had ever known. She always looked out for her officers, on and off the air. He often wondered what happened to her. He hadn't heard her voice since that day. He had to admit, most of the dispatchers were pretty good. The poor ones really stood out. They could cause a world of difficulty for the road sergeant and, depending on how far things went offside, create unnecessary costs and time spent in court for officers and investigators to try to explain the discrepancies between the audio recording and what actually happened. This one sounded like one of the good ones.

Mike stepped out of the car without responding and looked up. Sure enough, there was a man on what was probably the twelfth floor standing on the outside of the balcony railing.

Mike reached back into his car to update the dispatcher. "Buddy's on the ledge. Better have an ambulance attend, and do we have a negotiator working today?"

"Fire and ambulance are already dispatched. I haven't got a negotiator on my band, but I'll check the air citywide and get back to you. You are standing by until backup arrives, correct, IV2?"

Mike didn't respond, choosing to head up on his own instead.

* * *

"Hello?" Mike called out as he cautiously poked his head inside the apartment, having gently turned the door handle and opened the unlocked door.

"Don't come in," a man's voice warned.

"If you didn't want anyone to come in, why did you leave the door unlocked?"

"Because I don't want some stupid copper to blow his knee trying to kick in a metal door!" the man snapped back.

""Copper'? Only coppers say 'copper.' You a cop?"

"Thirty-eight years."

"And…?" Mike pushed at the apartment door with his elbow, hand still on the door handle, trying to get a better idea of what he might be walking into.

"And then I retired, dumb-ass."

"You still on the balcony?" Mike asked, scanning the area directly in front of him as he tentatively made his way inside the apartment.

"Yes."

"Then who is the dumb-ass?"

"And who the fuck are you to call me a dumb-ass?"

"Mike O'Shea. Detective."

Mike was inside the apartment entrance now. It was a standard layout, moderately decorated and absolutely spotless. Nothing remarkable. Mike paused for a moment to sniff: nothing. Everything immaculate. All beige. Anyone else who might have wandered in would have likely seen this nondescript presentation as a good thing. As a cop with a lot of miles on his shoes, Mike's skin began to tingle any time he was faced with such a sterile scene. Addicts, hoarders, and people unable to care for themselves because of poverty or mental illness were the ones he expected to be out on balconies, not guys like this. Except when they were. And it was these guys, who lived in a state of seemingly calm orderliness, who were the unpredictable ones.

And in Mike's world, unpredictable meant dangerous.

"Mikey? Mikey O'Shea? You still on the job?" the voice called from beyond the living room that separated the two men. Mike quickly scanned the room, looking for something to anchor his would-be jumper to this world. Not much to pull from.

"Apparently. Who are you?" he called back, not recognizing the voice. He intentionally let the door half close behind him so that his backup officers and the paramedics could get in, but gawkers wouldn't be able to catch a glimpse of whatever might end up happening here. An audience could change the dynamic of a situation like this, and Mike didn't really want to deal with that right now.

"Who do you think?"

"You tell me."

"Sunflower seeds."

"Enough with this bullshit. I've got shit to do, and I don't need a jumper on my watch." *What the fuck? Very few people knew about the sunflower seeds.*

Mike looked at the partially opened heavy blue drapes that were rippling slightly with the breeze. That meant his guy was likely a practical man who specifically chose heavy drapes to keep the morning sun from baking the apartment. He was frugal. And deliberate. Fastidious. And a retired cop.

Mike began mentally painting a portrait of his target to try to develop a game plan. He had to try to figure out the language to use to get this guy back inside the apartment. Unfortunately, those same heavy drapes that Mike was using as a markers of the man's character prevented him from getting a clear view of the balcony or of the man he was talking to.

"Come on, Mikey! Don't tell me you don't remember me?"

Mike felt his jaw tighten, almost wishing the man would jump.

"It's me—Robby Williams. Radio room should have told you that. Probably did and you didn't listen, you dumb shit. Nothing changes, does it?" Mike imagined the smile coming across his old boss's face.

"Robby? Holy shit! How long you been retired?"

"Ten and a half years. Thanks for checking up on me."

"Well, you know…" Mike fumbled for the words. Even though he was just a constable back then and Robby was his D/S, working in the JPTF made them close. And then, when Sal….

"Time flies, eh?" Mike continued, taking in a deep breath. "Seems like yesterday when you were watching over us, trying to keep things on the straight and narrow. You had one hell of a retirement party, though, eh, Robby? I'm surprised that *that* didn't kill you."

Mike lowered his guard, making his way past the predictably placed overstuffed living room furniture to the balcony doors and pushing the curtains back to reveal a much older version of the man he remembered, standing on the wrong side of the balcony railing.

"Me, too. I still can't believe how many of the guys came out for it. Some kind of fun, that was." The man on the balcony smiled at Mike. "I'm surprised you're not long gone, Mikey."

"Soon. Another couple of years left. So…" Mike resumed a cautious tone of voice. Robby wasn't crazy, but was he the kind of guy who was just crazy enough to jump off a twelfth-floor balcony? "What's with this balcony thing?"

"I'm done, Mikey," the old man confided, looking down at the parking lot below him.

"What do you mean, 'I'm done'?" Mike chortled. "What about June and the kids?"

"June died around this time last year."

"Sorry to hear." *Shit. Anniversary death. That raises the ante a bit.*

"Yep. Cancer. Hell of a way to go. She was a beautiful girl, and that disease ate her up, piece by piece, until there was nothing left but the sickness. Took five years to kill her."

Mike felt for his cell phone in the pocket over his heart, the text from his son vivid in his mind. He recalled the man lying dead on the floor in the coffee shop. And the picture of the man's little girls.

"What about the kids?"

"Grown up, Mikey. All of 'em are doing just fine, getting on with their lives."

"You know this plan of yours is just fucked, right?" Mike sighed, glancing over his shoulder at the photographs of kids and cottages and dogs and a much younger Robby in a cheap suit standing beside a beautiful woman in a wedding dress.

"No, it's okay, Mikey. It's time to go. I've had a good run. You and I and the boys and Julia: We all had a hell of a good time together, didn't we? I did my best for June. Kids are good. It's time."

"You're just talking stupid."

"Come over here and say that," Robby said with a smile, taking a half-hearted swing at Mike with one hand, the other one holding on to the railing.

Mike's body froze as the palms of his hands began to sweat, momentarily struck speechless, standing inside the apartment in motionless disbelief. The man who had gone to the wall for him so many times, the man who had stood beside Sal's mother when Mike had given her Sal's forage cap, that man here now, staring back at him from the other side of the balcony railing, looking right as rain. No crazy in those eyes. No confusion. No cloudiness.

"Well?" Robby turned his head to look over his shoulder as he flexed his knees, bouncing slightly as if limbering up for an Olympic-style backflip off the high board, before looking back at Mike. "Still afraid of heights, are you?"

"Fuck you," Mike said with a chuckle. He couldn't help smiling to himself when he recalled how, back in the day, he had pulled back from balconies like these hoping that he or Sal could either talk the pimp into changing his mind or they just pounce on the guy and beat him into submission before anyone got seriously hurt. But there were also the times—far too many times—that they arrived just a moment too late to pluck any of those girls off the railing before she could step into eternity. And each time, there was that unmistakable sound of the girl's head exploding like an over-ripe melon falling off a fruit truck on its way to the market when they hit the ground.

The smile faded from Mike's face as he realized that he might as well be back on any one of those balconies, except that this time, he was talking to one of his own. Not just his own, but one of the few remaining guys who remembered how it really was.

"So what the fuck am I supposed to do now?" Mike asked Robby. Nothing had trained him for this. There were no videos or scenarios that showed him how to keep a sane man from jumping off a balcony. Or a sane retired copper. Or your old boss.

"You're asking me? C'mon, Mikey. I'm supposed to be the one in crisis!" Robby laughed.

"Yeah. Real crisis. Thanks, asshole." Not since facing down Sal's killer had Mike felt so mortal, so small, so vulnerable. He knew that he was likely staring death in the face. He wanted to believe otherwise; he wanted to say something that would make it different, but all he had left was to try to convince himself that it wouldn't end up that way. Mostly, though, what he really wanted—no, needed—to do was stave off the feeling of utter helplessness that he had never known before Sal's death.

"I know what you're thinking," Robby said. "If I were you, I'd turn around, walk out, and close the door behind me. Go on. I'll be okay. It's what I want."

"Too late, Robby. They've marked me on the call. I'm committed," Mike's voice croaked as he moved onto the balcony, his eyes begging Robby to change his mind. "Do me a favour. Save me. Get off the fucking balcony. For me. Save me from giving them another chance to ask their stupid fucking questions that I wasn't able to answer the first time."

"I am going to jump, Mikey," his old boss said gently, his eyes softening, almost watering. "I don't suppose you'd like to see me do it, so just leave. You've seen enough blood and guts in your time."

"Then why the fuck did you call then?" Mike's anger flared as he realized all the loose ends and unfinished business of his own life. "You don't get to fucking check out without any remorse or responsibility for anyone at all. And I'm not going to be left trying to fucking pick up the fucking pieces. Again. Fuck you!"

The old man was easily within arm's reach of Mike. Mike thought for a moment. Of that afternoon, of that night. Of Robby, likely all tight-assed about it, likely standing there with his mouth hanging open when the warehouse was in flames, and Julia ran past all the big tough guys and pulled Mike out.

"Hey!" Mike said, reminding himself. "You'll never guess who's on the relieving shift."

"Nope, I won't. Don't know. Don't care."

"Julia Vendramini."

"Julia? Our Julia?" Mike could feel Robby's eyes truly focusing on him for the first time since the two had reunited. "She still a beauty? Man, she could turn heads back then! Best undercover we ever had. Helluva nice girl, too. Did she ever end up having kids? That was all she talked about back in the day. That and the outrageous amount of money she spent on shoes."

"Yep. She's still got it. We should all go for a drink one day."

"Yeah, let's do that. Only problem is, I won't be there." Robby looked out at the horizon just over his shoulder, fingers flexing on the railing in anticipation of the final release that would free him from the despair that had taken custody of him.

"Listen, Sugar Lips…" Mike recalled Robby's nickname, allegedly given to him by the girls on the street all those years ago for reasons likely less exotic than the rumours that swirled around it. "Squad guys like us don't jump off balconies. We retire to Florida and get drunk on the beach, telling boring cop stories to scantily clad bikini babes. Come on, get your shit together."

"Mikey, I'm seventy-three years old…" Robby's voice trailed off as he flexed his arms on the railing.

"Okay. So?"

"My wife passed last year." The old man sighed, and Mike saw him loosening his grip on the railing.

"Don't fucking let go. You got kids. Lots of them. And grandkids, probably?"

"Five kids, sixteen grandchildren."

Mike whistled. "That's a beautiful thing. And do you want them to remember you as that asshole who jumped?"

He tried desperately to think of options. He knew he couldn't watch Robby jump and would likely make a grab for him if he went, and then both of them would end up plunging twelve stories to their deaths. He wasn't comfortable with heights to begin with, and he sure as hell didn't want to end his policing career splattered all over a parking lot.

No, Mike had no intention of falling to his death, clinging on to some old man, even if it was Robby.

"Listen," he said, stalling for time. "I'm gonna make some coffee. Do you want some or not?" Given how much time had passed, it was increasingly clear that backup wasn't coming. He was it. He'd have to be the one to talk Robby off the balcony, and the only way he knew to do that was by engaging his old boss in something inside the apartment.

Mike backed up, stepping sideways into the galley kitchen to the right of the balcony, never taking his eyes off his old friend.

"Coffee?" Robby snorted. "Don't waste my time. There's a bottle under the sink in there."

"Even better. Want a shot with me?"

"Can't. I'm diabetic, and it throws my blood sugar off."

"You're going to jump anyway. What do you care?" Mike's head was starting to throb with fatigue and renewed annoyance.

"You never were very sensitive, were you, Mikey?" Robby laughed.

"Not according to my first wife, no. We'll see what the second says." Mike reached under the sink to retrieve an unmarked bottle of what could be any number of alcoholic beverages, careful not to turn his back to the balcony. "So? You coming in, or am I just going to pound this back on my own? You're not even suicidal, are you? Just lonely. What the fuck. Call your kids. Go to some of those goddamn coffee meet-ups all you old farts go to."

Mike relaxed a bit as he took a swig of the unknown liquid and immediately spat it into the sink. "What the fuck is this shit, you cheap bastard?" He looked back at Robby, then gave the bottle a smell and quickly pulled it away from his nose.

"Some wine I made a few months back."

"From what? Dog shit?" Mike gave Robby a look of absolute disgust.

"Not my finest batch, I'll have to admit, but it sure packs a punch."

"It'll probably make go you blind. Or crazy. You coming in to join me?" Mike reached into the kitchen cupboard for a glass in spite of his reaction to Robby's hooch.

"You always were a philistine."

"What the fuck is a philistine?"

"You, you fucking knuckle-dragger. Don't you want a wine glass for that?"

Robby asked.

"If it were wine, sure, but this is swill, asshole," Mike replied. He smiled: The two of them had revertinged to how they had talked with each other from the day they had first started working together almost two decades ago. Like any old friends getting together, it was as if nothing had changed, except that today, one was inside the apartment, and the other was outside on the wrong side of the balcony railing, twelve stories up, threatening to jump onto a patch of unforgiving pavement. Maybe some things had changed.

"It is not swill, and I do have better wine, you know."

"Oh yeah? Saving that for the coroner? Where?" Mike began to actively rummage through the kitchen in an effort to buy time, or to annoy Robby enough to give up his plan to kill himself.

"It's in my storage unit in the basement."

"Good call, fucker." Mike took a swig from another bottle he found, and then spewed that out in front of him. "Good God! This is even worse shit! I give up. Come in here and get me your good stuff from the basement."

"You are a very annoying man, Mikey. You always were," Robby said.

"You're channeling my first wife, aren't you?" Mike took another swig from the second bottle, this time swallowing hard, shivering as the plonk hit his belly. "Let's stop this bullshit and have a real drink, shall we?"

"If I come in, will you promise me we won't have to go through that hospital bullshit? I don't want my neighbours to see me, and I sure as hell don't want to talk to some little prick about *how I feel—*"

"Only if you promise me some good wine. My gut will rot with this swill."

"I'm serious."

"Me, too." Mike put the bottle down on the counter. He looked at it for a couple of seconds, trying to find words that would bring this incident to an end. Then taking a deep breath, he looked over at the man who he at one time thought knew everything about everything and began to talk.

"Listen, Robby. I'm not here to fix your world. I can barely handle my own. I just don't want you to jump, okay? I don't know where the wheels fell off for you, or if you're saner than me. Regardless, we both know that you'll make a hell of a mess, traumatize a few kids, and tie traffic the fuck up, and we're already busy at the station with a homicide investigation." Without thinking, Mike had picked up the bottle and filled his glass with the home brew as he chatted with his old boss, almost like old times.

"Really?" Robby sparked up. "Anything good?"

"Yeah, actually," Mike replied, moving towards the balcony, taking a drink from the glass. "One-legged guy found in an alley. Don't suppose he hopped there."

Both men chuckled.

"Interesting. Any leads?" Robby began flexing his arms on the balcony railing and bending his knees, loosening up his tired joints. It was as if Mike was giving him a pre-shift briefing. Just like the old days.

"Well, we've got one guy in custody that Old Clothes dragged in. Maybe he's our guy, maybe not. Find out soon enough. Hopefully, Old Clothes hasn't fucked it up too badly with their Ways & Means bullshit."

"Who's the lead from Homicide? Not that I'd likely know him, but still—"

"Her. It's a woman. Name's Amanda Black."

"You are fucking joking? They got girls in Homicide now?"

"Yeah. And the knuckle-draggers even let them wear pants. Wow, eh? Where the fuck have you been, buddy?"

"Retired. Living the dream. Remember?" Robby's body slumped.

Mike's heart skipped a beat as he saw Robby loosening his grip on the railing. *Gotta keep calm. Never show surprise. Everything is going to be just fine. And don't fucking let go!*

"Right. Hey, you should see about coming back as a civilian."

"Like fuck. To do what? Answer phones at a command post?"

"No, asshole. I mean like a consultant. With all of the useless shit you probably have crammed in that head of yours…"

"I dunno. Union issues. I can't see them going for it. Scab labour and all…"

The hopelessness of Robby's voice triggered more caution in Mike.

"Why not try? You wouldn't be the first retired copper to hang out a shingle."

The old copper laughed. "Sure. I'll get right on that. So, my friend," Robby shifted gears, "why are you here?"

"What? Stop bullshitting."

"No, I'm serious. Why are you here on this call?"

"Went for a coffee—which, by the way, is now sitting in the car, cold, thanks to you—and a call came over for a retired copper in need. Here I am, brother."

Robby nodded his head, appearing content with Mike's answer.

"Are you planning on hanging out there all day, or are you coming in to get me that bottle of half-decent wine you were talking about? You need to get your ass back on the saner side of the balcony railing, Robby. You gotta do it, okay?"

"Tell you what," Robby replied. "Call the uniforms and tree-hugging ambulance drivers off, and you and I will sit down and have a drink."

"Sounds like a great plan to me. Done," Mike replied, standing at the balcony doors, feeling more relaxed. "What are we going to have? Not more of this shit, I hope?"

"No. We'll have this Châteauneuf-du-Pape that I've got downstairs. I've been wanting to drink it for the past two years and—"

"Well, I'm willing to let this Chateau enough come to papa. This other crap is probably causing brain damage. What is it? Sixty proof? And since when do you wait two years to drink? Got no friends?" Mike returned to the kitchen to dump what remained of his swill down the drain, leaving the glass on the counter, his eyes momentarily diverted.

"No, Mikey, I don't. That's why I'm on this side of the railing."

"Stop talking stupid, and come on back over to this side so that we can have a drink together."

As Robby lifted his right leg up to straddle the railing, he looked down and saw a marked scout car, roof lights flashing, pulling into the lot below him.

"Still go to these calls with just lights, no sirens, eh?" Robby smiled sadly at Mike.

"I guess." Mike walked out on to the balcony. Robby was less than three feet away from him now.

Robby looked squarely at Mike and then seemed to pause before looking back down at the two officers getting out of their car. They might or might not have shouted something up to Robby, Mike wasn't sure. He certainly didn't hear anything if they did. Robby didn't make a move as he looked back at Mike, presumably, Mike later figured, to give the officers time to get into the building.

"I don't suppose they'd like to see me do it, do you?"

The rest happened very quickly. It looked to Mike as if Robby was beginning to shift his weight from his legs to his arms to hoist himself over the railing to safety. Suddenly, his left elbow buckled, and rather than steadying himself by dropping his right leg down and shifting the weight back onto his feet, the old man's entire left side collapsed. As hard as he tried to remember after the fact, it did not appear to Mike that Robby had made any effort to grab the railing with his right hand.

And then he disappeared from view. Before Mike could move that less-than-three-feeoot distance, the retired police officer had fallen twelve stories to his death. Mike didn't recall hearing the unmistakable sound of that over-ripe melon falling off a fruit truck on its way to the market, just the sound of the heavy drapes behind him rustling against the doorframe as the wind gently blew into the apartment.

He stumbled back into the living room, his eyes fixed straight ahead. A moment or two later, or maybe it was several minutes later, he was aware of the uniforms pausing inside the half-open door before rushing past him onto the empty balcony. The young officers looked down in disbelief and then back to Mike for direction.

"Write this one up as an accident. A horrible fucking accident."

"But he jumped, Detec—"

"Squad guys like us don't jump off fucking balconies, Constable. He fell."

Chapter Twenty-Six

Friday, August 24, 2018 - 9:15 p.m.

Hey. OT. Can't pick up. Sorry. Mike's text to his son was no briefer than usual. No need to say any more. Not much to explain in a text anyway. Everything from here on in 'may be given in evidence,' Mike reminded himself, quoting from the Caution To Charged Person printed on the back page of every memo book used by the Service and expected to be read to every accused at the time of arrest.

The blame game had begun. Again.

"You might want to call your wife, Mike," the unit commander said as he came into the office, his white senior officer's shirt crisp with starch, gold doodads all shined up, expensive cologne preceding him. He certainly painted a stark contrast to Mike's days-old suit, haggard face, and boozy breath. "It's going to be a while before they come to talk to you."

"I'm good, thanks," Mike replied, settling into one of the leather wing chairs that flanked the unit commander's oversized desk. He had reached that point in his years of service where the unit commanders were from either his recruit class or from classes a couple of years after. He had known most of them as front-line officers or through joint investigations they'd all been involved in. They were not mythical or larger than life, or anything like the giants of policing that the senior officers seemed to be when he first joined the force. No, these guys were just coppers who turned into administrators. As he got older, Mike was finding that there were very few people or things that were larger than life any more.

"Feel free to make yourself at home here in my office. There's a bathroom just over there. And you know the rules about phone calls. Just your wife. We've contacted the union for you. If there's anything you need, just knock."

"No, I'm good," Mike repeated to the closing door.

He glanced absently around the office at the plaques, police paraphernalia, and photos of smiling people in formal attire or in uniforms or on beaches. For all intents and purposes, despite the unit commander's cordiality, Mike was a prisoner, and this room was his cell. He was not free to leave. He was not free to speak with whomever he chose. He was a prisoner. And just like any other prisoner, if he wanted the attention of his captors, he could knock on the door. Was it locked? Probably not. They knew he wouldn't try to leave. He was a prisoner, and he, like all coppers, knew better than anyone else what that meant.

It was standard procedure to detain any officer who was present when someone died, whether it was at the hands of the officer or not. Even though they weren't under arrest, the protocol called for officers who found themselves in this unenviable position to be treated as if they were. As a result, they were detained in a room alone, separated from any other officers who were involved, and denied access to everyone except the union rep and their lawyer, except for one brief phone call home, if the officer wanted to make one.

Mike didn't see the point of using his phone call. Not much to tell right now. No sense getting things all stirred up. There would be plenty of time for that later.

Now, sitting alone, sequestered from the rest of his platoon, Mike was left to wait for the lawyer the union would send in to talk to him. And then a member of the Special Investigations Unit would come to interview him. Once that was done, he might or might not be free to leave, depending on how quickly and what sort of a decision was made. If the SIU determined that his actions were criminal, he'd be taken to the cells where Cockeye would likely still be. If his actions involved procedural issues, on the other hand, he'd end up talking to the unit commander and being suspended from duty until the brass could figure out what to do with him. Training issues or just bad luck could be sorted out another day. Of course, all these options presupposed that the SIU would be able to determine anything tonight. Otherwise, Mike knew he would be expected to carry on, business as usual, until he was either cleared or charged.

So he just sat quietly in the unit commander's well-appointed office, knowing that his entire career rested in the hands of someone who, with the luxury of time and objectivity, would determine whether or not an infraction of any sort had been committed when Mike did not grab Robinson Williams from the balcony if and when he had the chance.

Mike could feel the acid in his stomach beginning to churn. *Fucking Robby. Hoagy's gone. Just me and Julia left. After that, no one will give a shit about Sal. And they'll stop looking for the shooter, if they haven't already. Fucking plugs. Shoulda found Malcolm that afternoon. Doesn't make sense. Every cop in the city was looking.*

The unit commander popped back into the room. "Sorry, Mike, I forgot. I'm going to need your cell phone. I know this is difficult, but we want to make this as clean an investigative process for the SIU as we can."

"Yeah. Sure. No problem."

Mike reached into his jacket pocket and handed the phone over, not bothering to stand up. As the phone left his hands, he couldn't help but feel that he was somehow setting his son adrift.

"Don't say anything, Mike," the unit commander said in a low voice. "We've got a union lawyer on the way. Until then, I'll make sure no one gets to you, okay?"

"Thank you, sir," Mike said, awkwardly shaking the outstretched hand of his superior, who then turned abruptly and left the room, closing the door behind him.

Alone again with his thoughts, Mike realized that he had never really been in this office before. No reason to be. Only officers in shit or getting commendations came to see the Big Boss, and Mike was neither of those. He stood up, stretched, and wandered around the room like a tourist in a museum, looking a little closer at the numerous plaques and awards that represented a well-documented career. There were a few old photographs—from the good old days, Mike assumed—although the officers in the pictures looked more like parodies of cops than the real thing. There was a picture of a group of young men with handlebar moustaches wearing leisure suits and white shoes sitting around mounds of some pre-packaged substance, likely a memento from some huge drug bust. Another picture had a different group of men with similar moustaches, wearing long fur coats and holding shotguns; the picture was signed: *Thanks for Everything, Morton's Furrier.* The only constant in all these photos was the likeness of the unit commander as a much younger man, an age Mike remembered himself being not so long ago.

After a brief chuckle and another stretch, Mike flopped down in the chair he had previously occupied and closed his eyes. He was tired, too damn tired for this shit. He wondered how Ron was doing. He wondered what had happened with Cockeye, or more to the point, how Amanda Black was going to sort out what was going on with Cockeye.

He wondered about those little girls whose picture he'd found in the wallet of the dead man from the coffee shop. And then he wondered about the copper who would be delivering that compassionate message to the man's family. Would it be like the guys from his father's work who came to his mother's door when he was just a boy.

We're so sorry, Mrs. O'Shea....

"Are you Michael O'Shea?" a woman's voice cut through his thoughts.

"Yes. Yes, I am," Mike tried to shake the sleep off, instinctively standing up at the sound of a woman's voice.

"I am Shannon Somerville, the lawyer from the union. I'm going to be representing you." She extended her right hand to Mike, who, despite his efforts, found himself fumbling to shake it. When the unit commander said 'union lawyer,' Mike had expected some cantankerous old solicitor on his next-to-last legs with a forest of hair growing out of his ears, not this. She looked maybe twenty-five, and stood just shy of five feet tall, with black poker-straight hair styled in a blunt cut that went with her black suit. The thick glasses that she had already adjusted a couple of times on her plain face were the icing on the cake for Mike. A sub-basement laboratory, not a courtroom, was where Mike would have placed her.

He sincerely hoped he was wrong.

"If you're okay with that?" Shannon added, assuming that Mike's staring was due to the usual indignation she faced from cops-turned-clients that she'd grown accustomed to, rather than his genuine doubt in her abilities as a union lawyer.

"Yeah. Sure. Great," Mike mumbled, straightening his tie and pulling down on his jacket, attempting to sharpen up his appearance.

"Good. We don't have much time. I suspect that they'll be done at the scene shortly, and the SIU guy will want a go at you, so what do I need to know?"

"Well—" Mike began.

"Oh, and I'm sure I don't need to remind you of all people, Detective, but—"

"Mike. Call me Mike."

"Mike, but a couple of things: First, anything you say is confidential between you and me, and second, I need to know exactly what happened—the good, the bad, and the ugly—so that I can best represent you. I don't like surprises."

Mike nodded.

"Good. Let's sit down over here."

The lawyer motioned towards a small round table with four chairs tightly placed around it beside the unit commander's desk. Mike winced a little as he walked over to the table on legs that had stiffened up after a couple of long days with not enough sleep between them.

"Have you been drinking, Mike? I thought I smelled alcohol on your breath."

"Um... No, not really," Mike began.

Frowning slightly, Shannon adjusted her glasses as she looked up from the briefcase she had been pulling forms out of and stared at her client. Her question was simple, calling for a 'yes' or 'no' answer. She was not prepared for anything less, especially from this cop, given all she'd been told in her briefing prior to speaking with him.

"I mean, yes, but I can explain," Mike stumbled.

"Good. As long as you can explain everything, we're gold. Go."

The lawyer seated herself in one of the chairs and opened her laptop in front of her before tuckeding a piece of errant hair behind her left ear, not looking up at Mike.

Frozen, Mike stood by the chair he had been intending to sit in.

"Tell me why you were drinking, Mike." Shannon stopped what she was doing and looked expectantly at her client.

Her tone and the way she looked up at him were overwhelmingly familiar to Mike. He felt just like he did when he was fourteen, and his mother had heard that he and Bucky Rogers had drunk the flask of whiskey that everyone knew Father Richard kept in the back pew to lure the drunks in for Sunday Mass. Only this was worse: Ms. Somerville wasn't his mother, and he wasn't a kid any more. And this time, he had done nothing wrong. Nothing.

"Right," Mike said, sitting down in the chair. "I took the call for a man on a balcony threatening to commit suicide and—"

"Had you been drinking before that?" Shannon asked, glancing from her computer screen to one of the forms in front of her.

"No."

"Okay. Good. Continue." She looked up, acknowledging Mike briefly before looking back down at the form and pushing her glasses back up the bridge of her nose.

Rapid fire. Just as well. Get it done.

"And then I get there, and it's a guy I knew—"

"Did you advise the dispatcher?" Shannon interrupted, looking from the screen to the form and then back to Mike.

"No, I didn't have a radio." Mike met her gaze.

"Did you call for backup?"

Their eyes locked.

Mike broke first. "They were on the way," he said, sitting back and stretching his neck.

"But you're supposed to *wait* for backup," the lawyer pointed out as she pulled a copy of the force's policy on responding to attempted-suicide calls from her attaché case without looking down.

"Yes, but—"

"Exigent circumstances, Mike?" She looked directly into Mike's eyes. "Please tell me there were exigent circumstances."

"Yeah, there were. He was on the balcony. On the *wrong* side of the railing. He was hanging off, clearly about to jump."

Mike spoke slowly, nodding his head as he recounted his earlier activities. Shannon was nodding back in agreement, replacing that piece of hair again.

He paused for a few seconds. It all seemed so obvious to him: Robby was done. There was nothing anyone could do. Not even Mike could save him. There was nothing to save. And now, the more Mike thought about it, the more tired he became.

"I couldn't just wait around, you know." Mike could hear the pleading note in his voice.

"No, of course not. Go on," the lawyer encouraged, typing feverishly, her glasses sliding down her nose.

"So I go up there and find out it's a guy I knew: Robby Williams, a retired detective sergeant who was an old boss of mine." Mike looked away from Shannon and sighed. "There was nothing I could have done. He had made the decision before I got there. I just happened to be there when he did it."

"A conflict of interest. Did you wait for backup at this point?" Shannon pushed her glasses back onto her face as she looked closely at Mike.

"How was this a conflict of interest?"

"You knew him. Maybe you liked him. Maybe you didn't."

"Like I said, he was on the balcony. He was threatening to jump. I couldn't just walk out on him."

Simple answer. It was all so simple. Was he the only fucking person who saw that?

"And I like…liked…him. Very much."

Satisfied, she looked back down at her keyboard. "Did he jump right then and there?"

"No. He was talking to me for a while."

"How close were you to him while this was going on?"

The sound of her incessant typing was starting to get on Mike's nerves.

"I dunno. Three feet, maybe? Like this." Mike indicated the distance by placing his hands a little more than his shoulder- width apart.

"You were three feet from him, and you didn't grab him?"

Mike was startled by the incredulity in the lawyer's voice. "This isn't TV, sweetheart," he replied, wishing almost as soon as the words left his lips that he hadn't referred to his legal counsel as 'sweetheart.'

Shannon stopped typing and looked up at her client, giving him a glare designed to freeze his soul.

"Fuck. I'm sorry. What I meant to say was that this isn't like on TV, where one guy pulls another guy off a ledge. In real life, the jumper usually ends up pulling the copper over, and I wasn't going to go over, old boss or not. Besides, he made it clear that if I got too close or moved too fast, he'd jump."

"But he jumped anyway," she advised.

"No, he fell." As Mike corrected his lawyer, the same rush of weightlessness came over him that he had felt when he heard Malcolm's gun click after the fucker shot Sal.

"Okay, reasonable," Shannon concurred, nodding at him, tucking that piece of delinquent hair back behind her ear before returning to her keyboard. "So, when did you start drinking? After he jumped?"

"No. I was trying to coax him off the ledge by suggesting he have a drink with me." In his head, this made sense, but the words sounded absolutely ridiculous when he heard them out loud.

"Are you a trained negotiator, Mike?" Shannon had not considered earlier that he might be. How convenient it would have been for her if he was.

"No."

"But you figured this would be your chance to practise?" The lawyer stifled a chuckle.

"You don't understand." Mike felt the heaviness of the world fall back on his shoulders. "There was no time to wait for a negotiator. In fact, the dispatcher didn't even know if we had one working at the time—"

"Stop right there, Mike." Shannon held up her hand. "We did. He was on his way. You would have known this if you had a radio. The transcripts of the call have her stating this."

Mike heard the ice her voice.

"Fuck." He swallowed hard, loosening his tie. His eyes glazed over. *If I'd been faster, I'd have gotten to the door first. I'd have my gun out. I'd have shot that fucker, and me and Sal would be going for beers afterwards. If I had waited, maybe Robby wouldn't be splattered all over the parking lot now. That fucking negotiator guy would have talked him down. He'd have saved him. I couldn't fucking save either of them. Fuck.*

"Are you with me, Mike?"

"Yeah. Yeah, I'm with you. But you need to know something."

He took a deep breath while Shannon perked up her ears, hoping for some clear-cut excuse or confession or something she could use to help him.

"Life is live."

"What?" Shoulders slumping and hands dropped into her lap, the lawyer stared in disbelief at her client, ignoring, for now, both her glasses that had shimmied down her nose and that rebellious piece of hair that had fallen down in front of her face.

"You can't wait around for someone to show up to solve your problems all the time, you know. I've been a copper likely for as long as you've been alive. I've been to a lot of these types of calls—"

"I'd keep that knowledge to myself if I were you, Detective O'Shea. No need to look into those calls as well, I suspect."

Shannon had experienced this condescending attitude before, particularly with the clients she got through the police union. She knew that she was not the beauty her clients might have wanted to look at, but she was damned good at her job.

"The issues I see here are that you attended this call on your own, despite procedures and training to the contrary. You then failed to wait for backup. Again, lots of training and procedures covering this, which you, by your own admission, are familiar with." Shannon shot a glare at Mike. "You then failed to even attempt to stop this man from jumping off the balcony, despite being less than three feet away from him, and *then* you proceeded to consume a quantity of alcohol, perhaps even before he jumped to his death. That's the situation you've presented me with, Detective O'Shea. Anything else I need to know before I go that might help me to dig you out of this pile of procedural and potentially criminal doo-doo that you've landed in?"

Mike shook his head.

"Two other officers were there. Uniform guys," she said as she riffled through her paperwork to find their names. "Singh and Chu. "When did they get there?"

"Not until the end. They arrived after he jumped… fell," Mike corrected himself as he yawned. "Sorry. I'm just tired. Really tired. And I knew the guy. He was my boss. For years. He was my friend."

"Okay." The lawyer looked directly at him, and for some reason, Mike felt a glimmer of hope. "I'm going to talk to the SIU investigator and see what I can do for you. I'm not promising anything, but I'll try to get you out of here before long. Anything else?"

"No." Mike shook his head and watched the young woman pack up her papers.

"Great. I'll pop back in a few," she said, exiting the room.

Mike stood and stretched. Then he looked at the clock on the wall opposite him.

Twelve fucking thirty.

It felt later than that, if there even is a later than the middle of the night. He went back to the wing chair, sat down, leaned back, and closed his eyes.

Chapter Twenty-Seven

Saturday, August 25, 2018 - 12:50 a.m.

"I think we've got things pretty much sorted out for now," a voice broke into Mike's dream. "I spoke with their investigator. Guy named Beauparlante. I've dealt with him before. He used to be a truck inspector with the Ministry of Transportation but jumped ship a few years back. I imagine investigating police officers paid much better than kicking tires. He has requested a statement, which you will not be providing. You don't have to. We spoke, and after some discussion, he said that he's not looking into anything criminal."

The torrent of words assaulted Mike's ears as he was shaking himself awake. By the time he actually opened his eyes and could focus, Shannon Somerville was standing directly in front of him.

"That's great," Mike grimaced, fumbling to his feet.

"How drunk are you, Mike?"

"I'm not drunk. I'm fucking exhausted!"

"Fair enough," the lawyer conceded, not sure if she really wanted to know whether or not he was intoxicated. "In any event, you are free to go. I spoke to your unit commander. He advises that he isn't going to be pursuing anything policy-related at this moment, so my work here is done for now. He probably wants to talk to you anyway, but I don't have to stick around for that. Have a good night, Mike. And be safe."

And then she was gone, door left open behind her, leaving Mike to muddle around searching for his cell phone.

"Mike, sit down," the unit commander instructed as he walked into his office, motioning to the seat that Mike had just gotten out of. "Before I forget, here's your phone back," he said, pulling it from his jacket pocket and handing it to Mike. "I see you managed to get a text in before we seized... uh, took it."

"Yes. It was to my son advising him that I wouldn't be picking him up."

"I saw that. Not a problem. Just wish you had said something before so I didn't have to have someone check your entire phone."

"Check my phone? For what?"

"You know how these things go, Mike. We're not particularly worried about you. It's the young guys who end up taking selfies at crime scenes and texting everyone they know, telling the whole story, which of course means subpoenas and statements. Just a nightmare. Have to cover all the bases every time now. Texting your boy to tell him you're working late is no problem. Sure you don't want to call the missus?"

"I will speak with her when I get home."

"Good. We care about the members of our police family, you know. All of them."

He looked away from Mike, turning his attention to the photos on his desk. "I've been married to my girl for twenty-eight years next month. We have four children. She pretty much raised them alone. I couldn't have done it without her."

"That's great," Mike said politely, knowing that he couldn't care less.

"Yes, it is. Anyway," the unit commander turned his attention back to Mike. "There are a few procedural things that we need to sort out internally that may or may not have happened this evening. I've told Ms. Somerville that we're not going to worry about any of that now. I've notified Internal Affairs as I am mandated to do, and they'll probably want to speak to you in the next day or two. But for now, I need you back in my D office. Your partner is swamped, and Detective Sergeant Black tells me that you're an integral part of her murder investigation."

"Okay."

"In any event, if you're up to it, I'm going to hand you over to Detective Sergeant Black tomorrow to assist her with whatever she needs done. She's downstairs now, but I told her you may not be wanting to do anything but go home tonight."

"No," Mike said. "I'm more than willing to speak with her tonight and see where she's at."

"You're a good soldier, Michael." His superior beamed with approval. "Not many officers in your position would want to do more than go home and have a couple of drinks."

He got up from behind his desk, hand outstretched. Mike stood up and gave it an obligatory shake.

"Oh, and Mike?" the unit commander added as Mike turned to leave the office.

"Yes, sir?"

"Take a seat."

"Yes, sir," Mike said, sitting in the chair he had been sitting in when he first came into the office. The unit commander leaned against his desk, looking down at Mike.

"I knew Robinson Williams. He was my coach officer. He was a fine man. He had a lot of demons from before he worked with you. You remember that little girl who was murdered, and they found her in the rooming house fridge?"

Mike nodded. Everyone knew that case. There was no need to mention names or dates. It was one of those watershed moments for the city, when neighbours first began looking at one another as a danger rather than as a friend and when front doors were no longer left unlocked. Left-leaning dinner table discussions about inner-city poverty and inadequate housing gave way to hushed back-alley meet-ups by roving vigilante groups, intent on ferreting out local pervs, real or imagined. As well as running one of the largest investigations of its day, the cops had to ensure the safety of every balding pot-bellied man between the ages of forty and fifty who wasn't either a well-known fixture in the community or whose presence could otherwise be explained.

"Williams and his partner were the uniforms who found her."

Both men looked down in silence, remembering the little girl and her family and the number of newspaper articles that grew exponentially with each passing day as the police and community searches came up empty and the possibility of foul play loomed heavier and heavier in the case.

And then, after they found her body, there were the cautionary preambles before every news report that squeezed out every tiny morsel of information to the point of exhaustion until there were no more juicy details to be publicly revealed. The repeatedly shown footage of the body-removal men cautiously carrying the gurney, holding the tiny body down the rooming house steps into the waiting coroner's hearse, was a daily staple on the evening news for weeks.

Mike specifically remembered reading the details of how two uniforms responding to a 'bad smell' call had found the child's body crammed inside a decommissioned fridge in a ratty old house near the railway tracks in the Annex neighbourhood where she had gone missing. He remembered the talk among his fellow- coppers about how badly decomposed and beaten the tiny body was. The media advised that the body had likely been in that fridge for a couple of weeks, and that the lone occupant of the room-for-rent had split about the same time as the little girl went missing.

The case was the talk of the city for years, both inside and outside policing circles. At some point, Mike had probably even talked to Robby about it. He had no idea that Robby had been one of those officers, and Robby had never mentioned a word. Ever.

It was common knowledge that one of the officers quit the afternoon the girl's body was found, never to be seen or heard from again. Rumour had it that he'd hanged himself from a tree by the side of the road somewhere up north a couple of weeks after quitting. Word was that he had been having some personal problems.

And now Mike knew what happened to the other officer.

While the police were able to identify the murderer, they never did catch him, despite all the media coverage. Mike had heard that pictures of the killer could still be seen on the occasional milk carton, just in case. And if you mentioned his name to anyone in the province, cop or civilian, who was over forty, they'd likely know the whole sordid story. The lead investigator had long since retired, but he was still said to be carrying the banker's box of evidence around in the trunk of his car. No one was willing, or able, to let this one go.

"Pretty horrific, I'm sure," Mike said, almost wincing inside at his understatement.

"Never got over it. Surprised that you didn't know. You worked with him for a long time in that kiddie hooker squad, didn't you?"

"Yeah, a long time."

"Well, I guess your partner getting shot overshadowed a lot of that. In any event," the unit commander said, standing up and extending his hand before opening the door, "I'd like to personally thank you for doing your best to keep him from the pavement. We can't win every battle, but we never stop fighting the good fight, do we, Detective?"

"No, sir, we don't."

And with that, Mike stood up, shook the man's hand, and walked out of the office.

* * *

"Well, are you back or here to pick up your things or just passing through?" Ron chirped merrily amidst piles of papers strewn across several desks.

"Hard to say these days."

"Well, if you're back, I could certainly use the help. We had four bodies in this evening, not counting Cockeye; Amanda hasn't stopped bothering me all night;, and I'm on overtime that I don't want."

"Yeah, so fill me in. What happened to Cockeye?"

"Released. No charges," Ron said, continuing to sort through his papers.

"What?" Mike was amazed.

"Yes. Released, no charges. That idiot, Ricky Jergensen, had nothing on him, really, and Amanda was furious. You missed quite a show!"

"I'm sure I did." Mike sat down at his desk and logged into his computer.

"Yes. And I've been busy with the arrests the guys brought in over the evening. Here, would you mind reading over this Show Cause. I'll give you the case number once you're logged in."

Ron was moving along, business as usual, much to Mike's relief.

"No problem," Mike said, transitioning into work mode. "So what happened?"

"Oh, Cockeye was happy as a clam to be released, as you can imagine, and then the real show began. Once our wrongfully accused was released, the good Detective Sergeant Black just went to town on Jergensen, reminding him of what a lousy cop he is and how he's almost dirty—her words, not mine. Then he started swearing at her, calling her every name under the sun, including the 'C' word!"

Ron regaled Mike with his account of the events, inflecting his words and gesticulating wildly in a manner Mike thought not possible for such a reserved oddball.

"Not the 'C' word!" Mike laughed, finding himself getting caught up in Ron's animated reminiscence.

"Yes, the 'C' word! And then *she* threatened to document him, and then *he* threatened all sorts of indignities to her person, and then *she* called in the staff sergeant, and then Jergensen made some allegations about Staff, and then Staff called the unit commander, who was already here because of whatever happened with you—which, by the way, I don't want to know a thing about—and then *everyone* was yelling at *everyone*. Oh, it was a grand old time here in the D office, let me tell you. And there I was," Ron finished, taking a breath, "just trying to process my little Fail To Comply charges."

"Wow!"

"Oh, yes. It was quite the night, my friend." Ron's eyes twinkled and his eyebrows quickly shot up and down before he returned to his usual sedate state of being.

"Sounds like it," Mike said.

"I'm just glad you're back."

"Me, too."

"You are okay, aren't you?" Ron said, taking stock of his partner.

"Detective O'Shea?" Amanda Black's voice could be heard from just outside the D office.

"Yes?"

"May I speak to you for a moment? Here in the privacy of the hallway?" Amanda looked around her at the filthy, beige tiled walls. "God, I hate this building."

"Certainly," Mike replied, realizing that this wasn't a request. He got up from his desk and walked to where Amanda was standing in the hall.

"I'd grab an office or something, but everything is locked." She paused. "So tell me, what shit heap did you get yourself into this evening?"

"You know as much as I do." Mike shrugged, knowing full well that Amanda knew the whole story. She must have, otherwise, she wouldn't have bailed him out. Mike knew policing culture well enough to know that as a female cop, let alone a female detective sergeant, she faced too many natural obstacles to put her neck out for someone or something that she didn't know absolutely everything about and felt absolutely sure that she could safely put her name to. The professional world they shared may have appeared to have progressed, but the power and politics of policing hadn't, and the battleground was nowhere near a level playing field. If guys like Mike knew it, then Amanda most certainly did, too.

"In that case, let's get back to work. Every homicide investigation has its challenges, and this has more than it should. Are you back with me, or do you need some time?"

She surveyed Mike just as she would survey a crime scene, looking for answers to questions that she had to ask but was fairly certain that she had already figured out the answers to.

"I'm good. And before I forget, thanks for putting a word in for me with the boss." Mike meant what he said, but he fidgeted, hating to admit that he truly appreciated the intervention. Without her help, though, he could only imagine what an undignified shitshow this night could have become.

"It's no mere 'putting in a word,' Mike. I need your help. Ron is a great guy, but he's just not picking up what I'm putting down." Amanda shook her head. The possibility that she was much smarter than the average copper seldom presented itself as an option to her. Instead, she held fast to her stalwart belief that everyone else lacked commitment to the art of police work, even though this belief, however, was one that seldom served her well.

"Sorry to hear that."

"And Jergensen truly fucked up my plan. You know, the one where we'd actually gather some real evidence before arresting our suspect? Yes? Well, now I don't suppose Mark Johnstone will be hanging around town waiting for round two. So I need you."

Gloves off. No shit. No bravado.

"Okay. What do I do?" Mike knew he wasn't in a great bargaining position. He knew that she had been able to leverage her need for him against whatever the brass may have had on him to get him here, and now he had to deliver. He owed her, and she knew it.

"I'm putting a rush on Forensics to find me some DNA that can positively put our guy at the scene."

"But we know he was there."

"Look," Amanda shot back, "you and I both know that Cockeye Johnstone was there and is our man, even if he isn't the only wonky-eyed asshole in the city. But I still need a little more than the words of a couple of good-hearted landlords to definitively place him there. And while someone else may have murdered our deceased, Mr. Johnstone is a good candidate who certainly bears speaking with under the *legally* justified circumstances."

"After this little warning, if I were him, I'd be scrubbing my place down from top to bottom with enough bleach to kill an army," Mike pointed out.

"Exactly," Amanda agreed, reconciling herself to the fact that Ricky Jergensen's actions were going to cost her a great deal of clear and easy evidence linking Johnstone to the deceased. "He's probably working his ass off as we speak to make sure that any blood that splashed onto his clothes is gone, and then he'll fly. Ideally, I would have liked to have had all my grounds to arrest laid out before even the thought of running crossed his mind, but I don't think we'll have our results back soon enough. So this is where you come in."

Mike raised an eyebrow.

"If he runs," Amanda continued, "I need you to run with him. You know what he looks like, and you know where he is right now. I don't have time to get a spin team together or do a proper workup on him to properly know what he's about. I need you to follow this shithead until we can pinch him."

"Sure," Mike said, the muscles in his body waking up. Amanda was right. This was the Real Deal. This was the Big League. This was what policing was all about. And this was what Mike knew how to do.

"Great. I managed to pick up an old clunker from another district that doesn't actually look like a cop car. You live close by, don't you?"

"Yes." Mike could feel the adrenaline starting to pump. A plan was being hatched. This was fun, not work.

"Okay. I don't care how you do it, but I need you to be in that shitbox wearing something other than a suit and over to buddy's address as soon as you can. Watch him, Mike. Move with him. And for God's sake, don't lose him on me, okay?"

"Okay, but you know I don't have the mobile course, right?" He stopped short, both afraid and annoyed that his lack of formal certification might eliminate him from this detail.

"You're not playing that fucking game with me, are you? I didn't figure you to be like most of the guys around here who get all soft when the rubber hits the road." The angry flash in Amanda's eyes allayed Mike's concern.

"Just putting it out there so you're well informed. I'm more than good to go if you are."

"I'm going to pretend we never had this conversation, Mike, and if push does come to shove, I'll look after that end of things. You just get your little self home and into something other than your hundred-dollar suit, okay?" Amanda winked at Mike. "As long as you don't lose my boy, you and I will be fine."

Chapter Twenty-Eight

Saturday, August 25, 2018 - 2:37 a.m.

Mike turned the car radio up and rolled the windows down, in part to keep himself awake and in part to allow the stale stench that permeated the interior of the vehicle to escape. The steering wheel and the dashboard had been carved up, and both were disconcertingly gummy to the touch. The seats were torn and stained in a way that suggested that something more than a coffee or two had been spilled on them. Partial licence plate numbers had been written on the visors, and the floor was covered with discarded sunflower seed shells.

"Why you gotta spit those seeds everywhere, Sal?" Mike said aloud.

The exterior had a similar feel to it, with dented bumpers, scratches and gouges along the sides, and large patches of paint missing from both the hood and the trunk. The tires were as close to bald as was likely legal.

For all intents and purposes, this was an excellent undercover car, except for the telltale expiry date on the val tag. Every serious criminal in Toronto knew that licence plate validations for all city-owned cars expired at the same time, so all city cars had the telltale SEPT sticker in the corner. Mike was hoping that Cockeye Johnstone, like most of the people who wandered the streets in his neighbourhood, would be too preoccupied with his felonious machinations to notice.

According to Amanda Black, Mike had about forty minutes to get home, change, and show up in front of the squalid rooming house that Cockeye called home. A pied-à-terre for the down-and-out, Mike thought, amusing himself. It was likely rented weekly, cash only, for some exorbitant sum of money as compensation for the don't-ask-don't-tell occupancy policy. Not at all like the place the Majewskis ran, which explained why there should not have been any crossover in the tenants of the two very different houses.

Talk radio was a good choice, particularly the All News All The Time station that the car radio had been preset to. Annoying, repetitive, not at all soothing, plus that beeping in between the three- to five-minute segments would help to keep Mike awake.

"And finally, the victim of the city's sixty-third homicide has been identified. Sergei 'Sam' Kuzminov, a well-known former middleweight champ who fell on hard times a few years back, was found beaten to death in a Roncesvalles back. Sources say that Mr. Kuzminov had developed a severe drinking problem that led to serious medical conditions, including the amputation of one of his legs later in his life. Police advise that next-of-kin have been notified but do not wish to speak with the media. No information on any suspects has been released, but police advise an arrest is imminent. And that's the news on the hour every hour. Stay tuned for weather and sports."

Mike pushed one of the buttons to change the station as he neared his house. He didn't want to hear anything more about the murder, concerned that it might cloud his recollection of events before he had a chance to get them down in his own words in his memo book. It wasn't just what he knew as a detective, it was when he knew it, and how he came to know it that was an issue in any investigation when it got to court.

Shit. Mike thought, pulling this wreck of a car up in front of his dark house. *Forgot to leave a light on for Max. I guess he managed.*

After a quick cold shower intended to quash his own stink and wake him up, Mike scrawled a note to leave on the kitchen counter: **Working more OT tonight, buddy. Hope you had fun with your guys. See you in the morning. Love you lots. Dad.**

Brief text messages and notes left on the kitchen counter at home, pedophiles and burned-out coppers on balconies at work. *Is this really what my life is all about? There has to be something more. There is. Get going.*

Fifteen minutes later, Mike was back in the clunker, ready to be the eyes on Mr. Johnstone. Before pulling away, he looked back at the house, wondering if Carmen was really leaving him.

Fuck it, he thought, as he threw the car in gear and drove to the nearest coffee shop where he picked up an extra-large coffee and a second cup with a lid. He figured he'd need the caffeine to stay awake, even if all that liquid would initiate what had become a career-long juggling act involving coffee, bodily functions, and static obs. He had taken a good long piss at home and went for another squirt in the relatively clean washroom at the coffee shop, knowing that this would likely be the last time he'd see a legitimate washroom tonight. Familiar with this type of detail and understanding all too well the ultimate outcome of an extra-large coffee, Mike knew that it wouldn't be too long before he'd need to piss again, at which point he'd have the second cup with the lid ready.

And so, bladder empty, coffee in hand, Mike snaked casually through the Parkdale neighbourhood in the old clunker until he found a place to set up. He parked on the street behind another shitbox a few doors down from the targeted address with a relatively clear view of Cockeye's front door.

Ideally, he would have wanted to get out to get a better sense of what this street was about and to try to get a feel for the various hiding places that Cockeye might pop out from.

Even in his old jeans and stained sweatshirt, Mike knew he'd stick out like a sore thumb here. This was one of those neighbourhoods where everyone knew everyone else, and their business. Their lives depended on it. A new, different car in the area, no matter how dilapidated, would arouse suspicion. A new face would cause an even worse reaction, the automatic assumption being, Mike knew, that this was a cop. As a result, he had no choice but to turn off the engine, stay put inside the car, slink down in the seat a bit, and wait.

Let the games begin, he thought.

If not for the people who lived here, Parkdale would be a great place to live. The houses were all huge Victorian mansions that rivalled those found in the much-admired Rosedale area of Toronto. Prior to the city expropriating land to build the Gardiner expressway, this street had been on par with, if not more sought after than, the most exclusive of downtown neighbourhoods. Once the properties got separated from the lake, however, they diminished in value. The once-regal single-family dwellings became flats, and then rooms, as mortgages owing outstripped the crashing value of the properties.

The cheap housing turned this area into an ideal place for psychiatric facilities and their associated outpatient services, including numerous halfway houses, and that, Mike and probably most Torontonians knew, was a recipe for disaster. Poverty and violence soon followed. The area was improving with the inevitable gentrification now endemic throughout the entire city, but it was going to be a long, slow process. Mike looked at the still-beautiful architecture that surrounded him, its decay accentuated by the occasional flickering of the dying streetlight above him. What had been likely a majestic street was, at this hour, now barren except for the occasional stray dog or lost soul, both of whom moved with the same level of deliberation.

"Detective Roberts to Detective O'Shea. Detective Roberts to Detective O'Shea. Are you there, Detective O'Shea?" Ron Robert's crisp voice, sounding an awful lot like Joe Friday, seemed to blast out of nowhere. Mike jumped, realizing that the police radio was on, and then wanted to laugh at the ludicrous transmission. *Who the hell talks like that? What a weirdo! Fuck.*

"Yep. Go ahead," he replied, sounding more casual than usual as he turned the volume down on the radio and slunk further down into his seat.

"What's your 20?" With his use of an abbreviated police ten-code, Ron was sounding more and more like Jack Webb with every syllable.

"Outside of Cockeye's. Where are you?" *This better be good, or else you've got shitty timing. How the hell am I supposed to do obs if I'm flapping my gums on the radio to you? Jesus Christ.*

"At the station," Ron replied with a sigh. "Amanda wants a unit to drop a picture of Cockeye off to you. I suggested that that was a terrible idea, but she's pretty adamant. Can you drop by the station?"

"Remind Amanda that I know what he looks like. We all fucking saw him earlier tonight, remember? And I've seen him many times in court, both as an accused and as a victim."

"Remember, this is a monitored radio," Ron warned. "Watch the language, Detective."

"Then stop fucking annoying me. I'm trying to do covert obs here. Are you near a phone?"

"Yes. I can be at my desk in two minutes."

"Then I'll call you. In the meantime, tell D/S Black to take a fucking pill. She can text me a photo, but don't send any uniforms here. She'll fucking blow it."

"Monitored, Mike. It's all monitored. Call me in two."

Mike put the radio down and reached for his coffee, hoping that he hadn't already burned his cover. As he brought the coffee cup around to his mouth, a glint of silver caught his attention out of the corner of his left eye. He looked out and saw a man standing just outside the driver-side window, his body snugged up close to the car, with a shiny object in his right hand.

It took a second or two to register. Then, *game time*, he thought, as he dropped the cup of hot coffee onto his lap and lunged with both hands for the door handle, not feeling the scalding liquid burning his leg. He rammed the car door open with his shoulder, knocking the man in the knees and head simultaneously, and forcing him back a couple of feet. Mike's right hand grabbed at his belt for his gun, but his sweatshirt blocked the pancake holster. He tore at the sweatshirt, but it was futile. Somehow his hands could not pull it away from the holster. *Shit.*

He launched himself out of the car and onto the man who was still standing, albeit slightly off-balance. Mike continued the offensive, tackling the man and taking him to the ground. To his relief, his initial struggle to remain on top of his opponent was surprisingly easy, perhaps due to his comparative weight advantage or perhaps due to the survival instincts he had honed over the years. Whichever, he was thankful for both.

Gun. Gun. Gotta find the fucking gun. Mike knew that there was a gun somewhere, and he was fixated on finding it before it killed him.

The two men grappled and struggled, the other man seeming more intent on getting away than actually overpowering Mike. It was becoming increasingly obvious that this man had also spent a lifetime honing his survival instincts. The only difference appeared to be that Mike had trained to fight, whereas this asshole had been trained for flight.

Now, however, both men were playing for keeps. As the fighter his job had made Mike become, he hung onto the other man's neck while feverishly looking for the guy's gun. Had he been able to think about it, he realized much later, he could have grabbed his own police-issue semi-automatic from his waistband because, by now, his sweatshirt had billowed out, freeing the holster.

But he didn't think about it. He was in survival mode now, and all he wanted was that goddamned gun that he knew this asshole had.

The struggle seemed to last for hours when, in fact, less than a minute or two had passed. The man grabbed Mike's arm and twisted, pulling Mike underneath him while trying to straddle him. With his arm no longer a viable weapon and being forced into a disadvantaged position, Mike reared back and head-butted the man with the crown of his head, then climbed onto his opponent's heaving chest, screaming for the gun.

Suddenly, the tables were turned again, with his opponent on top of Mike. He had a clean shot and could easily have taken it, but instead, for some murky reason, the man seemed to be trying to use Mike's body as a springboard to bounce away from him. Mike held tight. *Give me that goddamned gun!*

The struggle continued until the man raised his hand and struck Mike full across the face with the shiny object. Mike felt what he was sure was his cheekbone shattering.

What the fuck. Why didn't he just shoot me? Afraid? Weak? No bullets?

And that's when he realized that the man didn't have a gun, after all. It was a metal pipe. *He's not a gun guy. There is no gun. He doesn't have a gun. No. He's going to beat me to death with a pipe. This pipe.*

There was a moment of grace before Mike's face exploded with blood. In that moment, Mike heard his old boss Robby talking to him: *You're a lucky bugger, O'Shea. Any higher, and he'd have hit the sweet spot. Knocked you out cold. Likely beaten you to death. Wake up, O'Shea. Find a break.*

Mike could feel the warmth of something liquid cascading down his face. He knew it was blood as soon as the intense pain hit, and it took every ounce of his diminishing stamina to remain conscious.

Robby was still there: *Wake up, O'Shea. Find a break. Make a break. Do not die now.*

For an instant, time and motion stopped. Both men looked directly at each other, both searching for their next move. Then as quickly as they had frozen, the other man drew back the metal pipe to strike Mike again.

Mike rolled as hard as he could to the left, causing his opponent to roll with him. He knew that his only hope was to somehow overcome this bastard. Then a wave of incredible crushing pain flooded over him, bringing with it the dread realization that he was losing this mortal contest.

The pain began to envelop Mike and numb him to everything except the instinctive understanding that he was dead if he did not get away from this madman. As he sized up his would-be killer, he suddenly recognized him as Mark Johnstone. Fucking Cockeye Johnstone.

No, dammit. Cockeye Fucking Johnstone is not going to kill me here. Or anywhere. No fucking way.

That was it. Mike knew, as only someone who had stood on that line between life and death would know, that one of them was going to die, and it damn well wasn't going to be him.

Now the only sound Mike could hear was the beating of his own heart. Everything else was gone. As his senses seemed to both shut down and sharpen, he lost any understanding of what was going on around him beyond Cockeye's face. The pain had transmuted into a kind of cool tingling; he couldn't even feel the blood gushing down his face.

His world had shrunk to just him and Cockeye.

Time slowed down. He watched Cockeye rear back with the metal pipe in his right hand, frame by frame, with the same critical detachment of a film director watching the day's takes in an editing studio. He watched that right hand rise across Cockeye's body until it was beside Cockeye's left ear. He saw in his assailant's eyes the exact moment Cockeye made the decision to hammer down with a full-force backhand across his face.

But he also knew that time would stand still for him until he was ready to finally put an end to this deadly encounter.

Mike pulled out his gun, long free from his sweatshirt's snare. He raised it and aimed at Cockeye's now-exposed torso, just underneath his upraised right arm.

Then he pulled the trigger.

Cockeye's body shuddered. Mike saw confusion and surprise in the man's eyes, but he also saw that Cockeye was still intent on crushing his skull with the pipe.

He pulled the trigger again.

Cockeye stopped and looked questioningly into Mike's eyes. He began to wobble a bit on top of Mike, and then he pulled his arm back again towards the left side of his head, still determined to strike the killing blow.

Mike pulled the trigger a third time.

Cockeye was becoming very unsteady. The front of his shirt was reddening. His mouth was open, and it looked like some sound might be coming out, but Mike couldn't hear a thing. Cockeye's eyes rolled back in his head, but still, he held his right arm up and ready to strike.

Then the gun jammed.

Fuck.

Tap. Rack. Tap. Rack. That's all Mike could think of. His years of training bounced and echoed around in his head.

Then he stopped tapping and racking as Cockeye fell back, his full weight cracking down on Mike's knees. The pipe dropped just to the right of Mike, bouncing away from the two men.

The world stopped. Mike couldn't feel or hear or see anything. Suddenly, the weight of Cockeye on his legs registered. Mike lifted his head a bit and could see the grotesque way Cockeye was lying, his legs below his knees tucked in neatly under his body, a deadweight on top of Mike. There was blood on Mike's sweatshirt. And chunks of flesh.

Sal? No. Not this time.

And then the pain from his face hit him like the proverbial ton of bricks.

He elbowed himself up as much as he could and noticed that the circle of blood on his sweatshirt was getting bigger and bigger. Any backsplash blood from the bullets he had just pumped into Cockeye should be over and done with. Fuck, this mess was his own blood. He lowered himself back down and looked up at the flickering streetlight just above him, shining down on him and Cockeye. *We're both just gasping for that last chance at life,* Mike smiled to the light.

He couldn't hear anything except a loud ringing in his ears. He couldn't hear Cockeye gurgling as the blood painfully entered his punctured lungs, drowning him slowly. He couldn't hear the rhythmic chiming of his door alarm, nor could he hear the voices of the crowd gathering, or the sirens in the distance as his panicked colleagues raced their way towards him.

If Mike had been more aware, he would have realized the havoc his fight was causing around him. Even in a neighbourhood like this one, gunshots ringing out attracted attention. After the second shot, drugs would have been pre-emptively flushed down toilets. Territorial lines would be drawn, and innumerable messages would have flown through the ether to confirm alliances in the event that this was a call to arms in yet another drug war.

Thankfully, no one in the gathering crowd had recognized Mike as a cop, which probably saved his life. Had they known, someone would have very likely stepped out from the crowd and shot him as he lay pinned beneath his wounded opponent before blending back and disappearing into the night. As it was now, this was just another tussle between a couple of rounders, one of whom everyone recognized. Luckily, Cockeye had more enemies than friends in the crowd.

As Mike noted people standing over him, he began to float in and out of consciousness. He felt dizzy, and his mind wandered away from that dark, dank street where he lay. *Digestives. Homemade. Leave at least one for your brother, Michael.* He could smell the cooked sugar and feel the warmth of the freshly baked biscuits as they melted in his mouth. Then, without warning, he was back watching the flickering of the streetlight. *'Watch me, Da! Watch me!'* Crack! *'Run, lad, run!'* The ball jettisoned out of the park as he hit his first home run. *'Watch me, Da!'* Then back to the incredible pain in his face.

'I'm right here, Michael. Don't let go. Yer Mam is waitin' on ye.'

Past and present no longer held any meaning for him. He needed to put his gun back in the holster. No, he had to call his son and give him shit for being out so late.

He wondered why all these people were standing around him and what they were saying. All he could hear was ringing. *Why am I lying here on the ground? I just want to go home to sleep.*

The crowd parted, and Mike saw a uniformed police officer standing over him. At first, the officer just seemed to be staring down at him, and then he saw the officer's mouth open really wide as if shouting, but he didn't hear anything. Then he saw the officer panicking and realized he knew the man: It was Preston McAfee.

He tried to open his mouth to tell McAfee that everything was okay, but he couldn't move his jaw. And then lots of officers and paramedics converged on him. He wanted to laugh: From his vantage point on the asphalt, it looked like they were running around like circus clowns, and no one knew what they were doing.

His initial impulse was to help, but he couldn't move. One of the paramedics seemed to be trying to talk to him, but all Mike could hear was ringing. And his face was throbbing. He'd forgotten all about being pinned, but once they pulled Cockeye off him and placed him onto a stretcher, Mike's knees began to throb. In a moment of clarity, he managed to raise himself up on his elbows to look down as he wiggled his toes, just to make sure. And that's when he realized something.

Oh, shit! I've pissed myself.

Chapter Twenty-Nine

Saturday, August 25, 2018 - 3:32 a.m.

"What the fuck do you mean: Mike's been shot?" Amanda Black screamed.

"I didn't say 'Mike's been shot,'" Ron calmly clarified over the phone. "I said Mike's been *involved* in a shooting. With Mark Johnstone. Happened a few minutes ago. They're both going to St. Mike's."

"That serious?"

"One's an emergency run."

Emergency run. Meaning nothing more paramedics can do except drive like hell and hope for the best. And St. Michael's Hospital was not the closest hospital, but the best equipped to deal with serious trauma. Amanda paused a moment to take in the gravity of the situation. *Shit!* Yes, she was an experienced homicide investigator. Yes, she saw dead people for a living and all of that, but this was different. This time, it was one of their own. *I can't do another cop funeral. I just can't. You better fucking hang on, Crumply-pants. Ho-ly Fuck.*

"O'Shea or Johnstone?" Amanda pulled her game face back on.

"I don't know. The whole shift is on the scene, no one is answering their radios, and if you watch the news, you'll see the loop of them loading Mike into the ambulance."

"I am not near a fucking TV. What the fuck happened?"

"I don't know. Nothing on the news," Ron replied, trying not to allow his own emotions to colour his tone.

"Us, Ron. Not the news. We drive the news, remember? What do we know? Does anyone there know what happened?"

Shotgun. Staccato. Authentic Amanda Black questioning. Ron could work with that.

"Well, like I said, the whole platoon is on the call, no one is answering their radios, Staff is on the phone to the Duty Desk, and the unit commander is probably on his way to the hospital. So in answer to your question, no. No one here knows what happened."

Ron was beginning to feel an increasing sense of annoyance, frustration, and fear blending in his mind, causing his chest to tighten. He took a deep breath, realizing that all of these emotions were just a mask for his own failings. He was responsible for all of this. It was his fault that Mike got made. He should never have called him on the radio. He should never have let Mike go out on this detail alone. He knew that Cockeye was a desperate killer who would likely have no qualms about killing again if that would keep him out of jail. Even if it meant killing a cop. He knew Amanda was going to put some crazy scheme in place, and he should have known that it would go sideways.

Ron took a deep breath. There was nothing he could do now except hold it together. Even that, he had to admit to himself, seemed really challenging at the moment. He wiped his forehead with his hand, thankful that everyone else was at the scene. No need for anyone to see him like this. Thirty-five years of policing. No need to fall apart now. Leave that for everyone else to do.

"Great. Okay. I am going to make my way to the hospital. Do you need anything there?" Amanda asked.

"No. I'm good."

Liar, Amanda thought, turning her attention to getting to the bottom of this shit show.

* * *

St. Michael's Hospital was in a state of chaos. It was a Saturday night and probably a full moon. Every crazy in the city was there. Add a seriously bleeding cop rolling in on an emergency run with every sworn officer within driving distance following, plus all of the media outlets in the city swarming Emerg, and the party just got more stupid.

Uniformed scout cars, beat-up old clunkers, and shiny sedans from HQ were already clogging the streets and laneways around the hospital. The red and blue of the roof lights reflected off the surrounding brick walls that also echoed back the screams of the odd siren that had been left on. The media trucks were vying for spots to set up outside, with pretty new talking heads trying to elbow out the seasoned hacks. Camera crews were pushing past each other in an attempt to be the first to get to the ambulance port for the money shot. And an increasingly large crowd of gawkers had begun to gather, some genuinely curious, others hoping for fifteen seconds of fame as they photo-bombed the live broadcast feeds.

There was mass confusion inside the emergency department as doctors tried to sort out fact from rumour. Did either party have life-threatening injuries? According to the unfolding media coverage, one man was going to be dead by the end of this evening. Was it going to be the cop or the other guy, or was one of them already dead? Was the cop going to be wheeled in first or second in an attempt to distract the media, and did it even matter?

"All right, everyone! Let's focus on what we have coming in instead of looking at the goddamn TV screen," an older Emerg nurse called out.

When Detective Mike O'Shea's stretcher burst through the doors, at least fifteen uniformed officers converged upon the waiting room from all entrances. The regular Emerg patrons became agitated by the huge uniform presence, and some made their way quickly down the hall to another exit, while others began to grumble loudly. One man who had been complaining of chest pains grabbed his chest and fell to the floor, but a nearby nurse advised him that he was not having a heart attack and that he would have to wait his turn to see a doctor. The man opened one crusty eye and looked up from the ground, disappointed, before getting up and stomping out of the hospital. The nurse called after him to tell him that she'd see him again next week. He told her to fuck off.

Mike's jaw was surrounded by gauze and taped to the backboard as a compromise between taping his still-bleeding head and causing him further pain, or leaving his neck insecure during transport and causing him further trauma. And pain. Under the bright orange sheet, his shoulders, chest, and legs were strapped down. Somewhere along the line, an IV needle had been poked into his left arm, and fluids were flowing into him—faster, Mike hoped, than the blood was soaking through the gauze around his head. A huge bandage had been taped over his face where it had been split open, but if he tilted his head slightly to the left, he could partially see out of the corner of his right eye.

Paramedics seemed to be talking to him, but he couldn't hear a thing. All he saw were their mouths moving and lots of gestures indicting that he shouldn't be moving his head at all. No big deal. All he could see without moving his head wasn't all that interesting anyway: just a blur of rows of fluorescent lights on the ceiling as they rushed him into the trauma room. He could feel a lot of hands on his body and see the shadows of what he assumed to be mostly coppers touching him as he was whizzed through the hall.

His head was throbbing now. Mike watched as the gauze on his face was removed. It was soaked in blood. Another piece of gauze was quickly placed on his face, and a paramedic took Mike's hand and pressed it against the gauze.

Looking up at the bright fluorescent lights, Mike held the gauze down and had to admit that he was afraid. It wasn't the bleeding that scared him; it was the resounding silence. Places like this were almost a second home to Mike, and he knew this particular Emerg like the back of his hand. It was loud at any time of night or day, and yet tonight, he didn't hear a thing.

A hand gently removed his hand and lifted the bandage from Mike's face, leaving the gauze around his jaw still taped to the backboard. There was a very bright light behind the face that belonged to the hand. Mike couldn't make out any details on the face because of the mask and cap, but he saw enough to know that it belonged to a woman and that she had very warm eyes. He could see that the mask was moving, but he still couldn't hear a thing. The woman nodded to him and then looked across to someone else.

Another masked woman was standing on the other side of Mike. Her mask was moving a lot. *She must be the doctor,* Mike thought. *She seems to be directing the show.* He tried to figure out somehow what she might be saying by her eyes, but he couldn't. And he was so tired. And a bit dizzy.

He felt a jab in his hand and saw that another IV needle had been poked into him. He followed the line that was attached to the needle and saw that he was going to be receiving something very soon. He hoped it was some kind of painkiller. He had no idea what the extent of his injuries were, or what was happening to him.

"I can't hear anything," he finally managed to say out loud.

Everything around him seemed to stop. The woman he had assumed was the doctor looked at the woman he'd assumed was the nurse, who in turn was looking over her shoulder at something or someone. It was taking all of Mike's waning energy to try to figure out what was happening around him. Then, just as he was losing focus, a sea of uniforms enveloped the gurney. Mike wasn't sure whether to feel relief or concern, when suddenly, Detective Sergeant Amanda Black parted that sea.

Amanda leaned over him, her uncovered mouth moving. She was saying something. He looked blankly at her.

Amanda motioned for something from someone behind her.

"Oh, for the love of God! Get me something to write on, people!" She had shouted, unbeknownst to Mike. She began writing furiously in a memo book, which she held up so that he could read it.

Can you hear anything at all? the words said.

Mike tried to shake his head to say no, but taped to the backboard as he was, he ended up more or less swaying his whole upper body.

Amanda scribbled some more. **Do you know where you are?**

Mike shrugged indifferently. He could feel himself slipping away.

Amanda scribbled for a long time before holding up the memo book. **You are at St. Mike's. You are okay. Stay with me.**

Mike grunted his okay.

Amanda scribbled some more: **Want me to call your wife?**

Before he could consider anything, she pulled the paper away, appeared to call out to someone, and then placed it back in front of him. The word 'wife' had been replaced with 'Carmen.'

Mike smiled slightly. No. No, he didn't. He did want Max to know that he was okay, though. That was important. Max needed to know, but not now. Mike knew that Max wasn't expecting him home, so there was no point in having someone try to find him just for this. No. Mike started to shake his head but thought better of it and just grunted.

Amanda nodded. Having done so many notifications in her day, she figured that she could read people's responses to that question like an old diary. This one was no different. Another cop marriage on the rocks.

Mike closed his eyes, ending the conversation.

Amanda stepped back.

Mike stretched his body as best he could within what was increasingly feeling like a body bag, but he stopped when the pounding in his head amped up even more.

Pain? one of the nurses wrote, taking over the roll of scribe.

Mike tried to nod his head up and down, much to the consternation of the medical staff standing over him.

Allergies? the second note-writer asked.

Mike tilted his head side to side. He was beginning to worry about Max. If only he could phone his son.

No pain meds until examined, the note flashed as the nurse stepped away from him.

Amanda Black moved into Mike's view with another note. **Union lawyer en route. Don't talk to anyone,** her handwriting directed.

Mike saw the note blur out of existence as he lost consciousness.

* * *

"I'm looking for Detective Michael O'Shea."

"I'm sorry. We're not allowed to give out information," the Emerge nurse at the desk stated, not bothering to make eye contact with the unkempt man standing in front of her.

"I'm George Beauparlante from the Special Investigations Unit. I believe that you have Detective O'Shea in your unit here, and I need to talk to him." He set down the briefcase he had been holding in his right hand and began to reach behind into his back pocket for his wallet and official ID.

"Good luck with that, bud," a voice just to the right of the nursing station challenged.

Beauparlante looked over and saw a uniformed officer leaning against the doorframe of the only glass cubicle on the floor.

"Excuse me?" Beauparlante asked, hoisting his pants up, a thumb tucked in the belt loop on either side, as a subconscious show of authority.

"You heard me," the officer challenged, a swagger in his voice.

"Is Detective O'Shea in there?"

"Damned if I know, and fucked if I'm going to tell you."

"You know that you are required by law to cooperate with the SIU, don't you?" Beauparlante replied, attempting to sound challenging.

"Go fuck yourself," the officer replied, smirking as he rolled his back around the doorframe and disappeared into the room.

Beauparlante began to move towards that same door.

"Excuse me, sir, but only immediate family are allowed in," the nurse's voice announced sharply.

Beauparlante looked incredulously at the nurse, who seemed equal parts authoritative and intimidating. He thought about heading in anyway, but realized that this battle wasn't worth fighting. Besides, the nurse looked as if she had her finger on the buzzer for security. Or she just might tackle him herself.

Beauparlante picked up his briefcase with as much dignity as a man forced to retreat could muster and took the only available seat in the waiting room down the hall, right beside a raggedy woman who was insistent upon eating whatever entity inhabited her unruly hair.

Chapter Thirty

Saturday, August 25, 2018 - 6:25 a.m.

On another floor in the same hospital, two uniformed officers sat next to a hospital bed in a room subdivided by bile-yellow curtains. They were crowding a scrawny man whose handcuffed wrists clinked against the metal rails on either side of his bed. Their prisoner, barely covered by a sheet over his skimpy hospital gown, had been tossing around since his arrival in the ICU, despite the pain medication being pumped into him through the IV drip in his left arm. He seemed oblivious to the heart monitor tabs stuck on his hairless chest and to their wires, which loosely tethered him to a machine behind his bed, but he was quite vocal with the nurses who routinely removed and reapplied the gauze over the still-oozing hole in his gut where the bullet had been dug out.

"Mark Johnstone?" Amanda Black yanked the curtain back, disrupting the rhythmic sound of the monitoring devices and almost causing the younger of the two officers to kick over the half-empty paper coffee cup by his boot as he rapidly stood.

"Who wants to know?" the scrawny man opened one eye to look down the bed, answering with a yawn that culminated in an unsavory burp.

"My name is Detective Sergeant Amanda Black. Gentlemen," Amanda nodded to the two uniforms before turning her attentions back to Cockeye Johnstone. "Mark Johnstone, I am arresting you for the attempted murder of Michael O'Shea."

"Who the fuck is Michael O'Shea?"

"The cop whose head you fucking bashed in, you shithead," the uniformed officer who had stood up when Amanda entered the tiny space snapped at his prisoner.

"Officer? If you don't mind…?" Amanda looked over the reading glasses she had just put on, cautioning the significantly younger uniform.

"Yeah, fucknuts. Let the bitch speak."

"Fuck you," the rookie whispered as he sat back down, his coach officer shaking his head with a smile.

"It is my duty to inform you," Amanda looked down at the printout she had pasted in the back of her notebook, "that you have the right to retain and instruct counsel without delay."

"Is this your first rodeo, princess? Gotta read this shit from the book there? You look a bit old to be playing cops-and-robbers," Cockeye sneered, turning his body casually towards the left side of the gurney where the officers sat, before blocking off one nostril with the hand affixed to the railing and blowing a wad of snot out of the other, narrowly missing the knee of the younger one.

"Aw, shit." The young man recoiled in disgust, much to the amusement of his prisoner. The officer tasked with training the young cop rolled his eyes apologetically at Amanda.

"You have the right," the detective sergeant read, "to telephone any lawyer you wish. You also have the right to free advice from a legal aid lawyer—"

"I got a lawyer. Don't get your pussy all wet worryin' 'bout me." Cockeye chortled, shaking the bed as he made some half-hearted attempt to tear the handcuffs off his wrists. The younger cop started to get out of his chair again but stopped when the older one gave him a tap on the elbow.

"He's strapped in pretty good, Kev. He's not going anywhere."

"If you are charged with an offence," Amanda continued, glancing again at the baby-faced officer before returning to her script, "you may apply for legal assistance—"

"I said I got a lawyer, bitch." Cockeye hissed, sitting as far forward as his restrained wrists would allow him, the gown that had been precariously covering him now dangling from one shoulder.

"Do you understand?" Amanda asked quietly, unmoved.

"Fuckin' bitch is *dim!*" Cockeye flung his body back and looked over at the two uniformed officers for confirmation, his gown now held in place by the sheet tucked in at the bottom of the bed more than anything else.

"Do you wish to call a lawyer now?" Amanda's voice was icy.

"Yeah. Sure. With my fucking CELL PHONE THAT THIS ASSHOLE STOLE!" Cockeye rolled over one side, putting his back to the officers, his handcuffed wrist forcing him to leave one arm behind him.

"A telephone can be arranged," Amanda continued, undaunted by the theatrics.

"What part," Cockeye flung himself around and back up, his eyes locking with Amanda's, "of get the fuck out of here, don't you understand?"

Amanda jotted something down in the notebook before flipping back to her printout and continuing. "Now, Mark Johnstone, you have been charged with attempted murder. You are not obliged to say anything unless you wish to do so, but—"

"Speak to this," Cockeye turned onto his side again, this time pushing the sheet away from his body to expose his skinny legs and boney ass before releasing a loud stinking fart.

"Oh, fuck!" the older officer said, bringing the crook of his elbow up against his mouth and nose while his partner gave a slight cough. "Now *that* was nasty."

"Whatever you say may be given in evidence. Do you understand?" Amanda did not move.

Cockeye rolled back over on his back, smirking in apparent satisfaction at the uniformed officers' response.

"Do you wish to say anything in answer to the charge?"

"Wanna suck my dick?" Cockeye kicked off the sheet to expose his naked body before thrusting his pelvis in her direction.

"Mr. Johnstone, you do know that you're handcuffed to this bed, right?" This being far from her first rodeo, Amanda found neither humour nor pathos in the accused's behaviour and was quickly running out of patience.

"You wish it was the other way around, don'tcha, you fucking whore? Come a little closer, and I'll give you some of this." Cockeye sat up, throwing his head forward, tongue wagging.

Being even less amused by Cockeye's antics than Amanda was, the older officer suddenly shot his arm out, and with the palm of his hand against his prisoner's forehead, pushed Cockeye back down on the bed with such force that the locked wheels skidded on the laminate flooring, sending the bed into the wall behind it.

"Delightful," Amanda commented.

"Wait till I give you the real thing," Cockeye continued, rocking his pelvis a couple of times while defiantly looking at the old cop.

"Mr. Johnstone, I'm from Homicide."

"Ooh. So your cunt is—"

"Of no concern to you," Amanda snapped back, much to the surprise of the two uniformed officers, who quickly glanced at one another. It was unusual for any female officer, let alone a detective sergeant, to even acknowledge such a comment, never mind respond to it. "I am telling you I am from Homicide because I will be back, likely within the hour, to charge you with the murder of Sergei Kuzminov."

"That so?" Cockeye's demeanor suddenly became quite civilized, the notion of being charged with something as serious as murder seeming to straighten him out. "I have no idea what you're talking about."

"We can place you at the scene," Amanda sniffed.

"Lotsa people probably knew the guy.," Cockeye said lightly as he began surveying the curtains that surrounded him, avoiding eye contact with anyone.

"I now have the lead pipe that you used to try to murder Detective O'Shea," Amanda continued.

"I never tried to murder nobody." Cockeye looked down at the fingernails on his left hand before bending his body over to bite on the middle fingernail, his head once again precariously close to the rookie.

"I believe I will find Sergei Kusminov's blood on that lead pipe."

"Lucky you." Cockeye shifted the piece of fingernail he had bitten off to his tongue and blew it onto the rookie's shirt. He looked down at his naked body, past the sheet bunched up at his feet, towards Amanda. "Maybe I found the pipe by the side of the road."

"Fucking animal!" the rookie muttered, flicking at his shirt several times with the back of his hand.

"And I sincerely doubt that you are the most hygienic man on the planet, Mr. Johnstone," Amanda added as she did an slow, deliberate scan of Cockeye Johnstone's body before removing her glasses and smiling at the officers to her right.

"Maybe if you suck my dick, you'll find out," the handcuffed man thrust his pelvis towards Amanda again.

"Settle down," the senior constable advised, giving Cockeye a quick but effective shot to the side of the head.

"I believe I will find bloodied fibres from Mr. Kuzminov's room in the clothing that I have seized as evidence in relation to your attempted murder of Detective O'Shea," Amanda continued implacably.

"I believe you're fucking bluffing," Cockeye countered.

"Mr. Johnstone, Sergei Kuzminov owed you a lot of money, and you got tired of him, so you beat him to death with the same lead pipe you used to beat Detective O'Shea," Amanda concluded as she dropped her designer glasses into their case and then into her purse. "Isn't that right?"

"You can think whatever you want, precious, and I can say whatever I want because I ain't got no lawyer present, I ain't waived no rights, and I'm on enough legal shit to fly me to the moon. So yeah, I killed that fucking crip. And I killed Jimmy Hoffa. And I'm fucking your mother and likely gonna kill her, too. Any other unsolved mysteries you want to clear up, there, Detective Bumbaclot?"

"Watch your fucking mouth, asshole!" the senior cop cautioned, constrained by the omniscient video cameras that saved this rounder from the serious beating he would have received back in the day, even if he was chained to a hospital bed.

Cockeye blew the older man a kiss.

Amanda inhaled deeply and closed her eyes as she exhaled. In that moment, she hated Cockeye Johnstone almost more than she had ever hated anyone, not because he had almost killed a police officer in the line of duty, nor because he had murdered another man, but because he reminded her of someone else. Knock a few years off him, and Cockeye Johnstone could be Randy Valencourt, the punk who had severed her sister's spinal cord in a botched holdup twenty years earlier. Same arrogance, same lack of insight into his behaviour, same reptilian look.

"You guys need anything?" Amanda offered, after taking a few more deep breaths. "Another coffee? A bite to eat?"

"I'd love a coffee," Cockeye jumped in. "With a little Baileys in it. Isn't that what you faggots have in your coffees?"

"Let it go," the senior man advised his charge without even looking over at him.

"Oh, and Mr. Johnstone?" Amanda turned her attention to the man in the bed. "I have DNA from a footprint we lifted from the sidewalk outside your rooming house."

"Alert the fucking media."

"And I have your shoes—"

"Mama's got new shoes, boys!" Cockeye laughed, looking over his left shoulder.

"…that made that footprint."

"Hoo-ha!"

"I believe we will find Mr. Kuzminov's blood on the soles of your shoes."

"Well, there ain't no diamonds on 'em!" The rookie moved away from the bed as Cockeye shifted his head to the side to look down at Amanda's shoes. "Do you fuck your husband wearing those shoes?"

"Thanks again for your help, guys. I've got my partner trying to track down a judge to set up the telephone remand so we can get someone from the court to guard our friend over here so you two can get out of here sooner rather than later."

"Aw. And we were just starting to bond," Cockeye winked his good eye at the rookie.

"Hopefully, by that time, Amy will have had a chance to look at the shoes, and I can come back and charge this… individual… with murder. I'll keep you posted."

Amanda pulled the curtain behind her open and closed as she disappeared, leaving the two officers at their post.

* * *

Mike was blissfully unaware of everything that was happening around him. After a series of X-rays and pressure-resistance testing, an agreeable amount of drugs were pumped into his body. Whether or not he had been informed of what was happening via a series of notes was debatable, but once the painkillers kicked in, he had no idea what was happening. Nor did he care.

He didn't feel a thing until he awoke several hours later, still wearing his bloodied clothes. His face still hurt, but not as much. More importantly, he wanted to check his hearing. The ringing in his ears had subsided somewhat, but there was a hum. Hospital machinery, perhaps?

"How are you doing, partner?"

Mike's eyes snapped open. There was Ron smiling almost warmly down on him.

"Ron. Good, my friend. Good. You?" Mike was relieved to be able to hear Ron's voice.

"Well, better than you. Not much better, but better."

"What time is it?"

"It is…" Ron pulled his arm in front of himself, checking his watch, "a quarter to ten."

"A.M. or P.M.?"

"A.M. It's Sunday morning."

"Oh, okay. Everything get sorted out from last night?"

"I don't think we should talk about that here," Ron said, looking over his shoulder. "It's not that I don't want to tell you. It's just that there are a lot of… undesirables… in this place, know what I mean?"

"Gotcha." Mike tried to smile, but the right side of his face tightened and began to hurt.

"Looks like you got quite a whack," Ron said, moving closer to the bed.

"Yeah. I guess. I don't know if anything is broken—"

"Cheekbone's a bit of a mess, but you're pretty lucky otherwise," Ron replied. "Mind if I have a look?"

Mike grimaced.

Ron reached over and delicately peeled back the gauze. "Huh. Looks like they did a bit of sewing and then just kind of taped everything else up. Huh." Ron put the gauze back and stepped away from the bed.

"Excuse me, sir, but are you related?" the nurse entering the room asked.

"I'm his partner," Ron announced, standing tall.

"Oh, I'm sorry. Can I get you a chair, then? Has the doctor come by to update you?"

"No. Why?" Ron asked blankly.

"We just like to keep family members informed, you know."

Despite the pain, a slight smile came to Mike's face.

"He's my *work* partner," Ron corrected.

"Oh. Well, in that case," the nurse's warm tone became cold and formal, "could you please not remove the dressing from your colleague's wound?"

"Certainly," Ron replied as she walked out of the cubicle. "What would make her think—"

"Can you find out when I can get out of here?" Mike interrupted.

"Oh. Right. Yes, I was about to tell you. The doctor said they just wanted to ask you a few questions, make sure you can manage the concussion and that sort of thing, and then you can go. Is Carmen coming to pick you up?"

Ron poked his head out of the cubicle to try to spot a woman he'd never met.

"No." Mike looked away.

"Do you want me to give you a lift home once you're discharged, then?"

"Sure."

"Kinda like old times, isn't it?"

"Not at all like old times, hopefully."

* * *

Less than half an hour later, Mike was standing, stoned and alone, in the hospital parking lot waiting for Ron. His shirt was still crusted with his own blood, and his face was swollen and beginning to discolour like a week-old Halloween pumpkin.

Shit.

Chapter Thirty-One

Sunday, August 26, 2018 - 10:43 a.m.

Mike put his key in the lock and waved Ron off as he opened the front door to his house.

"Jesus, Mike!" Carmen gasped as she looked over from the couch. A young man he recognized as one of her colleagues pulled his arm away from her, casually reaching for his beer—Mike's beer. "I thought you were—"

"At work? I was."

"What happened?"

"Had a bit of a run-in with a lead pipe."

"Pumpkin," the young man smirked.

"Shut up, Ash," Carmen ordered as she got up and rushed over to her husband.

Mike held his arm out, motioning her to stay back.

"Mike, I can—" Carmen began.

"Explain?" Mike offered, certain he was the odd man out on this Saturday-morning rendezvous.

"It's not like—" Carmen began again.

"Who the fuck are you?" Mike said, looking at the little shit.

The boyish man stood, smoothing his lavender dress shirt. He smiled at Mike.

Mike looked around and noticed the man's jacket casually tossed across the table in the entry way.

"I think you should leave," he said, walking over to open the front door, the cool autumn air wafting its way into his home. He glared at the Little Shit.

The young man looked to Carmen, who nodded.

"I'll wait outside, then?" he asked, stretching as he stood up.

Mike took a deep breath. *In like the vacuum. Out like the wind.* He picked up the soft leather jacket from the table and threw it outside.

"Your jacket is waiting for you."

The Little Shit smiled as he walked within punching distance past Mike and down the stone stairs and retrieved his jacket. Mike slammed the door closed.

Carmen walked over to the door. "What is *wrong* with you?" she spat, as if Mike had punched the interloper and dropped him cold, which was what Mike had played and replayed in his mind's eye many times already.

"My head hurts, my mouth tastes like dried blood, and I'm wearing the clothes that I pissed myself in yesterday. How's *your* morning going?"

Carmen pushed past Mike and reopened the door. "I'll just be a second," Carmen called out to the Little Shit. She slipped on her black flats and grabbed her purse and jacket that she had close by.

"And the boys? Where are the boys?"

"Max is with your mother. Lucas is at his father's."

"You're a class act, Carmen."

"Don't—"

"I didn't."

"It's just easier if I leave now, Mike," she said as she looked down at the boyish man waiting outside for her. He nodded up at her with a silent understanding

"Easier than what?" Mike's eyes darted between his wife and the Little Shit, his fists clenched.

"Than leaving later today. Or," she went on to suggest, pulling her hair back casually as she tied it with the band she had on her wrist, "do you want until all of this heals?" She nodded towards Mike's face.

"Whatever," Mike sputtered, sucking the wind back into himself, seeing the world he had come to know—the world he had built with her—slip away from him. "Where will you go?"

"I'm moving in with Ash," his wife—ex-wife, he corrected himself—remarked casually as she looked around her, making a mental note of what she would need sooner than later.

"What about the boys? Are you leaving them, too?" *You're The Man now, Michael,* he remembered his mother telling him. *With your Da gone, I'll be needin' ye to help me run the household and look after the wee ones.*

"I'll take Lucas. Max will stay here with you, of course," she replied with a sigh. "Leave with what you came with and all of that."

"Yeah. All of that." Mike looked at the family photos on the walls before looking back at his soon-to-be ex-wife. Even at her age, her skin was flawless, as if she'd just stepped out of a magazine.

In fact, Carmen's whole life could have come from a magazine. Unlike him, she had come from privilege and pedigree, both of which served her well. The only fly in the ointment had been meeting him—that 'rugged police detective,' as her friends had initially half-facetiously referred to him—at some gala he had been cajoled into attending. Her friends' chuckles quickly turned to sneers when she left her cookie-cutter corporate husband behind to marry him, a high school graduate from a poor immigrant mick family who didn't appear to know a soupspoon from a ladle. To Carmen's friends, Mike was more to be played with than brought home. Especially if bringing him home meant destroying the home Carmen already had.

"Lucas will stay with my parents until Ash and I get settled," Carmen explained.

"You mean until you convince your boytoy that he wants to be the father of a teenager?"

"He'll get used to the idea. He likes kids."

"Thought of everything, haven't you?" Mike mumbled. What had he missed? Was she *that* unhappy? Unhappy at all? Was that Little Shit standing out there in his front yard a thing, or was he just a convenient exit? Had he himself been anything more than a convenient exit? Shit.

"No. I just don't want to drag this out any longer than we have to. Do you want me to look after the paperwork, or will you?"

"So that's it, then? Sign, stamp, and file. Done?"

"Never mind, Mike. I'll call Dad and have him get things going. Excuse me," she brushed by him, the smell of another man's cologne wafting from her.

She stood in the doorway for a moment.

"We need coffee, don't we?" she called to the Little Shit. He nodded, flicking the ashes from the cigarette he had lit onto the front step. Mike cringed.

Carmen came back into the house and flitted past Mike into the kitchen. He followed her.

"I thought you were leaving." He rubbed the scruff on his face with his hands, still in disbelief.

"I'll be back later today to pick up what I can and make arrangements to pick up the rest, maybe tomorrow," she said, pulling out the bag of fresh coffee beans from the cupboard.

"Carmen…" Mike began, not wanting to sound desperate but also not wanting to give up without…what…a fight?

She closed the cupboard and waltzed back to the front door, bag of coffee beans in hand, Mike a few steps behind.

"Mike," she whispered, turning quickly back to him just before stepping outside, "you're a good man. An excellent father. A great cop. It's just—"

"Is he the only one?" Mike asked, motioning towards the Little Shit with his head as he stepped further inside the house, distancing himself from his wife.

The pause was enough. He watched her go before making his way to the cupboard in the kitchen where they—he—kept the good whiskey.

Mike heard the bolt in the door turn as the bottle rattled his glass. Shaking now, he poured generously, remembering the exact moment he had answered another door so many years ago. He was supposed to be at school that day, but he had lied about being sick because he hadn't studied for a test. Mike moved to the living room, glass, and bottle in hand, and sat. He closed his eyes. The man at the door that long-ago morning was the union boss at his father's work. The man had asked Mike to get his mother and then told her to sit down, that he had something important to say. His mother sent Mike off to the kitchen to plug the in kettle for some tea, but Mike hung back, standing on the other side of the wall, trying to hear the words.

It was the wailing that he remembered most. Muffled at first, but then full -on howling. When he came back into the living room, he saw his mother hastily wipe her eyes before telling him to run upstairs and get dressed. Then more orders: Put something on against the rain. Go get your brother and sisters from school. Don't ask. Just do.

He remembered running as fast as he could through the hard rain that pricked at his face, wondering if whatever had happened was his fault, what his Da would say when he got home from work, if God was punishing his family for his lie.

It wasn't until many years later that Mike was able to convince himself that his lying had nothing to do with God killing his father. Nor did God, he knew, have anything to do with him and Carmen.

Why the fuck did I marry her anyway?

She was beautiful. Manufactured mostly, but she was beautiful nonethe-less. And stable. Or so he thought. And came from a good family. She seemed to be everything his first wife was not. Everything he wanted.

Apparently not.

Likely, she'd been at this game for a while now, and Little Shit likely wasn't the first. But if he was being honest with himself, Mike realized, if he had loved Carmen half as much as a husband should, he might have fought for her. Or maybe it just wasn't in him any more, that ability to love and fight for love. Or maybe it had been erased by age and work and family and the burden of responsibility.

He looked at his empty glass and then over at the bottle of Midleton. The good whiskey.

No. He'd save it. For another day. Another momentous event.

Under the right circumstances, anyone is capable of anything.

Mike could hear Robby Williams's voice as clearly as when he'd first heard him say this, back when Mike and Sal began working together, wearing tight jeans and cowboy boots, their handlebar moustaches lighting them up as cops trying to be blend in with the hookers and their pimps.

No matter who they are or where they came from, Mikey, under the right circumstances....

Mike looked past the living room and up the stairs, a fog hanging over his eyes, his ears still ringing from the sound of the gunshots that had taken down Cockeye. The walls were a soft shade of yellow, the colour the previous owner had chosen. There was a ding in the wall from moving Max's dresser upstairs that he hadn't plastered over yet. Goddammit, it was too soon for her to have decided that they were done, that their marriage was dead.

Mike stood up and pulled out the tiny white envelope they had given him at the hospital from his pocket. He tapped a couple of the painkillers from it into the palm of his hand, trying to recall how many and how often.

Enough adventure for one day.

Chapter Thirty-Two

Sunday, August 26, 2018 - 3:46 p.m.

"Surprised to see you here, Mike," Ron said, sitting back until his partner could get to his desk and sit down.

"Yeah, well, I was going to take the night off, and then I couldn't sleep, so I just figured…" Mike mumbled, not because he particularly wanted to, but because that was all his face would allow him to do.

In fact, he had slept very little since leaving the hospital. And sitting alone was just too…alone.

As he sat down at his desk, however, he began to wish that he had stayed home. His pounding head told him that he was almost at that magical four-hour mark when he could take more meds. And while it was great to see everyone, he had found his reception at the station a bit overwhelming. He could have gone to his mom's just as well. She would have lost her mind.

Oh, God. The thought of it, her seeing his mangled face. And what she'd have to say about Carmen. 'She left you? Really? The nerve of it all! She'll never find anyone better. You were a godsend for that boy of hers. Poor lad.' Her brogue would thicken, the more emotional she got. All the O'Shea kids, even now, always knew when Mom was pissed. Ha! Stop it, Mike. Focus. Do what you've come here to do. 'Work is my salvation.' Yes, Father. Focus.

"I suppose you'll want to know what's going on with your situation?"

"Yeah, if you have any news. No one has contacted me." Mike could not have cared less at this moment.

"We just thought you'd need a bit of space. The union lawyer was by the hospital last night, but you were out cold. Told me it's all pretty straightforward. Not much to worry about. The SIU investigator spoke to the lawyer, and it sounds like they're going to more or less sort everything out around you."

"Great.," Mike replied after a pause. His head was hurting. A lot.

"The jumper—" Ron continued.

"Robby Williams."

"What?"

"Williams. Robby Williams. He had a name."

"Yes. Williams…"

"He was my boss, back when Sal—"

"I didn't know that. Sorry. I mean—" Ron was interrupted, saved by an in-coming call.

"Doesn't matter," Mike slurred to no one in particular as he stared blankly at the screensaver on his computer screen.

"Mike, Christopher Williams is at the front desk. He's here to pick up his father's effects. He'd like to talk to you specifically. You don't have to. I told them I'd talk to him. If it's easier." Ron's clipped words came across as cold when, in fact, he wanted to protect his partner, but didn't have the language to explain.

"I'll go." Mike heaved himself up from his chair. He straightened his tie and fastened the top button of his suit jacket. Duty called. "It's the least I can do."

The three Ws—wallet, watch, and wedding band—were usually the only things of value a person had on his or her body at the time of death. It was routine for these items to be removed by the officer at the scene, and if there was no family to give them to at the time, they would be held at the station for pick-up by extended family or a friend sometime later. This usually happened within a day or two, unless there was no one, in which case the property was shipped off and stored indefinitely at the centralized property bureau.

Generally speaking, the responsibility of returning the three Ws fell on the shoulders of whichever D was working at the time, regardless of his or her involvement in the actual call. A brief read-through of the occurrence and the plastic bag of property was usually enough to get by. Quick and easy for everyone.

Even though Ron had offered, Mike wanted to do this one. Despite his throbbing headache, Mike felt a sense of responsibility to Robby's family to make sure they knew what had happened. That it had been an accident. That their father was a fine man. That he had not committed suicide.

He rounded the corner to the front desk and abruptly stopped. Had he not known better, had he not seen Robby fall to his death, he would have sworn that it was Robby Williams standing on the other side of the counter. Mike found himself catching his breath before moving forward. Yes, Ron had said that Robby's son, Christopher, had come to collect his father's effects, but at this moment, the resemblance of the man at the front desk to the man Mike had worked with fifteen years before was uncanny, right down to the slightly cocked head.

The younger Williams was equally shocked. While he had never actually met Mike, he had heard more than enough stories to give him a fairly accurate description of every member of the JPTF crew on their final night working together. Even so, Christopher was in no way prepared to see Mike in such a battered state.

The two men stared at each other for more than a few moments before shaking hands across the cracked and stained old counter. Christopher shook Mike's hand heartily, acknowledging the toll that police work took on the soul, while Mike mumbled something about having been in a fight to explain his present state. The two men looked awkwardly at one another again until Mike picked up the property bag that had been retrieved for him.

Usually, in Mike's experience, this would be the end of it. The bag would be opened, its contents removed and accounted for, and the recipient would sign for it and be gone. This time felt different. Looking at the young man in front of him, Mike stopped just before he dumped Robby Williams's personal effects onto the counter, the thought of the indignity of such an act cutting through his chest.

"Would you like to come around?" he offered, inviting his old boss's son through the same doors he had led the Majewskis through only three days before, down the same stairs, and into the same interview room. This time, there would be no cameras to worry about. It would be just two men talking about a man they both thought they knew well.

"I know Dad jumped," Christopher began, not waiting for Mike to sit down.

"No. No, he didn't. I was there. He slipped," Mike gently corrected, fiddling with the ring on his own finger as he saw Christopher pick up his father's wedding band.

"Detective O'Shea, my dad jumped."

"Call me Mike, Christopher. And he didn't jump. I saw him. I was right there." Mike looked up at the boy—no, the man—and then back down to his hands, his shoulders slumped, his head exploding. *I was right there. I could have grabbed him. I could have saved your dad. I didn't. The coffee shop man. Mrs. O'Shea, we're so sorry...*

"Mike, I know you and Dad worked together, but that was a long time ago. You didn't know him very well."

Mike felt an electric current shoot through his body that almost caused him to spring out of his chair.

"Dad had a lot of... issues." Christopher let the words hang in the air, torn between his need to preserve family secrets and the opportunity to finally tell the truth.

"Listen, Christopher," Mike said, putting on his best *Father Knows Best* face as he leaned in towards the young man. "I know this must come as quite a shock to you—"

"No, Mike. It's not a shock at all. We're all just surprised that he waited this long."

"What do you mean?" Mike sat back, wide-eyed, licking his bottom lip, his mouth suddenly very dry.

"He was on the take. Told Mom about it after your partner was murdered. And then things got worse. She said he wanted to come forward. Wanted to tell, but there was no one, and they really leaned on him."

"Pardon?"

"So many coverups. It got to him. He began to drink. A lot. I remember that part. Mom kicked him out," Christopher released his words cautiously, almost in a whisper, knowing that each one was chipping away at the wall of lies he had grown up with and leaving him more and more exposed.

"She said he told her it started just after they found that little girl. She says it broke Dad. Did you know that he stopped hugging or kissing or even acknowledging my sister after that, Mike?"

Mike continued to stare across the table.

"Did you look in his fridge, Mike?" Christopher had seen this look of disbelief before.

"No. I didn't have time."

"It was empty, Mike."

"That doesn't mean anything."

"We never had a fridge in our house. Dad wouldn't have it. Didn't even use the space for shelves. Just an empty hole in the kitchen that no one was ever allowed to even step into."

Mike felt trapped. Nothing Christopher was saying made any sense to him. None of this had anything to do with the man he knew. But Christopher continued talking, telling Mike about the day-to-day life in this dysfunctional household, about the fear he and his younger brothers and sister had grown up with, about the insanity they saw in their father.

"What does this have to do with Sal's murder?"

"That little girl in the fridge was a discard."

"What?"

"Dad was a uniform guy. Why do you think they put him in charge of you guys in the Juvenile Prostitution Task Force?"

"You tell me."

"He figured out that this little girl wasn't a random kill. She had been targeted by a ring—the same ring you guys were investigating when Sal was shot—but she didn't work out. So they killed her. Made it look like some pervy hound had done it."

Mike's jaw dropped as much as his sore face allowed.

"Dad was starting to do some digging. They didn't like it—"

"*They* who?"

"The brass. They were in on it."

"In on what?"

"It wasn't supposed to go that way. The ring was just supposed to move drugs across the border, but somebody got greedy and figured running girls would be easy—"

"Fuck off."

"Why would I lie?"

Mike just stared at his old boss's son.

"Dad was beginning to connect the dots. The girl in the fridge connected to a prostitution ring that connected to a drug ring that connected to a bunch of senior officers. Dad was way out of his league running your crew, but he didn't know it at the time. They gave him that spot because they figured he'd keep guys like you on a short leash. They didn't expect you to actually get so close to their ring."

Mike studied Christopher. He'd done enough interviews to know when someone was full of shit. This kid was coming across as the real deal.

"Everyone knows who killed Sal. You and I both know that. So why haven't they caught him?"

"You tell me."

"No, Mike. You tell me."

Mike glanced at the camera behind him, wishing he had turned it on. And he began to feel sick. Really sick.

"I'm not really telling you anything you haven't already figured out, Mike, am I? They could have arrested Malcolm Oakes for the murder years ago. But they didn't. Because he knows even more than Dad knew. They paid Dad a lot of money to forget. But Dad was a cop—a good cop—first and foremost. So he took that money and bought booze and likely drugs to forget."

Another jolt went through Mike's body.

"Your mom. She died last year. Cancer. Took five years," Mike said, grasping at straws.

"No, Mike. She's outside in the car. Alive and well. Remarried. Helluva nice guy. My kids call him 'Grandpa.'"

"No. That's not so." Mike heard the childish words fall from his lips.

"She called the station to pick up Dad's stuff, but when they said you were working, she thought it would be easier for me to come in. She's in the car right now, Mike. I can bring her in…if you want?"

"No.'Sokay. Yer right."

"I wanted you to know, Mike. About Dad. About the coverup. About Sal's killer. I haven't been there yet, but knowing Dad as I do, I wouldn't be surprised if he's got something that might be of interest to you in his storage locker."

Like a helluva good wine.

The two men sat quietly across from each other, one relieved that the truth was finally out, the other reeling from that truth. Mike continued to alternate between looking at his hands in his lap, the ugly picture on the wall in the interview room, and the ghost of his boss seated across from him. Christopher's gaze never left Mike's battered face.

"I… I'd like to see whatever you have ," Mike finally said.

"I wouldn't be surprised if he kept all of his memo books and documented everything. I'll give you a call when I find out."

There was a pause that compelled Mike to ask, even though he had already heard too much.

"After that little girl—"

"It was like therapy for him. Checking every possibility. Speaking to anyone…everyone…about her. That's how he figured it out. And that's when they realized that he knew. So they promoted him out of that division, then promoted him again to a nice warm spot inside, then dropped him in your unit to make him feel like he was doing something about it, then finally gave up and just started threatening him."

"With what? What did they have on him?"

"Nothing. But he figured he should have blown the whistle sooner and that he was not complicit—"

"But he was." Mike's words slapped the air.

"Yeah. He was. And now…?"

Mike could not hold it together any longer. He felt his throat tighten as his eyes began to well up. *Shit.* He didn't even cry at his own father's funeral. *What the fuck!*

"I think I should go," Christopher stood up, feeling as awkward as Mike did.

"No. I'm sorry. Please sit. Tell me about your mother. How is your mother?"

"Mom's great. She'd like to see you." Christopher looked hopefully at Mike, who now appeared to him like an old man in a suit that was too big for him.

"Sure, that would be nice. But maybe not today." Mike gestured at his face.

"Right. Well, I'll call you after I go through Dad's locker. I know there's going to be a box or two there."

Mike walked Christopher out, giving him his father's wallet and watch, just before the young man left the station.

As Mike made his way back to the D office, he could feel his mind slipping away. His head was pounding, and he was finding it increasingly difficult to stay focused. He made a short stop in the washroom, where he took a couple of painkillers.

"Just got some intel on the down low," Ron advised as Mike swayed his way into the office. "The neighbour who called in your jump—uh, Robby Williams.… Well, the caller left their balcony door open after you arrived, and from what I've been told, pretty much heard the conversation back and forth between the two of you."

"Great."

"Regardless, I don't think you have anything to worry about. Meanwhile, Amanda Black is tickled pink at the arrest. Turns out there's DNA on the pipe Cockeye hit you with that matches our one-legged man."

"So she's got her man." Mike didn't hear himself slurring quite as badly now. "And our landlords?"

"Totally on our side, which is not surprising but nice to see for a change. Their testimony will more or less give Johnstone a motive, the blood will place him at the scene, and the DNA from the pipe will give us the murder weapon."

"Sounds like a slam dunk."

"Should be, but you never know."

Chapter Thirty-Three

Sunday, August 26, 2018 - 6:03 p.m.

Mike took a deep breath as he knocked on the front door of his childhood home. What had been a proud house back in the day now looked more like a hobbit's cottage, standing as it did amid newly built monster homes. Nevertheless, aside from the shamrock-green paint on the shutters needing a touch-up and the cement crumbling between some of the red bricks on the side wall, the old homestead had aged better than he had, even with its fifty year or so head-start. Even the chair on the front porch was still there, exactly as it had been back in the day when his mother had spent countless hours watching him, his sister Teaszy, and his brother Petey playing. Presumably, Katie, too, although she came along later and became more Teaszy's responsibility.

"Jesus, Mary, and Joseph, Michael," Mary-Margaret O'Shea gasped, her outstretched hands hesitating, afraid to touch his mangled face. "What happened, luv? Max told me you had been in a bit of a dustup, but I had no idea—"

"Oh, Mom, it's not that bad—"

"Ach. Tell that to the blind cobbler's thumb. Never mind. Come in. You're out." Mike's mother started to walk back into the house with Mike on her heels, then stopped and turned abruptly to look up at him.

Mike glanced over his mother's left shoulder at the table that started in the tiny dining room and went through to the slightly larger living room every

226

Sunday to accommodate the family dinner. If she didn't insist on setting a place for Mike's dead father, another for his long-vanished brother Peter, one for the Unexpected Guest, and now, Mike was sure, one for the new wife his mother probably already conjuring up for him, then she wouldn't have needed to use all of the table's leafves. The likelihood of that, however, was akin to Mary-Margaret giving up the Church.

"Everyone has already sat down. We've got a full table tonight. Even our wee Katie and her Ahmed are here, but we'll make a quick stop in at the kitchen before you scare the living shite out of the rest of them."

More by habit than desire, Mike followed his mother down the hall to the tiny kitchen at the back of the house, his presence unnoticed amidst the multiple conversations bouncing around the table in the other room.

"What in God's name is goin' on with ye, my Michael O'Shea?"

"I told you, Mom. Work."

"If not for yer lovely eyes that are so much like yer Da's, God rest his soul, I'd hardly recognize ye under all that of that mess. Tell me ye went to the hospital, at least?"

"Yeah. They told me to take it easy for a few days and I'll be fine."

"Horsefeathers. More like come back in a few days if ye are not already dead." Mary-Margaret examined his face again, holding her hands back from reaching out to touch the various gashes on his face that had been stitched over, the antibiotic ointment on them glistening from the light over her stove. "Son, not a day has gone by since ye signed up that I haven't worried meself almost to drink. Don't get me wrong, Michael. I do enjoy me half pint of Guinness with the fish and chip down at O'Leary's on Friday after Mass, and I'm as proud as a mother could be that ye are a policeman, what with all the good work ye have done and all, but this is too much. If not for yerself or me, think about young Max."

"I should never have come today."

"Don't be startin' that line o' chatter. And there's Max out there—not that much older than ye were when yer Da died, God rest his soul, but at least ye had me and the others. Who does Max have? And now with Carmen leavin' and all—?"

"She hasn't—" Mike began, wanting to leave but knowing he couldn't.

"I'm yer mother, Michael. I'm not anyone's fool, and I know what I saw yesterday mornin'. That wife of yours has left ye."

"Mom—"

"You and Mom are always having these little side… Holy shit!" Mike's Irish-twin sister, Teaszy, stopped short inat the entrance to the kitchen, the colour draining from her face. "What the hell happened to you?"

"Ach, it's the damned policing's got to him," Mary-Margaret said in disgust, giving Mike the look and adopting the tone that he recalled well from his younger, wilder days. "We'll talk later, Michael. Right now, just sitcheedoon at the table with the rest. Ye are looking worse by the moment. Dinner's been set out, but I'll make up a plate for ye."

"I've got it, Mom," Teaszy offered, looking at Mike and then her mother, shaking her head in disbelief. "Both of you, go sit down. Jesus, Mike. Really?"

"Work," Mike mumbled as he made his way to the dining room, pulling out the chair in his usual spot to the right of the unclaimed setting where his father would have sat at the head of the table. Mary-Margaret returned to her place at the other end of the table, the ssshhh ssshhh of her wringing hands ominously clear against the silence that suddenly choked the room.

"Well, look at you, Michael," Alan rocked forward from his place two down and directly across from where Teaszy, his wife, always sat, his arm reaching across the starched linen tablecloth. "Never a dull moment with you, is there?"

"I guess not." Mike shook his brother-in-law's limp hand before sitting down.

"Just set yer little self down, Michael. Alan," Mary-Margaret smiled pleasantly at her son-in-law, "would ye pass the salt, please? Not unlike yerself every Sunday, I'm finding me dinner a little on the bland side this eve. Anyone else?"

"Wow, Uncle Mike," Paulie commented. "You look so… butch!"

"That's a good thing, right?" Mike smiled, albeit carefully, at his nephew, remembering a time not so long ago when Paulie, his older brother Richard, and Max were all just little boys. "Katie, long time no see. Ahmed."

Mike's younger sister's boyfriend stood up, reaching over Alan and across the table to give Mike a warm handshake.

"Michael, sit. Yer noggin must just be pounding five beats to the four," Mary-Margaret commented.

"Not really. It looks much worse than it is."

"Well, ye may be able to pull the wool over the eyes of a blind man, but not your mam. Yes," Mary-Margaret continued, taking a mouthful of cabbage and moving the conversation along as she realized that everyone was silent and staring at Mike, "just a pinch of salt and we're away again."

As if on cue, forks began clinking on plates as food was hoisted into mouths, the numerous side-conversations sparked up again, and except for the odd comment, Mike was no longer the centre of attention.

"I bet they gave you some killer drugs," Griffin, Paulie's on-again, off-again boyfriend, commented.

"Pretty much."

Clearly, Paulie and Griffin were on again. The general consensus within the family was that Paulie's Griffin was not a bad kid, just a bit of a lost soul. His Doc Martens and facial piercings had taken some getting used to and were in stark contrast to Paulie's clean-cut look, but he always seemed to have a job and never missed a Sunday dinner, provided they fell when he and Paulie were on.

"Hi, Dad," Max called above the hum of multiple conversations.

"Look who's got the place of honour next to Gran!" Mike looked down the table to his son, who always had the place of honour at his grandmother's right.

Mike looked down at the plate with the ends of the corned beef, a mountain of mashed potatoes swimming in butter, and some cabbage that had been boiled in with the meat that was in front of him.

"You really look like shit, Mike. Are you going to be okay?" Teaszy whispered to her brother as she took her place beside him at the table.

"Once again, I failed to see any of you at Church this A.M.," Mary-Margaret called up the table, her voice easily heard over both Paulie's giggle at Griffin's latest comment and the scraping sound of Teaszy's chair as her daughter pulled back into the table after picking up the fork she had dropped on the floor.

"I think the Catholic Church is on its way out," Alan commented with a sarcastic smile. "I bet you've investigated a priest ofr two in your day, eh, Mike?"

"Alan!"

"Well? Tell me I'm wrong, Theresa."

Uh oh, Mike thought. Calling his sister Teaszy by her actual name was not a good sign.

"Oh my God," Paulie sighed, rolling his eyes at his boyfriend. "I swear, I'm adopted."

"Ye are no such thing, my lamb," Mary-Margaret cut in, ignoring Alan while restoring decorum at her table. "We were all there the moment yer mother birthed ye, weren't we?"

A general consensus made its way around the family, as did the plate carrying Mary-Margaret's homemade buns and the bowl that still seemed full of mashed potatoes despite nine diners having taken at least one helping from it already.

"I wasn't, Gran!" Max said.

"No, ye weren't even a glimmer in your Da's eye that day." Mary-Margaret smiled lovingly at the lad, who was arguably her favourite grandson. "So, Michael. About this head-bashing business ye have engaged yerself in: I don't want to know the details, but what happened?"

"Well," Mike began, having to renegotiate the fork loaded high with potatoes that he had just tried to shove into a mouth whose jaw muscles were still seizing as a result of said bashing.

"Mom, please. We're eating," Katie jumped in.

"Ach. Ye are just like your Da, God rest his soul. Never one for the gore, neither the two of ye." Mary-Margaret paused for a moment to look up the table to the seat that Jimmy O'Shea had not occupied for the last thirty-five years. "Not that I was expecting ye to tell us the details, mind ye."

"Carmen not feeling well again, Mike?" Alan asked smugly, looking over at the empty place setting to his right, knowing as well as the rest of them about Mike's pending marriage collapse.

"She left me, Alan."

"Another one?" Alan looked around the table with a wink.

"Alan!" Teaszy shot him a look to kill, not maim.

"I *am* fucking adopted," Paulie announced.

"Mouth, Paulie," Mary-Margaret cautioned, looking over at Max. "And, where I come from, it's pronounced '*fecking*.'"

"Sorry, Gran. Not like Max never heard the word before, though, eh, Maxie?" Paulie grinned at Griffin and then down the table to his younger cousin.

"Yes, Alan, another one. Great job on the mashed, Mom."

"Thank ye, luv. I put a wee bit of oregano in them this time. Sally next door was sayin' how her lot go gaga over her mashed. Now, Michael, I've just this moment had a thought —"

"Oh no," Teaszy groaned, smiling knowingly over at her older brother.

"This involves ye as well, missus," Mary-Margaret nodded to her older daughter, then looked back at her son. "I'm looking at the mess of a mug you're wearing, and if I understand correctly—and as much as I don't want to discuss it at the dinner table, Michael—Carmen has just left."

Mike nodded in cautious agreement.

"And if what I'm reading in the papers is true, they're laying off computer fellas right, left, and centre these days, which means that it's just a matter of time before you're jobless, Alan." She glanced over at her son-in-law before returning her focus to Mike. "So I think the best thing for all of us is for me to move in with ye and Max and have ye," Mary-Margaret looked at Teaszy, "and Alan move in here."

Alan dropped his fork with a crash loud enough to shatter his plate. Luckily, it did not.

"What did you tell your mother, Theresa?"

"Nothing. I didn't say a word."

"Well then, how would she know that—"

"Because, despite what ye may think of me, I'm not deaf, blind, nor stupid to the world around me, Alan," Mary-Margaret cut in. Then, not missing any opportunity to knock down by a notch or two the man whose only saving grace was providing her older daughter with a steady household and two lovely boys, added, "And we all know ye have always had a bit of a big front and a sloped back. I don't suppose ye have much of a nest egg saved up, now then, Alan? Now. Think about it, Michael, but that's the plan."

"No, that's *not* the plan," Mike corrected.

"C'mon, Dad. It would be great." Max's eyes were already lighting up with the prospect of his ever-indulgent grandmother being in his house every day.

Mary-Margaret rubbed Max's arm, smiling warmly at him.

"No, it wouldn't be," Mike and Teaszy simultaneously corrected.

"Well, then, Mr. Humpty-Dumpty-After-The-Great-Fall, ye come up with a better one, then," Mary-Margaret challenged, her lower lip protruding in a massive pout.

"How about you stay in your house, I stay in mine, and Teaszy and Alan stay in theirs?"

"Mom, I know you're trying to help," Teaszy began, trying to soften Mike's words to avert an all-out battle while bolstering her husband's ego. She looked across at Alan and then down the table towards her mother. "But Alan is not losing his job."

"And you're not moving in with me," Mike stated firmly, placing his knife down on the table with more force than he had intended and bringing the banter in the room to an abrupt stop.

"Don't be so quick to bite the hand that feeds ye."

"I have to get back to work, Mom."

Mike attempted to wipe his face with his napkin and winced.

"Ye canna go in looking like that."

"Where do you think I came from?"

"Michael, that's daft! And this is why ye need me to move in with ye. Clearly not an ounce of common sense in yer shot glass. Sitcheedoon, and I'll have Max get ye a strong cuppa."

"Anyone need a lift?" Mike asked, ignoring his mother's comments.

"You haven't looked this bad since—" Alan began.

"Maybe I'll move in here by myself," Teaszy said, folding the napkin on her lap before setting it on the table beside her.

"Max, you staying here or coming home tonight?" Mike asked, ignoring Alan as he reached into his pants pocket for the key to the unmarked police car that he had parked out in front of the house.

"He'll stay here with his Gran," Mary-Margaret stated.

"You spend more time in my old room than I ever did," Mike smiled at his son, thankful in spite of himself for his mother's stability.

"And don't worry about a thing, Michael. I'll make sure he gets to school in the morning."

"We have to get going, too," Katie piped up. "I've got a big launch coming up and a pile of emails to shoot out first thing tomorrow."

"Well, think about what I've said," Mary-Margaret reminded Mike as she walked with him to the front door.

Mike just shook his head, thinking it wise to say nothing.

"Don't be too hasty in making yer decisions, Michael. Such haste clearly hasn't served ye well in the past. And, luv?" Mary-Margaret stopped, her voice dropping to a near-whisper. "Keep an eye out for our Peter, won't ye?"

Mike stood at the front door and turned back to his mother, surrounded by the family that she held together so lovingly. Regardless of what looked like a full house, he knew that she could never fill the emptiness left inside her by the death of her beloved Jimmy or the absence of her long-gone son. In his quieter moments after a long day and a couple of pints, he was inclined to believe that he shared the burden of that same void.

"I always do, Mom. I always do."

Chapter Thirty-Four

"Why the hell are you here, Mike?" Amanda Black's voice broke into the comfortable banter between Mike and Ron, a mixture of confusion and warmth crossing her face as she waltzed into the office. "Christ, you look like shit."

"And I was just about to say how lovely *you* look, Detective Sergeant," Mike slurred, the painkillers taking hold of him.

"This is me on Day Three of no sleep. What's your excuse? Get hit in the head with a lead pipe or something?"

"Hanging out with hard-living broads, I guess."

"Yeah. Oh, and thanks for keeping an eye on my man for me. Maybe I should have been a little clearer. I just wanted you to *watch* him, not get into an all-out brawl with him."

"How is he doing?" Ron asked.

"You know how those guys are. If it was you or me, we'd be dead four times over. The doctors pulled the bullets out of him, and he's being released into our loving care in a couple of days. More importantly, how are *you* doing, Mike?" She looked him over. "And are all your pants wrinkly, or just the ones you wear when I'm around?"

"Excuse me, but did you know that guys don't like being looked up and down?" Mike tried to smirk, but his mind was beginning to drift. "I'm fine."

"Well, you don't look fine. I couldn't believe it when Staff called me and said you were here. What are you—mental? Where's your wife?"

"Gone."

"Oh." Amanda knew that something else had to be going on here. There was no way that anyone would let their spouse go to work in the condition that Mike was in. "Okay, so haven't you got a girlfriend on the side to take care of you?"

"You offering?"

"I do like them big and dumb, but I've already got one, thanks. And he can fix shit. Like an iron. To iron his pants. Seriously, though, why aren't you at home?"

"He came in to see me," Ron said, also sensing that something more might be going on in his partner's life, but wanting to shield Mike from Amanda.

"That's even more pathetic." Amanda shot a deadpan look at Ron, then turned to Mike. "Anyway, enough about you two. Update: Cockeye has been charged with attempted murder on you, Mike, and first-degree murder on our friend. He's looking a helluva lot better than you are and will likely have an actual bail hearing soon. I don't expect any judge will let him out, but welcome to Canada. I'm going to need a statement from you sooner rather than later just to demonstrate what a danger he is to you and society in general for the bail hearing. I know," Amanda signed and rolled her eyes dramatically, "the murder charge should be enough, but I'm not counting on anything with this one. I'm also going to need some photos of your injuries. You're looking pretty rough now, but you'll probably look worse tomorrow, so let's make arrangements to get Amy or somebody good from Forensics over to get some shots for me, okay?" All business.

"Okay. Clothing optional?"

"That's a sight I wouldn't want to subject myself to. I also need a copy of your notes—"

"Got none."

"I realize that. When you get back to work, as in *really* back, I need you to sit down and write up. Take as much time as you need. No rush. I'll just tell the Crown that you'll have then as soon as you can. Not a problem. Finally, while it's not my problem, you're going to have to address the issue with the jumper—"

"Robby Williams," Mike corrected.

"Wait. Detective Sergeant Robby Williams?"

"Yeah."

"Oh, shit. That's too bad. He was a really good copper. Anyway," Amanda plowed on, "you're going to have to write up about that sooner rather than later as well. Shannon Somerville gave the case to Grant Hooper. Good guy, knows his stuff. Done lots of work for the union in the past. Does some criminal defence work, too. Not bad. Shouldn't be too much of an issue, but it's something to keep in mind. In the meantime, lie low. Don't go anywhere. Don't speak to anyone. Don't do anything. God, I feel like I'm talking to my kids. You have kids don't you?"

Amanda's mind on the best of days was like a thousand hummingbirds going in all directions. With minimal sleep, it was as if those birds were all on crack.

"Yes," Mike said simply. *Go away. Stop talking at me. Let me sleep.*

"Tell me you didn't drive in, Mike, right?" Amanda asked, the lines on her forehead deepening.

"Wha'?" Mike squinted and rubbed his head.

"You're not looking your best there, Crumply-pants. How about we get you back to the hospital?"

Mike stared blankly at her, his jaw dropping, his eyes vacant.

Amanda sprang into action. "Ron, give me a hand. Something's going horribly wrong here!" She tried to stay calm, professional, but her voice was getting shrill.

Ron was at Mike's side almost before the words had left Amanda's mouth. Without speaking, the two of them had Mike hustled out of the station and into the passenger seat of Amanda's unmarked car. Ron buckled him in while Amanda ran around to the driver's side.

"Call St. Mike's and let them know we're coming," she hollered out the window to Ron, tires screeching as she sped off into the night. St. Joe's would have been closer, but St. Mike's was a clear run right through the city, and they had Mike's file. Sunday morning. Not the worst time for it, but

Amanda knew she'd be running every red light to get there…with no police escort and no lights or sirens.

As the car sped off, Mike began to slump towards Amanda. *Coffee. A good fucking cup of coffee. Wallet. Pictures. Little girls. Teaszy and Katie? We're so sorry, Mrs. O'Shea. Da? I'm sorry, Da. I wish…. Robby. Hold on a bit longer. There you are. And look. It's our Sal. Our stupid fucking annoying Sal. I've missed you, Sal. Robby, look. It's Sal. And sunflower seeds. I'll find him, Sal. I promise. I'm so tired—"*

"Mike! Mike!" He felt someone elbowing him. "Tell me something. Anything."

"Horrible. Losing Da. So hard. 'Specially on me. Fuggin' Petey. Broke Mom's heart. Still lookin' for you. Promised I would. You still out there

But for the screeching of the tires as Amanda wove in and out of traffic, the car was silent again.

"Michael!" Amanda yelled. "Fucking talk to me, Michael!"

"Huh?"

"Your son, Mike. Tell me about your son. Yeah. I know. go FUCK yourself!" Amanda yelled out the window as she narrowly escaped being t-boned by a car that had the right-of-way, as she raced through yet another red light. "Where the hell is a cop when you need one? An escort would be nice about now," she muttered to herself. Then, "Tell me about your son, Mike. What's his name?"

"Max, zizz name is Max," Mike slurred.

"Okay. Tell me about Max."

Nothing.

"Don't you fucking die on me, Mike! Stay with me! Max? How old is he?" Amanda was practically screaming at Mike.

"Seventeen."

"What colour is his hair?"

"Red."

"His eyes. What colour are your son's eyes, Mike!"

"Blue."

"How tall is he?"

Silence.

"Mike! Tall. How tall is Max?"

Mike was losing consciousness fast. Amanda shoved his slumping body off her in a last-ditch attempt to find that goddamn police light that she knew must be somewhere in this car. She reached behind her, but found nothing.

"How fucking tall is Max, Michael? Michael, wake up!"

With the next turn, Mike's body fell back onto Amanda's right side. He wasn't answering any of her questions now.

"Holy fuck, Mike! Talk to me!!"

Amanda's foot was as far down on the accelerator as she dared press it. With both hands on the wheel, she maneuvered the car through the streets, over sidewalks, through red lights.

"Holy fuck! How far away is this goddamned hospital? Fuck. Don't die, Mike! You can't die. None of us signed up for that. Don't let those bastards win. We're the good guys. We win. We gotta win. You gotta live. I cannot bury you. I will not bury you. I will not let them bury you. Fuck you, Mike O'Shea. Fuck you!"

Amanda could hear sirens. Lots of sirens. The road seemed to clear ahead of her. She raced through red lights, marked scout cars now blocking on-coming traffic. She was going too fast for a marked car to get in front of her as an escort, but she could see officers in the distance on foot, waving cars and pedestrians out of the way as she approached. As she got closer to the hospital, every intersection was closed so that she could get through. It was officially another emergency run.

"Don't you die on me, mister," Amanda whispered, releasing one hand from the steering wheel to gently rub Mike's head, leaving the other glued to the wheel as she sped through traffic towards the hospital. "We're all out here for you, buddy. You gotta live, okay? You gotta make it. You're too good a cop to go out like this. Not now. Please, not now."

The car screeched around the final corner before Amanda fishtailed into the ambulance bay. A group of scrubs surrounded the waiting gurney. The team quickly removed Mike from the car and whisked him inside, leaving

Amanda alone, sitting behind the wheel of the car, shaking, tears streaming down her face.

"Don't die, Mike. Please don't die," she whispered through her tears. "Every time one of us dies, a piece of each of us dies. And I'm running out of pieces.

Chapter Thirty-Five

As Amanda sat weeping in her car, a tap on the window made her jump. Before she could move, the car door was being opened.

"It's time to get out of the car, Amanda." Ron's voice was unusually smooth and calming, carrying with it the authority of a man who had helped many people out of cars in his career. He gently peeled her frozen fingers from the steering wheel, enveloping them in one of his warm hands while placing his other hand under her left leg to carefully swing her out of the car. Without thinking, Amanda placed her arms around Ron and allowed herself to stand up with him. For a moment, the two of them were face-to-face, inches apart.

"This is awkward," Amanda blurted, wiping the tears and snot and smudged mascara from her face with the back of one hand, clinging to Ron with the other.

"No, this is normal. Get your balance, and then let's go inside and see how things are going with Mike. Come on now. You can do this. You're going to be fine. I promise."

Amanda steadied herself against him, knowing that she could not have wished for a better man to have by her side, until she was ready to walk through the hospital doors, head held high, and in command. No bullshit. No smart remarks. No gossip later.

"How long was I in the car? Did anyone see? Did anyone say anything?"

"I have no idea how long you've been here. Long enough for me to get here. As far as being seen, everyone is inside with Mike. Sorry to say, Amanda, you're not the star of this show. Yet."

Amanda let Ron go, standing on her own. She looked down.

"Amanda," Ron said, leading her towards the emergency department doors, "you did the right thing. You did the only thing. If you hadn't acted when and how you did, who knows what would have happened to Mike? You did the right thing."

Amanda at Ron briefly and then looked away, trying not to show him that she had begun to cry again.

"There's no crying in Homicide," she said with an awkward smile, thinking of the advice the unit commander gave her when she first got transferred and was the only woman in the unit.

"Suit yourself," Ron said. "In any event, ready to go inside to see how Crumply-pants is doing?"

Amanda stopped short and turned back to Ron with a smile. "Can you talk to him about that, Ron? I mean, good God. We're professionals out here, not bums!"

"I'll be sure to mention it to him, Detective Sergeant. You know how these old squad guys are. Not like us Traffic men."

* * *

By the time Ron and Amanda got to Mike's side, the organized madness around him had settled down as his condition stabilized. Some tests, a catheter, and a cocktail of medications later, he was conscious and practically ready to receive guests. In fact, he felt like a million bucks and was quite surprised when the doctor advised him that he would be spending at least the night, if not longer, in their care.

"It's for the best," Ron stated matter-of-factly.

"Yeah. I don't think my car can take another run like that. I'm pretty sure I've ripped something off it during one of those curb- jumps," Amanda joked, shivering as she forced herself to refrain from holding Mike's hand and rubbing his forehead.

An orderly arrived to move Mike's gurney into the hallway. Even Sunday evenings were busy at St. Mike's.

"Mike?" called a female voice.

Mike, Ron, and Amanda looked around and saw Bridget Calloway approaching them.

"Yes?" Mike recognized a familiar voice.

"What happened?"

"He's been in an accident. Can I help you?" Amanda replied curtly.

"No. Not at all. I just saw Mike and thought—"

"You're going to have to adjourn your case for a couple of weeks, Bridget. Mike isn't going to be able to testify for a while, as you can see." Even Amanda was surprised at how hostile she was sounding towards a woman she'd fought several cases with over the years.

"Bridget?" Mike muttered, a few steps behind the conversation.

"Hey there, Ziggy Stardust. You look wrecked, buddy. I'm just here with my father and kind of saw you passed out in the hall here." Bridget shot a guarded glance over at Amanda.

"Oh," Mike sighed.

"Perhaps we can step over here for a few minutes," Ron said, taking Amanda by the arm and ushering her to a sitting area not far from where they had been standing.

"I didn't know that she was your wife." Bridget lowered her voice, practically whispering to Mike.

"She's not my wife," Mike attempted to whisper, dribbling spittle down his chin as he fought to keep his eyes open.

"Well, I think she'd like to be."

"Fuck off," Mike commented, working to focus his eyes on her.

After a couple of blinks, he gave up.

"Got my sexy on," Mike muttered, feebly lifting his hand to gesture to the catheter tube dangling from his IV pole.

"I'll leave you to your friends," Bridget said, rubbing Mike's leg as she turned to walk away.

"Hope Da gets better," Mike mumbled.

Bridget turned back. "He's terminal."

Mike stared at her with increasingly glazed-over eyes. The drugs exacerbating the exhaustion while trumping the pain.

"I've been doing this hospital run for a long time. Sooner or later," Bridget said as she turned back, sucking in a deep breath of air, "it has to come to an end. And then what?"

"Dunno. What?"

"My dad is going to die, Mike. And I'm going to be alone. Old and alone. Old and alone and… alone. And you know what?"

Mike just grunted.

"I've probably seen more of you in the past five years than any guy I've ever dated. And the ones I have dated all dump and run at the first sign of trouble. At least, you come back."

"Uhhuh."

"Even if it is only because you have to. Shit, that's pathetic. I am officially pathetic. Thanks, Mike. Once again, you have made me consider things I never wanted to consider."

"Hrmph."

"Well, at least I have my work, eh?"

"Uhhuh."

"I don't know what happened to you, Mike, but I need you to get better. You're the only solid guy in my life." Bridget laughed to herself. "God, that's depressing."

"Yeah. Depwwesssss…" Mike began waving his arm with wild abandonment as the heavy-duty meds took hold of him, knocking the pole with the urine bag on it and pulling the catheter tube slightly as he did so. "Fuuuuuuuuuck. Huuuuuuuuurt."

"Oh, I'm so sorry, Mike!" Much to her own surprise, Bridget giggled.

"O'Shea? Head injury?" an orderly called down the hall.

"He's over here," Amanda Black's voice could be heard along with the *click click* of the heels of her shoes as she and Ron made their way back to Mike.

"Listen," Bridget leaned in to Mike, "I'm going to get Dad settled in, and then I'll check back to see how you're doing in a bit, okay?"

"Always picking up guys in Emerg?" Mike managed to say clearly enough for Bridget to understand.

"Just you, Mike. Just you," Bridget replied, gently kissing him on the forehead in spite of herself.

"Sorry, ma'am. We have to move your husband now," the orderly said as he moved in to prepare the gurney and its occupant to be taken to a room.

"Oh, I'm not his wife," Bridget replied, almost springing away from Mike as the orderly commandeered the gurney.

"I think she'd like to be," Amanda muttered to Ron, glancing back at the young crown attorney as they followed the bed that carried their fallen colleague down the hall towards the elevators.

"It was never like this in Traffic," Ron muttered.

Chapter Thirty-Six

Three Days Later: Wednesday, August 29, 2018 - 5:07 p.m.

"Do you have any decent coffee in this place?" Mike asked as the orderly brought in his dinner tray.

"Sorry for your luck, boss. Just this delicious meal especially prepared for you by our very own chef!"

The orderly placed a tray on the wheeled table beside Mike's bed and then rolled it over to him.

"Bon appetit!" the orderly called out as he walked out of Mike's room.

"Hmmm," Mike replied, lifting up the burgundy plastic cover to look at the meal that had been placed in front of him.

Sealed plastic cup of water. Sealed plastic container of peaches in sugar water. What looked like playdoh but was probably mashed potatoes and some sort of mystery meat with pieces of what might be carrot around it.

And a thick mug of hot brown water.

"Fuck this," Mike said. He placed the lid back on the tray and pushed the table away from his bed. Then very carefully, he lowered himself onto the floor and stumbled over to the closet. He pulled out the brown paper bag that held his clothes and slowly dressed himself, taking care not to lose his balance. Then taking a deep breath, he shambled into the bathroom and looked at himself in the mirror.

Not bad. The suit he had come in with wasn't any more crumpled than usual, and the shoes were shiny. He, on the other hand, hadn't seen anything more than a sponge bath since he was brought in, and his hair seemed to have grown an inch in the last few days.

Mike splashed some water on his face and ran his fingers back through his hair.

"Good enough," Mike said to the man in the mirror. "You're looking for coffee, not a date."

He went to the door and peeked down the hallway to make sure the orderly was gone. No sign of him, so Mike walked towards the elevators. There were a few other people who were leaving at the same time, and Mike fell into step with them.

Once on the ground floor, he walked as briskly as he was able towards the main exit, trying not to look like a fugitive while being aware of the security cameras that recorded everyone's movements.

At the door, he took a deep breath—the first breath of outside air he had had in more days than he could remember. Then he strolled intentionally past the coffee shop he knew all the cops went to when they were near St. Mike's and found one that he never knew existed just a few doors down.

The place was empty. Good.

Mike walked in.

"You look like you could use a coffee," the young man at the counter said.

"Yep, I could."

"You're in the right place, then. What can I get you?"

"Americano."

"You got it, buddy. That'll be four bucks."

Mike reached into his suit pocket for his wallet. It wasn't there. He reached around to his back pocket. No wallet there, either. *Shit!* He began to frantically pat himself down.

"I've got some change in here somewhere," he muttered, realizing too late that Ron or Amanda had likely removed his wallet and anything else of value, including his badge, when he was admitted to the hospital. He hoped they dropped the stuff off at his house.

"I-I'm sorry, but I don't seem—"

"Joey, make me one, too," Julia Vendramini said from behind Mike.

"Friend of yours, Julia?" the young man asked, looking Mike up and down.

"He's a cop, Joey. One of the best. Mikey," she said, "why don't you go over there and grab us a table. Not like there isn't any place to sit, but you choose."

Mike nodded and chose a table for two near the front window.

"So, is this that really good cup of coffee you said we'd have one day?" Julia asked with a smile as she set the two cups down and then looked for another stool to place her purse on. "Joey keeps a clean shop, but I swear, there's more germs on these floors than you can imagine."

"More than on a washroom floor?" Mike said, raising one eyebrow.

"Probably," Julia replied, pulling a stool over from another table.

"You have impeccable timing." Mike took a long sip of his coffee.

"Or you're just one lucky guy." Julia looked at the screen of her cell phone before tossing the phone into her purse, which was now sitting on the third stool.

"Perhaps. How did you know I was here?"

"I didn't. I was actually coming to visit you. I had no idea you were in the hospital. I was on my days off when all of this happened, and no one bothered to call me. You'd think Amanda—"

"Detective Sergeant Black, you mean?"

"She and I go back a long way, Mike. In fact, I think she's one of the only women from my recruit class who's still on the job. What does that tell you, eh? Anyway, I would have thought that she would have called. I sure wasn't waiting by the phone for Ron—"

"He's not half bad, you know," Mike pointed out.

"No, he's not. He's just not someone I can warm up to, which for me says something. But I'm not here to talk about Ron. I was just popping in here to pick you up a coffee because I figured you'd want one, and here you are."

"Hey, Julia," the young man called out from behind the counter. "Want some biscotti? I've got some good stuff in the back that I was going to wait until tomorrow to bring out. I'll cut you and your friend a couple of slices if you want."

"Always so generous, Joey. Thank you," Julia said, smiling.

"How often do you come here?" Mike said.

"Any time I have to come to St. Mike's. Or go shopping downtown," she replied, taking a sip of coffee from the white porcelain cup. "You think I like that crap Dave brings in every day? You know, he reminds me so much of Sal sometimes."

The two of them took another sip of their coffees and stared out at the crowds of people walking by.

"Yeah, I can see that."

"Here's your biscotti," Joey said, setting two plates gently down between the two cops. "Let me know what you think. I'm using a new supplier."

"Mmm. Thanks, Joey. I'm sure it will be fabulous. How is your sister? Still in treatment?"

"She's good, yeah. Thanks for asking. Been clean and sober for ten weeks now. Thanks again for getting her into that program, eh?"

"My pleasure, Joey. And let your mother know that I pray for your sister every day." Julia reached up to the cross around her neck and rubbed it.

"I will. Thank you," he said, walking back to the cash register as he noticed another customer coming through the door. "And let me know. About the biscotti, that is. Yes, sir? How can I help you?"

"In all these years, we've never talked about that night, have we, Mike?" Julia said. Then, not waiting for a response, she continued. "You know what I remember most? Sitting alone in some office at 54 Division waiting for the SIU and watching Sal's blood dry on my sweater."

They both looked out the window.

"I don't know what I remember most," Mike said in a low voice.

"It wasn't your fault, you know."

"Yeah."

"Truly. I was there. Almost. He didn't stand a chance. And you were just lucky."

"Kinda like now." Mike held up his coffee cup.

"Sure." Julia smiled.

They sat for a few moments, looking at each other but not seeing one another, lost in their own thoughts.

"I gotta get going," Mike finally said with a cough. "Before they notice me missing."

"Who are you kidding, Mike? You weren't going to go back. I know you. When did you ever play by the rules?"

"Me? Always."

"Please. How long have I known you? You have always been a get-the-job-done kinda guy. I mean, come on. Look at Ron. Are you like him?"

"No."

"Well then? *He's* a Rules & Regs guy. You? You're a copper's cop. And you know it."

"Thanks for that, I think."

"I mean it. If I ever needed anything back then, or now, even, I'd call you. As my Uncle Carm used to say, 'A dog doesn't change its spots.'"

"Isn't that a leopard?"

"Likely, but my Uncle Carm never spoke of something he didn't know about, and I don't suppose he knew too much about leopards. Anyway, all I'm trying to say is that you are practically a rock star back at the station now. And you were back then, too. As for me? I am so glad you're going to be okay, but let me tell you, two near-death experiences, that I know of, is enough already. You got, what, two years to go? Maybe you should think about taking some—"

"Desk job? Sure. Thanks."

"Seriously, Mike. You've done some really great work over the years—"

"And now I should be put out to pasture? Come on, Julia—"

"Think about your son, Mike. If I had a son, I would be off the road now. This is a young—"

"Young man's game? Thanks."

Mike pushed the stool away from the table and got up to leave.

"Mikey, it's over," Julia said, gently touching the sleeve of his jacket. "You caught this one-legged guy's killer. You have a million great arrests under your belt. Maybe it's time—"

"If this was coming from anyone else but you, Julia—"

"What? You'd punch me?" She laughed.

Mike smiled, too.

"Listen," she said, her voice softening. "Why don't we go back to the hospital, you try to do what you're told, and then take some time off to consider your options?"

Mike stared at Julia as she reached into her purse and pulled out her buzzing cell phone, and read the text message.

"Sorry, Mikey. I gotta go. Hey, Joey," she called to the counter man, "buy more of these biscotti. They're good."

"Like Nonna Tramantozi's?"

"Don't push your luck, but close enough. Anyway," she turned her attention back to Mike, "think about what I said. Sorry I can't take you back to the hospital myself, but I know you'll go now. Keith's car died. Again. With a trunk full of fresh meat. I gotta go pick him up. Well, the fresh meat, anyway. Keith? He can go with the tow-truck driver for all I care right now. You know, I keep telling him, 'Keith, honey, I know you've had that car for fifteen years, but Keith, honey, you've had that car for fifteen years. Enough already.' Okay. Gotta go."

Julia stood, grabbed her purse, and kissed Mike on both cheeks in one movement. She was almost out the door when she stopped and turned.

"Oh, and say hello to your mother for me. Tell her I'll be over for dinner again one Sunday."

"Will do."

"And go back to the hospital."

"Yeah."

Mike watched out the window as Julia left and was swallowed up by the parade of people passing by. Then he took a deep breath and walked out the door, giving the young man behind the counter a slight wave.

As he got to the sidewalk, he reached inside his front pocket and pulled out a crumpled twenty-dollar bill.

Grinning, he stepped to the curb, raised his right hand, and hailed a taxi.

A Note from the Author

Death Before Coffee is special to me because I wrote it during the time I was a detective with the Toronto Police Service. While the names, events, and most of the places are fictitious, the feel of all of them is not.

I would like to thank the officers that I have worked with over the years for their commitment to and compassion for the people in the communities that they have served.

I hope you enjoy the book.

Acknowledgements

Thank you, Cindy Bullard at Birch Literary, and to Cathy Chow and Cheryl Freedman.

About the Author

For almost thirty years, Desmond P. Ryan worked as a cop in the back alleys, poorly-lit laneways, and forgotten neighborhoods in Toronto, the city where he grew up. Murder, mayhem, and sexual violations intended to demean, shame, and haunt the victims were all in a day's work.

Whether as a beat cop or a plainclothes detective, Desmond dealt with good people who did bad things and bad people who followed their instincts. And now, as a retired detective, he writes crime fiction.

Desmond resides in Cabbagetown, a neighborhood in Toronto where he is currently working on *The Mike O'Shea Series* and *The Mary-Margaret Series*, both published by Level Best Books.

SOCIAL MEDIA HANDLES:
Twitter: @RealDesmondRyan
Facebook: RealDesmondRyan
Insta: desmondpryan

AUTHOR WEBSITE:
www.RealDesmondRyan.com

Also by Desmond P. Ryan

10-33 Assist PC